L · O · V · E
UNKNOWN

L · O · V · E
UNKNOWN

by

A. N. WILSON

VIKING

VIKING
Viking Penguin Inc.
40 West 23rd Street,
New York, New York 10010, U.S.A.

First American Edition
Published in 1987

LIBRARY OF CONGRESS CATALOGING IN PUBLICATION DATA
Wilson, A. N., 1950–
Love unknown.
I. Title.
PR6073.I439L6   1987   823'.914   86-40511
ISBN 0-670-81758-9

Printed in the United States of America by
The Book Press, Brattleboro, Vermont
Set in Sabon

L · O · V · E
UNKNOWN

Prehistory

Once upon a time, some twenty years ago, there were three nice young women, who lived together at 73b Oakmoor Road, London N.W.2. Memory obscured how they all came to share the flat, but when the lease ran out (they were only there a year) the three had apparently become friends for life.

In Monica Cunningham's recollection it had, while it lasted, been a conspicuously unenjoyable year; heaps of congealing saucepans in the untended kitchen, squabbles about telephone bills – but myth had sublimated these sordidities. In Belinda's memory it had been a period of happy innocence. They were all girls together and the world was young. Belinda was still, in those days, Linda. She had not been married so much as once; her hair was only beginning its romp through the colour spectrum; her complexion was nothing to boast of, and Wolverhampton still lingered in her tones. Now that she spoke so Sloane, Oakmoor Road had become a lost Eden, and whenever she saw either of the others she would refer to 'Oakers' in terms of such rapture that they were ashamed not to feel the same. Gradually, the myth encompassed them all. Oakers had been an idyll – for Richeldis at least. Perhaps it was *her* idyll that the others chiefly remembered. For it was during their days in Oakmoor Road that Richeldis had met, and married, the Man of her Dreams.

Belinda, as we shall later call her (for our tale belongs to a period when Linda was as far forgotten as her mini-skirts and her black beehive), was the chief oo-er and aa-er in the matter of Richeldis. She regarded the marriage of Richeldis to Simon Longworth as the most romantic fact of which she had been a first-hand witness. Everyone else, somehow, made a mess of life, or, like Monica, failed to have a life at all. But Simon and Richeldis had done what we all feel we are supposed to do, what we all dream of doing, what the modern world makes so nearly impossible. Simon and Richeldis had lived happily ever after.

It was during their first winter in the flat that Monica and Belinda had become so gigglingly aware of Simon's importance. Talk, in their cornflake-colloquies, ironing-intervals and hairdrying-confessionals, was, between the three, chiefly of Men. They endlessly assessed each man who came their way. How attractive did they find him? When his un-satisfactoriness had been made manifest, what was to be *done*? When he rang up, what excuses would be made? ('I'm afraid Linda's out,' Monica got used to saying as her friend silently gesticulated that she had no wish to speak to any of them: to John, to horrible Edward, to Cyril, or to George.) Initially, Richeldis had been prepared to fall in with this line of talk when Simon became an object of general fascination. There was no need to debate his looks. Anyone could see that, in the term still current, he was dishy. Linda led the field in the more problematic areas of inquiry. What was his history? What did he *sell* on those visits to Egypt about which Richeldis had been told on their first introduction? Then, not long after his first real 'date' with Richeldis, was he going too far, or not far enough? Was it fun? How much did he mean to spend on her? (They had eaten pizzas – then, how exotic!) Was he serious about her?

But very soon it became apparent that they should not be talking about Simon so frivolously. It was quite all right, somehow, for Linda to have the other two in (admittedly coarse) 'fits', as she regaled them with something which had transpired in the back of her current paramour's Humber. It was somehow all right for Monica to read aloud love letters from 'horrible Edward', to amuse the other two, or for Linda to let herself be taken to *Lawrence of Arabia* by the same Edward and squeal with revolted glee as she recalled his sweaty palm on her lap during Peter O'Toole's heroic walk through the desert. But somehow Simon was different. Simon and Richeldis – that was the point – were different. Once felt and apprehended, this fact became immediately noticeable. When wedding plans began, Monica remembered Linda saying, with uncharacteristic solemnity, that you suddenly saw what was meant by 'the holy estate of matrimony'. Simon and Richeldis, in those days, gave off an extraordinary feeling. Their love was so powerful, their happiness was so pure, that it awed those who saw it.

I am sorry to say that it is left to me, their chronicler, to record that happy time on their behalf, because in both their minds it is now so blurred that they cannot properly remember it. Monica can remember it, but it is all too painful for her to recall. She won't open up on the subject. Belinda remembers, but she does not realise how her memory distorts.

So let us, briefly, before our story starts, go back to some early scene in the lives of Simon and Richeldis. They have been 'going out' now for a very short period, and going out is all that has taken place. There have been two Cypriot meals in Camden High Street (Simon had *been* to Cyprus for his National Service) and an outing to see *Dr. Zhivago* at the cinema. This is a juncture before Simon became too special to talk about. Belinda has expressed interest in what it was that the Longworth family firm *sold*. Richeldis did not, or would not, reveal. Simon was presumably one of the *Sons* of Longworth and Sons, a firm based 'outside London'. Bedfordshire had been mentioned. He also seemed to do something in the City. It all seemed more grown-up than the fledgling accountants, junior civil servants and half-trained medics who regularly called as wooers at the flat.

Where in Bedfordshire? Richeldis only knew the name of the house, Sandilands, and its proximity to Dunstable. There was apparently a batty older brother who was too 'hopeless', in some capacity, to take over the business when Pa Longworth retired. The mother was already dead.

At this stage, there was more information about the Longworths than about Simon himself. Linda had privately advanced the view that the man might be kinky. People who were very family-orientated were. Look at *Psycho*. But then Richeldis was mother-dominated, so perhaps she did not mind. (They were all, come to that, dominated by Richeldis's mother; to dominate was Madge's normal mode of conducting a relationship.)

Look at them, though, Simon and Richeldis. He is twenty-five years old; according to Linda, a sort of English Omar Sharif, unfairly handsome. Richeldis is three years younger, and her appearance immediately brought to mind the epithet 'sweet'. She was moon-faced, and she kept her light blonde hair so neat and clean that no one really noticed how fine it was. She wore Alice bands above her high childish forehead, and she looked, 'horrible Edward' had once remarked to Linda, like the sort of girl who gets her photograph at the front of *Country Life*. She wasn't out of that class. Her background was pure 'Hampstead intellectual' (though actually her mother lived in Putney). Her father had been a wastrel left-wing poet who had died early of drink. Her mother was a publisher. But Richeldis still looked like a smiling English rose. Simon – Belinda excitedly conjectured – looked as though he wanted trouble. He looked as though he might take you to the races, or even treat his women rough. And yet, in the company of Richeldis, he was a doting child.

Richeldis never heard her friends wondering if she was *right* for so exotic a man. By the time Monica and Linda were reaching their verdicts over the Nescafé and the Marvel Milk, Simon was at the wheel of his Mini, and Richeldis was at his side, quietly confident that she was the possessor of his future.

She knew that he was in love with her. Not only had he told her, but she felt it instinctively. Girls who saw life in competitive terms might well have supposed Richeldis conceited: she took the fact of his love for granted. But vanity and conceit were not truly part of her nature. Never in her life had she ever supposed that she was the sort of girl with whom men might, as a matter of course, fall in love. Still less did she think of herself as a good 'catch'. There was nothing calculating in her attitude, still less was there self-contemplation or self-regard. It was much more as though he were already her familiar, as though, when they first met, she had known him already.

'Oh, it's you.' That's what she felt when he first came upon the scene. 'There you are. Always, without quite articulating to myself such an optimistic thought, I have known you would come along. It is a little sooner than I expected. I *am* only twenty-two. But how nice that you have arrived.'

That was what she felt, when the first social nonsenses were exchanged. She felt a deep joy, but curiously little of the over-excitement which, in those initial weeks, was evident in *his* manner. Simply, she knew, here he *was*, the stranger who was not a stranger – for whom, ever since she was a little girl, she had been waiting. Whenever she heard stories read aloud to her about princesses who lived happily ever after, Richeldis had always known, as a child, that she was such a princess. There was no vanity in this conviction. She merely knew that love and marriage would never be complicated for her. She knew that, when The Man came along, she would recognise him and that their pathway would be smooth. These absurdly formalised preparations were sweetly adorable: these nervous 'dates', these restaurant meals, these love letters, these beautiful cut irises. But there was really no need for these formalities. She had made up her mind.

And that was the evening when they were to make love for the first time.

Sex, as a subject, was all-absorbing to Linda. The stories which Monica and Richeldis had listened to in front of the electric bars! Linda knew the most astonishing things about coils, pregnancy tests, what not. She seemed able to make some distinction between different weights of 'petting'. None of this was of any great interest to Richeldis. She was no prude. There had been men, politely designated boy friends, with whom she was still on good terms. She had experienced all the things which a girl at that period of history was supposed to

have experienced. But these episodes in her past were no more serious
to her than the occasional joint, smoked when passed round at parties
to show she wasn't a spoilsport. There had been no real seriousness in
her love life. She knew that, when she met the man who was to be All in
All to her, it would be obvious both when and how everything would
proceed. Tonight, as the mini wheeled past King's Cross and into
Bloomsbury, she knew that they were going to make love and it was
obvious that he was in a flap about it. It was evident that he would
suggest at a certain point their going back to his flat, which in those
days was in Great Ormond Street. She felt charmed by his shyness,
sorry for his plight, but anxious that it should not spoil the whole
evening.

'I haven't really thought what film we are seeing – that is if you want
to see a film.'

'We don't have to see a film each time we go out.'

'Of course not. To tell you the truth I'm in no mood for a film,' he
said.

'Why don't we just go to your flat?' she asked.

He stared at her to see if he read her meaning aright; and she stared
back at him, with a smile, before squeaking: 'Simon; I say!'

The mini lurched dangerously into the middle of the Euston Road,
and he had missed his obvious left-hand turn. The near accident made
him even more agitated, and when he finally parked, outside the flat,
he was shaking. It is true. Simon Longworth did shake. When she
squeezed his arm in the darkness of the stairs, he wondered whether to
tell her that he was a virgin.

She never asked – not in a whole lifetime. An hour or so later, he
said, galumphingly, 'I just think I must be dreaming. I never expected
you to . . .'

'To what?'

'To *let* me!'

They were naked now. She had seen the pupils of his eyes quiver and
dilate as he leant over her. She had stared deep, deep into his eyes as
they made love, and it was as if she could see the whole of him, peer
into his soul, and, like God, love him through and through, all in all.

She only whispered, 'I love you.'

'Do you really?'

She did not answer him with words. Later, he began, 'I thought . . .'

What he had been going to say was, 'I thought you were such a *nice*
girl.' It was always his belief that nice girls did not really like doing
what *men* like doing. She seemed, by her almost motherly powers of
sympathy, to understand this, but she stopped the sentence with a kiss.

Later, laughing innocently, they gathered clothes from the rug in front of the gas fire and made their way into the bedroom for a tender repetition of this magical proceeding, a repetition which carried them to further heights of ecstatic wonder and joy. And then they lay there, for how long neither knew, in a state of the most perfect contentment.

'I wonder if it was as nice for you as it was for me.'

'Much nicer,' she said.

'Couldn't have been.'

'Could. You didn't know I'd let you. I've had all afternoon to look forward to it.'

His body now had become for her a thing of wonder, its muscular shoulders, its shaggy chest, its strong beautiful legs. He, too, looking down on the wonderful smooth pallor of her flesh, the marbly roundness of her, felt something like awe for what this body of hers had been able to do to him. (We, as guilty onlookers, have no business to be there; but knowing Simon and Richeldis as we do – or shall do – how touching it is to see how young they are. Their youth is the most beautiful thing about them.) There is no word strong enough to describe the intensity of delight which they had both felt. Nor is there language to express how completely mysterious they both felt it to be, as though these two naked bodies had led their possessors, by their strange conjunction, into the sort of mental state more usually spoken of by mystics, druggies, nutters. They had been to Heaven. It was wilder, more exciting, than any trip which a joint or a fix or a course of meditation might have provided. Moreover, unlike the drug-induced or religious ecstasy, it all felt so profoundly elemental and natural. In the very rhythmic movement of their bodies it was as though they were in touch with the deepest forces of Nature, with the turning of the spheres, the motions of the seas, the great and perpetual revolution of their friend the Earth itself.

No wonder, that, when speech returned, they had to take refuge in a light irony.

'If I'd known it was so nice, I wouldn't have wasted all that money on kebabs last week,' said Simon.

'You mean pig. Aren't you going to buy me a meal?'

'At this hour?'

'What hour?'

It was nearly midnight. He mustered what provisions he had. Some milk was heated on a ring. A packet of ginger nuts was consumed. Then some toast filled the room with its comforting, but inescapably matutinal odour. Marmite was spread on it. Somewhere, in the bottom of a drawer, some Turkish delight was rooted out. This was their meal on that momentous first night: it was really their wedding breakfast.

After, with all her instinctive desire to fuss, she had made the room neat, washed a pan, wiped some plates, she said, 'Let's go and look at the stars.'

'Won't you get cold?'

All she was wearing was a red jersey of his, picked up from the bedroom floor. The garment barely covered her but she didn't answer his question.

'Do let's,' she repeated.

'I thought you were going to stay the night.'

'Bed's too small. You need your beauty sleep.'

'Don't leave me, Richeldis. Never leave me.'

'Let's see the stars. Please.'

He could tell that it was a serious request, so they dressed, and went downstairs. She was still wearing his red jersey, but now she wore her own clothes beneath it, as, hand in mittened hand, they stared up into the bright frosty air and contemplated all the immensity and eternity of the night.

'Oh, Richeldis, I love you so . . .'

'Ssh!'

But London will never be shushed. There was no point in shushing: the shouts of revellers in Lamb's Conduit Street, a car rushing down to Queen's Square, they all destroyed the silence after which she strained.

'Do you think there is a music in the spheres?' she asked.

'Funny question.'

'I think there is,' she whispered, 'even though we can't hear it.'

'Stay with me, Richeldis. Love me forever.'

'The second request, kind sir, I shall do my best to satisfy.' She kissed him. Though younger than he, she was so much in control. 'But as to the first, no, I must get back. The others will be wondering what on earth has happened to me.'

'Let them.'

But he did drive her back to Oakmoor Road in the green Mini. She kissed him lightly and went indoors without looking back. When she came to undress that evening she found herself still wearing his red jersey, and she put it away as a keepsake. Six months before this story begins Richeldis came across the garment, and gave it to a jumble sale.

This chapter is all prehistory. Forgive me for not giving all the details of the year in Oakmoor Road. You will pick up all you need to know later on in the story. The three girls grew fonder of one another as the months went by. From time to time Richeldis's mother would 'blow in' to the house, making exclamations of amazement at the squalor of the flat. These 'raids' (as the girls felt them to be) were as embarrassing to Monica as they were to Richeldis.

'You're only her daughter,' Monica would say, 'I work for Madge, which is much worse.'

Richeldis's mother was, at that stage, besotted with Monica, whom she called Tatty Coram. The obsession gave way to another, but it was infuriating while it lasted, particularly since Monica seemed to regard the Old Woman – as she called her – as little better than a menace.

'My darling Tatty Coram, how can you live in this filth?' was so often the question. Never 'my darling Richeldis'. 'And what on *earth* are those things hanging over the bath?'

They were Linda's of course, who had her abortion in the May. Monica was beginning to see a lot, by then, of Professor Allison, but she continued to be more Monica-ish than ever, frowning over Katherine Mansfield's short stories, and drinking a lot of instant coffee and coping with perpetual, very mild depressions with a breezy lack of surprise whenever they descended.

Richeldis gradually forgot, as the years receded, how annoying she had come to find Monica. At the time, unable to articulate, herself, the fear that Monica Cunningham had alienated Madge's affections, the mildly jealous daughter took refuge in fury at smaller failings. How maddening had been Miss Cunningham's little gallicisms, even, then, her *je ne sais quoi* and *tant pis*; and her failure, *always*, to wash up her coffee mug until *la fin du jour*. Then there had been (Belinda reminded Richeldis about it only the other day) the time of Monica's sudden and unannounced decision to give a party in the flat. It was amazing now to think that Monica had once known enough people to give a party. Who on earth were her friends? (Talking about it at the time, the two others had concluded they were people from the Hobbit Society, chiefly, and perhaps a few librarians or publishers' readers. Old Professor Allison had been there. Had Madge come? Richeldis could not remember now.)

The other girls became less important. Richeldis was taken to Bedfordshire, shown the sand quarry on which the Longworth fortune was founded. Simon had explained the business story to her but in such matters she was a bad listener. Longworth and Sons Ltd. were about to be bought up by a much larger conglomerate, old Mr.

Longworth (Simon's father) was on the point of retirement but Simon could still hope for a place on the board. Little it meant to Richeldis then. She found the factory side of Simon's life a little frightening. Likewise his moustachioed father who dressed like a bookmaker and called her 'my dear'. She preferred (secretly) Simon's 'dotty' brother, Bartle.

The idea of allying herself, in perpetuity, to the Longworths and their fortune based on sand gave her many moments of alarm, as did the dinners with her *own* mother, with whom Simon never quite saw eye to eye. But through none of these prosaic preliminaries to connubial happiness had there flickered a single moment of doubt about her feelings for Simon. She knew herself to be adored, and she wore on her face the unmistakeable look of almost terrifying joy which such certainty brings and proclaims. She was Simon's; he was hers. So would it always be.

Children came – Daniel, Thomas, Emma. Richeldis gave herself up to motherhood with a ready, natural joy which was all of a piece with her felt love for Simon. There must have *been* a time, aeons since, when she was *not* a mother, nor a wife. She did not visualize this time because she so rarely thought about it. When Monica, or Belinda, said, 'Do you remember such and such?' about their year together in Oakmoor Road, Richeldis never really did, though she would nod and hoot to oblige Belinda. She lived entirely in the present moment. Sorrows and rages, when they came, were absolute. Since she was incapable of comparing her present mood with previous ones she did not notice that she was in fact imperceptibly unhappier than she had been as a young woman. Simon was cross quite a lot of the time. Much of her energy in the first decade of marriage was devoted to stopping the children cry. In its second decade she spent an equal amount of time trying to keep her husband sweet-tempered. It was such a perpetual struggle that she no longer noticed herself doing it. She still loved Simon. She retained her physical passion for him. They had come to inhabit one another's bodies as if they were interchangeable. She had no more grief in her own spare tyre of a belly, her browning teeth and homely chins than in Simon's grey hair and wrinkled brow. They were among the lucky ones. Their marriage had, triumphantly, survived. People spoke about making love, and often the phrase had a hollow ring to it. When, for instance, Belinda spoke of making love to a man she had known for only a few hours, the expression meant nothing to Richeldis. Nothing at all. But when she was curled naked in her husband's arms through the long marital hours of night she felt, quite simply, that they were both enfolded in love. When, during the day, he had one of his childish outbursts of irritation against her or the children, she only had to nuzzle against his shoulder, or run one of her plump moist fingers through his grizzled hair, to feel a recurrence of that Love, that warm enfolding delightful Love they had made together so many countless times in the previous twenty and more years.

Most miraculous of all was that this most joyful of human activities should have led to the existence of more people, and of such delightful people. Again, how wrong people like Belinda got it. The idea of an 'unwanted child' (one of the cant words in those days) was incomprehensible to Richeldis. On each occasion that she had known herself to be pregnant she had experienced an immeasurable extension of happiness. Her joy in Simon was not merely something between the two of them. Too big to be contained, it led to the creation of another life. Contemplating another life within her, with all its opportunities for joy and all its mystery, had always left her awestruck. And, as the children emerged from infancy, their personalities were of all-consuming interest and concern to her.

She was perfectly aware that she was a 'bore' about her children. She knew that Monica, for example, when she came on visits from France, had grown to pity her. As far as her friend was concerned, Richeldis had thrown away her life by becoming a wife and mother. She had subsumed her own personality, her very existence, into that of her husband and children. Richeldis knew that the received Wisdom of the Age was against her. She should have been striving for independence from these ancient and ignominious roles. She should have been Using her Brain, Having a Career, Fulfilling Herself. There were moments when it looked perilously as though she had no self to fulfil. There were times when she recognised that she had really had no life apart from this man, these children, this house, these relentlessly repeated domesticities. She saw what angered the feminists. But it did not anger Richeldis because she was for the most part so happy.

There *were* weeks of exhaustion when colds and influenza swept through the family leaving them all weary and pale – there were hectic weeks when happiness appeared to depend on the proper functioning of the washing-machine. There had been several alarming spells before Mrs. Turbot became full-time when they had had to manage without help in the house. But what Monica would not perhaps have understood was that Richeldis enjoyed all this. That is to say, none of it affected her fundamental underlying joy. Through all the changing scenes of this life – the measles, the influenza, the agonising drama of Daniel's milk teeth, the worry that Emma wasn't forming relationships at Primary School – her children's childhood unfolded, spread itself, and then, like the personality of her husband, thoroughly engulfed her. Of course there continued to be an independent existence called for the sake of convenience Mummy, Darling or, on Madge's lips, Richeldis. She was still the charming moon-faced blonde girl whom everyone loved. She continued to have her own thoughts, her own separate and independent physical existence. There was even a week, in 1978, when she had a cold all of her very own which she had not caught off one of the children. Sometimes she would wake in the morning and have a thought which did not relate to Daniel, Thomas, Emma or Simon. Sometimes there were moments of it just being Her and Nature. Her in the garden, taking in the flat view beyond the mellow bricks of Sandilands, breathing the sweet odours of the rose garden. But for the most part, the most considerable part, she had no existence outside the role of wife and mother. And so it all went on, as year succeeded year, until Daniel had wobbled through the Common Entrance, and Emma (thank goodness) had a few little friends and it was Thomas's turn for the agonies of a metal brace on his teeth. And then Marcus was born, poor little Marcus.

His birth was the worst crisis in all their lives.

It was worse, Richeldis thought, for Simon. He minded so very much. For her, the deep sadness of his affliction quickly evaporated into simple joy that another child of hers had been born into the world. In fact, they were given to understand that Marcus only had Down's syndrome in a very mild form. Just as, years before, Richeldis had been certain that Simon was Her Man, so now she felt equal certainty that everything would be All Right about Marcus. She knew that he would be an enriching companion for all of them, not merely a difficulty. But for Simon this was not so. For his father, Marcus *was* merely a difficulty. Richeldis knew that this attitude would soften and alter. She loved in Simon his profound vein of paternal pride. He minded much more keenly than she that the boys should get into Pangham and Emma into Wycombe Abbey. When they were babies he had not been so interested. By the same token, she felt that Simon's love for Marcus would grow, unfold.

In this prehistory, we will conduct the reader up to the day before the action begins. The scene is in the marital bedroom at Sandilands. Simon has emerged from their bathroom at about half past eleven. He is wearing a pair of pyjamas but his chest is bare, and Richeldis admires the rug of grey hair which grows on it. Going over to him, she strokes his chest and smiles. Simon seems mildly irritated by this attention and says, 'Have you ironed those shirts?'

'Mm . . .' she kisses his ear. 'I've packed them for you in your bag.'

'You're sure there are four?'

'I told you there were four, darling. Mrs. Turbot ironed them specially for you this morning. And I've put your socks in the bag, darling, and four pairs of pants and your spare suit. I took out those pale trousers, you're not going to wear those at a meeting.'

'You are a *wonder*!'

'Am I, darling?'

Within twenty minutes, they are in bed together. Twenty-two years have passed since their first magical conjunction in Great Ormond Street. Daniel has left Pangham and is having a year in Canada. Thomas (horrors!) failed Pangham and is at Allhallows. Emma is at Wycombe Abbey and hoping to try for Oxbridge. Only Marcus is at home with them now. How strange, all those years ago, as they sailed into Paradise on the hearthrug of a rented flat, there had been no thought of whether they had cleaned their teeth or been to the lavatory or switched out the lights in other rooms. Now, neither of them went to bed without rehearsing these thoughts.

'Darling,' said Richeldis.

'Yes.'

'You put out the lights in the kitchen?'

'Yes.'

'You'll buy something nice for Marcus in Paris, won't you?'

'Course. Something nice.'

'It doesn't have to be expensive. Anything.'

'I know. I'll get him something.'

'He's so happy at the playgroup, bless him.'

'Hm.'

'Did you see his tortoise?'

'*What?*'

'In the kitchen. Don't worry. I used Blu-tac.'

'Oh, a *picture* of a tortoise.'

'So sweet.'

Simon emitted what Richeldis interpreted as a grunt of paternal pride.

'Try to see Monica in Paris, darling.'

'I'll see.'

'She says she's not lonely, but she must be.'

'Goodnight, darling.' He kissed her. The asexual, condescending sort of kiss you might bestow on a child. 'That's enough prattle from you,' it seemed to suggest. 'Now let's get some sleep.'

He turned his back to her and put out the light on his side of the bed. She too switched out her light and for a while she held his shoulder. But he appeared to be asleep.

I

Monica Cunningham had become accustomed to solitude. The arrival of anyone else, especially of an old and much-loved friend, was to be viewed with a mingled pleasure. The tranquillity of existence was easily disturbed.

It would be wrong to say that Miss Cunningham was set in her ways since, for the last fifteen years, she had strenuously avoided having any ways to be set in. Within a very short period of emigrating to Paris, she had made her liberating discovery about life. You don't have to take part. People don't go on bothering you indefinitely. You can say *no* when they ask you out.

The pain which she had left behind in London receded from consciousness almost as soon as she became a Parisian. Noiselessly it vanished in the grey French air, which looked as though it contained quite a lot of pain, pain that no one cared about because it was other people's. Her family, her former flat-mates, Madge, all expressed their anxiety when they found that rather than merely going to Paris for a fortnight she had *bought* an apartment there. Madge of all people was indignant.

'This notion, d'you see, that persons can simply take off into the blue,' she had said, as if this in itself were both a convincing argument and a sentence. 'But, you see, in London you have me, and Richeldis, and your various other friends.'

That was the trouble, the various other friends.

'I always think it is important to have a few stalwarts in your life that you can drop *in* on,' Madge had added.

Certainly Madge was a great dropper-in, an inviter of herself to Sunday lunch. Monica Cunningham was not. The various friends and the dropping in led in one direction to boredom and in another to heartbreak. By the age of twenty-five she had had enough. The pleasures of solitude had, ever since, more than compensated for its sorrows.

There were such trivial considerations as food. Alone, one could eat what one liked when one liked. With another there were always their tastes to consider. And the fewer people she had to stay at her flat, the more out of practice she became.

The previous week had been of unrelieved happiness. She had just shaken off a cold, and there are few greater pleasures in life than emerging from a very mild illness. None of the fear of serious sickness and none of the pain: but that delicious sense of the body functioning once more, and the world being again delightful. Her Russian, too, was coming along. Having mastered a reading knowledge of German and Italian, Miss Cunningham had paused. For a while she had thought with some pleasure of Greek and the Dialogues of Plato. But then whim prompted her in the direction of Slavonic tongues. For the previous six months she had been making weekly pilgrimages to a lady called Agafya Mikhailovna Bogdavich. She had wanted a toothless crone murmuring before her glowing icon her nostalgia for the days of the Tsar. It was Agafya Mikhailovna who was recommended at the British Council Library. She turned out to be a pasty, rather fat woman from Tula, with no poetry in her face. Her husband worked at the Soviet Embassy. Agafya Mikhailovna was bored. Absolutely no small talk ever passed between teacher and pupil. It was entirely a matter of Aspects, Genitive Plurals, vocabulary lists and an increasingly enjoyable and less painstaking read-through of *The Captain's Daughter*. There was nothing like learning a language to pass the time. It was, in Monica's experience, the highest form of pleasure. There was a sense of leaving oneself behind, of having an adventure, of charting new waters. It was quite as exciting as what others – Belinda, say – looked for, and so rarely found in love.

Russian, therefore, for the time being, was the main thing. And her tapestry had continued – a large thing, which she had devised herself in imitation of French seventeenth-century originals. Mornings of Russian and evenings of tapestry were punctuated by calm unhurried walks through the pale light of the Jardins du Luxembourg (it had been a blissfully 'bad summer') and well-chosen solitary meals. There was a restaurant she particularly liked a mere olive stone's throw away from her apartment near Les Invalides. Alternatively she could eat all the things she best enjoyed in the apartment itself. On sybaritic days, a jar of caviar could be taken to bed with a teaspoon and half a lemon. There were at least a dozen other things which tasted especially good when eaten in bed: biscottes (from a packet) spread with anchovy; boiled eggs; pasta shells with a delicate sauce of cream, chives and basil; cold quails; Mars bars; frankfurter sausages; baby turnips (which she served whole in a lot of garlic butter); junket (just plain, with a sprinkling of nutmeg); *purée de pommes de terre* (what nicer?)

with the gravy of yesterday's *daube*; tinned lentil soup; baby Brie; a bag of cherries; a banana. All admirable bed-snacks. With a guest in the flat, one could not live in this way. Supper, instead of half an hour eating bananas while laughing over Carlyle's *Frederick the Great*, had to be tables, chairs, shopping, cooking, *talk*: and never any certainty that the other persons were enjoying themselves. One good thing to be said for sex was that it soon became obvious if the other person was only pretending enjoyment for the sake of politeness. Then one could stop. But other forms of shared pleasure – meals, playgoing – could be continued for years with neither party happy and both too nice to say.

Not that Lady Mason was anything but the perfect guest, the kindest friend. Yet, after only four days of her animated presence, Miss Cunningham had begun to feel restless. Surely one couldn't be *bored*? In *Paris*? But the suspicion threatened to form itself that Lady Mason *was* cheesed off. Given her gusto there had been little time for actual boredom to set in. She had queued for Douanier Rousseau at the Grand Palais, queued for Impressionists at the Jeu de Paume, queued for Watteau at the Grand Palais (again) and then, not really sharing Monica Cunningham's passion for the great painters, she announced that she had queued enough. Monica had then accompanied her to the shops and felt uneasily that extravagance on the Boulevard Saint-Germain had not provided her friend with that inner calm which in her own case it always guaranteed. A few meals had compensated: in particular, a sublime bit of fish at La Marée, for the price of which, in London, they could have bought a serviceable second-hand car. And there had been the usual consoling dinner at Maxim's. But, throughout, there was the sense of *ennui* threatening. It vexed Miss Cunningham, who loved her old friend with an uncomplicated love. She knew that Belinda had come to Paris to be comforted, and that she herself was failing in her consolatory obligations. Since the break-up of the second marriage, Lady Mason had lurched from one unsuitable attachment to another. The most recent had been, predictably, the married man.

'But I wasn't going through all those hoops again with *anyone*,' she said with a wave of her Falstaff – how they polluted the atmosphere in the Rue de Bourgogne flat. 'For the first time in my life I know that I've done the right thing, the sensible thing.'

Lady Mason certainly did not look as if she had ever done a sensible thing, even once. The immediate impression was of platinum blonde hair framing a long face which was beginning, somewhat alarmingly, to be ravaged. Ultra-violet rays (a lamp?) actually increased the sense that she had been through much, though her bronze features were a good way from being leathery. In spite of the little cigars, the large teeth were in pretty good shape. The eyes were covered with dark glasses to disguise an unhealthy yellowing of the whites. She was expensively gloved and coated in light grey leather. Brilliants gleamed from lobes and throat. Her companion by contrast looked so untouched by experience that one would have wrongly guessed her to be ten years Lady Mason's junior. Her cotton skirt and lambswool crimson cardigan, the flat-heeled well-made shoes, the short nearly mousey hair and the absence of make-up suggested the history mistress at a rather good private school.

'Sensible, Belinda! You! How does it feel?'

'Terrible!'

There was a lot of grinning but there could be no doubt that a sacrifice had been made, one that caused Lady Mason pain. Monica was now acquainted with the whole three months of it: Belinda's first encounter with the man (something quite ordinary, an anaesthetist) at a dinner party; the flowers next morning; the luncheons and raptures; the secrets and the little lies; the near-misses when his coat or her car or someone's cigarette lighter was seen by someone else. The whole cloak and dagger of adultery.

'It was just seeing him that day in Harrods with his *children*.' She had said this before, but Miss Cunningham allowed her to repeat herself. 'He didn't see me but . . . it just *finished* me. You understand?'

'I think so.'

'You're so sensible. Why is my life such a mess? Always?'

'Perhaps you like people? More than I do? Perhaps my life should be in more of a mess than it is.'

'No it shouldn't,' said Belinda. 'We need you . . .'

'So!' interrupted Monica. 'What did you resolve, both of you? Finally, if it was finally?'

'I made the bravest speech of – my – life. I simply told him that we aren't going to meet any more.'

'He won't believe you.'

'He didn't. But I mean it. Monica, I can't put his children through all that unhappiness. I can't, however much I love him.'

Seeing her friend reach quiveringly for an ash-tray, Monica said, 'Poor Belinda.'

After an awkward pause, Lady Mason resumed. 'Your life's so wonderfully spare, uncluttered.'

'You mean empty.'

'You know when you go to see some funny old relation . . .'

'I don't have any old relations.'

'Who's never managed to throw anything away, who's inherited all her mother's things, and all her sister's things, and the room is simply *stuffed*. You're falling over things. There are potted plants, and harps and a pianola, and dogs, and a sofa that's much too big for the room . . .'

'What exotic relations you have.'

'Well, that room is my life. It's so overcrowded that I can't get into it any more. It's too full of things, of people bursting in.'

'No one ever burst in on my life,' said Monica. 'No one, that is, whom I have liked.'

'But that's just *it*, Monica. You see the pitfalls before you start – so you don't start. For me, when someone new comes into my life I always trust they won't be like the others. I'm too come-hitherish.'

'And then they crash in like hooligans and smash all your lovely harps and pianolas,' said Monica.

'Oh you know what I *mean*. It was just so nice to leave all that *mess* behind me and come into this. Your rooms, my dear . . .' The metaphor was uncompleted, as, with the wave of a brown hand, she indicated the silvery damask of the curtains, the gleaming cherry-wood of the escritoire, the lush trees in the garden beyond the long windows. 'How *is* it that you are so sensible?'

'As I said,' Monica confessed, 'things simply don't happen to me in the way they just keep happening to you. I'm not made unhappy by solitude.'

'But that's just *it*. There's nothing wrong with *you*. My own company drives me bananas. And I'm not unique. Nearly everyone else seems to be drinking themselves crazy, or stuffing drugs into their systems, just because they can't stand being on their own. That's why people feel so threatened by unemployment.'

'Can't they sit at home and read books, knit?'

'I'm serious.'

'That's what I was afraid of.'

'You are – awful! Quite honestly, Monica, I sometimes think that is the only thing you really and truly *are* afraid of – being serious. Everyone else in the world, except you and a few Buddhist monks, hates his own company. What's your secret?'

'We shall be late,' said Monica, who had never asked herself the question. Perhaps *that* was the secret. By late, she meant late for the 'bus to Fontainebleau.

Lady Mason, at heart a Pelagian who believed in taking matters into her own hands, had been all for the hire of a motor. Monica urged that the 'bus would take them there just as fast, for a tenth of the cost and with none of the anxiety. The walk to the Rue de Rivoli took half an hour, through perfect weather. It was August, but it felt like late September, with a hint of cold and a touch of mist which were purely pleasurable. Above their heads in streets and boulevards the trees were still green, bunchy and luxuriant. Belinda Mason could see the delights of Paris, but she could not imagine choosing to live there. It was so stately, so heartlessly formal, so grey. As they crossed by the Pont Royal they felt as though they could take in the whole of Paris at a glance. On the opposite bank, shimmering with smudgy mist, and with sunlight on water, the Jardins des Tuileries stretched into a blue distance which seemed purely painterly, made, imagined. To the messy eye of a Londoner it all seemed curiously unreal, but they were both silenced by the vision.

They had both agreed that, if it did not actually pour, it would be nice to have an expedition. Belinda had never seen Fontainebleau. She accepted that Monica knew how to organize things, while fearing the side of her friend's nature that liked Mars bars and Walt Disney. Belinda's heart missed a beat at the sight of all the bus-queues in the Rue de Rivoli.

'They're all guided,' Monica sprung on her, 'which language would you prefer?'

'English is the language I speak. In case you hadn't noticed.'

'I suppose there isn't a *Russian* aftobus,' said Monica, maddeningly Slavonic in her intonation.

'But, darling, I'd never understand . . .'

'The English-language buses become crowded with the Japanese,' explained the Parisian with no apparent surprise at this paradox. It was indeed the case that well over one hundred Japanese tourists were queuing for a 'bus with an English-language guide. Belinda bowed to Monica's suggestion that they should join the shortest queue, regardless of its linguistic affiliations. This turned out to be the French one. The 'bus, when they had clambered aboard and paid, was comfortable enough, cool, air-conditioned. Since neither Monica nor Belinda suffered from nausea they stationed themselves 'well back' to be as far as possible from the guide. For ten minutes, they sat contentedly with their own thoughts and some dozen French-speakers: two old ladies with an even older gentleman who discoursed in harsh Burgundian accents about the expense of Metro fares; a pair of men with shaven heads, spectacles, thick Rudyard Kipling moustaches and almost identical suits of pale green denim; two priests murmuring of dinner; and a gaggle of *tricoteuses* who might have been an old folks' outing. Just as the engine began to throb, and it appeared they might be about to leave on a blissfully empty bus, they were joined by about twenty Italian girls, very noisy, very brightly dressed. The guide, a beaky woman with dyed black hair scraped ruthlessly back from the brow, said through a microphone that they had just been joined by a youth club from Milan. She would therefore give her commentary in Italian *and* in French.

'Christ, Monica,' exclaimed Lady Mason, when she had had the message translated for her.

'There's no need to listen. The main thing will be seeing the forest.'

This made sense. It was one of those days when there could have been no better place than the middle of a wood – and, though this seemed a perverse way of getting there, it had its charms. After the tedious traffic jams of Montparnasse, it was refreshing, even in a 'bus, and even with a bilingual commentary which Lady Mason could not understand, to be bowling along the straight road which cuts across the *pays de Brie*. In not many moments, they were informed by the flat inflexions of the voice coming from the loudspeaker over their heads, they would be visiting the village very famous for its great inspiration of many painters of the nineteenth century. In the main street of Barbizon, there was time to disgorge. Some of the sillier girls bought ice-creams. One of the priests and most of the old ladies queued up to urinate and one of the Rudyard Kiplings took a photograph of the other Rudyard Kipling posing – no other word would do – in the doorway of Corot's studio. And then, after anxious head-counting which recalled a school outing, they were all back on the 'bus penetrating a landscape more beautiful and the midst of the wood. It was almost overdone. As far as the eye could see, on every side, interminable avenues of deepest green stretched into a bright distance, dappled with perfect brushstrokes of sunlight.

'And it was here that the kings of France came to hunt,' said the dull voice, twice.

Ever since their conversation of an hour or so before, concerning the rival merits of solitude and society, the topic had hung about the two friends. All else was said in parenthesis. Hurtling along in the air-conditioned 'bus, Lady Mason returned to the theme. How did Monica contrive to stop things happening?

'Oh, I don't contrive. It's ages since anything happened to me.'

'But the difference is that you don't want anything to happen.'

'Difference? Between whom and whom?'

'You and normal people. Richeldis, say.'

'Richeldis really *is* normal. That I grant you. But are the things which happen to her exactly interesting?'

'My dear, why should they be interesting? Richeldis is too happy to need *interests*. It is only unhappy people like me who want to be interested by experience. Richeldis has got the children, the house, Simon.'

'I know!' There was a tiny bit of despair in Monica's voice.

'It's beautiful,' Lady Mason asserted. 'People talk such *rubbish* about married women not being fulfilled unless they get out and have careers and quite honestly just *look* at how happy Simon and Richeldis have been.'

'I know!' If anything there was a yet sharper note of desperation in Miss Cunningham's tones.

'Don't start making jokes about Richeldis, I can't bear it. Be unkind about anyone else.'

'I'm never unkind about Richeldis. I adore her as much as you do.'

'You said she never reads.'

'Ages ago.'

Eighteen months previous, to be precise. Monica had expressed a doubt whether Richeldis, in recent years, had kept abreast of literature.

'Reading isn't *everything*,' said Belinda.

'I never said it was.'

'Richeldis is actually a very intelligent woman.'

'I agree,' said Monica. 'That's why it seems a bit of a pity to lose herself entirely in domesticity. I mean, there will come a day when the children don't need her. Then what?'

Belinda was silent. She could not read the future. Then she gave a little laugh.

'What's funny?'

'Just thinking of Oakers.'

'You always are. The three of us, burning saucepans, and quarrelling about who used up the last of the milk.'

'Monica, you *know* it wasn't like that. Do you remember that marvellous man who was chasing Richeldis when I first brought Simon to the flat?'

'Jonathan Martindale,' said Monica. She had, or believed she had, total recall of everything which had happened in Oakmoor Road. How could she have forgotten so crucial a detail as the arrival of Simon? 'Are you sure it was you who brought . . . ?'

'Goodness he was good-looking. Do you remember?'

'Yes. And I remember what happened to him.'

'My dear, you are *awful!*' Belinda guffawed. 'He seemed so jolly serious about Richeldis. He can't have been queer in those days.'

'It was Cedric who was queer,' said Monica, as though no more than one member of the human race at any moment had such proclivities. 'Jonathan changed sex, which is different. But, Belinda, you can't be serious. Did you say it was *you* who introduced Simon to Richeldis? I never knew that.'

'You can't have done, darling. I must have told you a thousand times,' said Belinda unconvincingly. 'We met at a dinner party.'

'That's the title of your autobiography.'

'And Simon asked me out. You must admit he was pretty dishy in those days. Well he still is quite a wrinkled charmer.'

'But he wasn't . . . Simon was never your . . .'

'We only went out a couple of times,' said Belinda, covering whatever tracks there were to be covered. 'You remember what we were *all* like in those days. We thought nothing of having four or five boyfriends all dangling around at once.'

'Some of us.'

'Anyway, I asked him back to Oakers – my dear, you *did* know all this! I refuse to believe you can have forgotten anything so important. Well, he met Richeldis and it was well and truly a case of love – at – first – sight.' When Belinda drew out a well-oiled cliché from the word-hoard she liked to emphasise it by leaving long pauses between each word.

'How are they?' Monica asked.

'Simon and Richeldis? They're really extraordinary those two. The way they – coped. The way they rose – to – the – occasion over that *Tragedy*.'

'Poor things. Marcus is something that's *happened*, and no mistake.'

'Do you know, my dear, I have never *once* heard Richeldis speak about Marcus as if he was a disaster. She just loves him. If it had happened to me, I'd have just gone potty. I *simply* wouldn't have been able to cope.'

They stopped their conversation and listened, first in French and then in somewhat uncertain Italian, to the story of how François Premier came to Fontainebleau. Moreover, they were informed, each room in the palace would give an impression exceptionally vivid of the changing styles of the painting and the immovables since the Rebirth of Learning to the Second Empire. The Italian girls, who weren't listening, had started to flick each other with the sharp ends of their ice cream cones. It was some relief when the great gates of the château came in sight, and they were allowed to disembark. There were to be four hours of freedom, and it was not obligatory for all members of the party to stick together.

'Could we have lunch first?' said Monica.

'Or at least a drink.'

'I always forget about drinks; it's one of the consequences of living alone.'

Glasses of kir preceded a clean, happy little meal at a curiously old-fashioned café some way off the square: a heavy fish soup, a fricassée of chicken in a delicate lemony sauce, served with a mountain of boiled rice in a mould; an excellent Brie with the salad; pear sorbets; coffee.

'I think we're both rather envious of Richeldis,' said Monica over coffee, 'and it isn't her handsome husband or her house or her children that we envy.'

'I envy them enormously,' said Belinda.

'It's her virtue I envy,' said Monica.

'Ah! And we both lost ours years ago?'

'I don't think I ever had that sort of virtue, that sort of automatic niceness,' confessed the solitary.

They paid, rose, made the stately little walk to the château and attached themselves (you had to) to an English-speaking guide. Within, the place was splendid enough, but routine splendid, production-line splendid. Good tapestries, but not great tapestries. Dull High Renaissance paintings. Heavy gilt furniture. But there was splendour enough for an afternoon's ambling; good views from high windows of lake and trees; a strong feeling of history having been enacted here, even if, as in Lady Mason's case, it was history of which you felt incurably ignorant. She was one of those who simply got lost among all those Louis and brightened at the arrival of Napoleon not because she had a particular admiration for the Corsican Emperor but because at least he could be placed. Josephine and so forth.

'And here,' said the guide, 'is the throne room. Napoleon, you will remember, did not live at Versailles. This, then, is his throne room, where you see the throne. Notice the initial N above the throne. This stands for Napoleon Buonaparte. Notice too the glass bauble on the great chandelier which weighs . . . '

'My dear!' Belinda suddenly gripped Monica's arm. Monica made her sighting a split second sooner. Simon Longworth, the husband of Richeldis, whose connubial happiness had been the subject of so much conversation, had entered the throne room by the opposite door. To judge from the concentrated air of abstraction with which he was looking out of the window, it seemed certain that he had already spotted Monica and Belinda. Nor was it hard to guess why he did not wish to greet them. There was a very young woman with long yellow hair holding his arm.

Instinct forced Monica and Belinda to retreat. While the rest of the party pressed on around the palace, they retrod their steps through gilded ante-rooms; a dining-room heavy with ormolu; until they reached the landing of their first lecturette, its hunting tapestries and middling-good Italian pictures.

'It really *was* him, wasn't it?' asked Belinda.

'And they were arm in arm, and no, I don't believe it was his niece. Of course it was him.'

'It's all right for you, running in those sensible shoes. These heels will kill me.'

'I'm not running. Just walking briskly.'

'He's the one who should be running.'

'Don't let's talk until we are outside.'

'Monica! Slower please on these stairs.

'Why *wear* heels like that?'

They were both breathless when they reached the lake and paused to consider their excruciatingly embarrassing situation. They had just seen the husband of their best friend arm in arm with someone who looked little better than a tart. They had just spent the day holding up to each other the example of Simon and Richeldis as a marraige which embodied happiness, stability and virtue. At best, one felt foolish.

'What makes it worse is that I'm sure he saw us,' said Belinda opening her bag and fidgeting for cigs. This was no time for a Falstaff.

'What makes it worse,' said Monica, 'is that it happened.'

'I dare say all men . . .' Lady Mason's sentence drifted off into the first inhalation of cigarette smoke.

'But *Simon?*'

'There might be some perfectly innocent explanation.'

'There's no such thing. If you need an explanation for your behaviour, then it isn't innocent.'

'Smoke a Marlboro, it will calm you.'

'Why did we have to come here? I could have shown you Chantilly, Versailles . . .'

'So you agree with me. What makes it worse is that we saw. Now, my dear, I think that *much* the best thing we could possibly do is to ignore it, pretend it hasn't happened.'

'But, Belinda, don't you *see* . . .'

'That way, at least one person will be spared. The person who really matters, after all.'

'I know you're right. But that hurts. Oh, it hurts. I think I *shall* have one of your cigarettes.'

Monica peered at the Marlboro as though she had never seen such a thing before. A casual observer, noting her raised brow, her puzzled fingers, her examination first of the cork tip, then of the tobacco end, could be forgiven for guessing that she was about to eat it. But she did the commonplace thing and, when it was between her pouting, cross lips, Belinda lit it for her.

'So,' said Monica, 'we just behave as if we don't know? Oh, what does he think he is *playing at*?'

'That, my dear, is all too obvious.'

Monica looked very very angry. She said, 'He's . . .' then she paused as though no word were bad enough. After another puff of the unwonted fag she cast it away and could come up with nothing stronger than, 'He's a *fool*.'

It was too awkward that the friends evidently felt so differently about the episode. Lady Mason could see that it was embarrassing, but, for that very reason, it was also mildly farcical. Well-accustomed to the agitation of the betrayer, the grief of the betrayed, she did not underestimate the sorrow of Richeldis should this afternoon go, as she thought, 'any further'. But at the same time she could respond to the archetypal joke involved in the discovery of a philanderer. It was mildly troubling that Monica should be so prudishly disapproving, so shocked, so totally, as she put it, *bouleversée*. It made Belinda feel that Monica's habits of solitude would not quite *do*, if they incapacitated her in a crisis. She simply did not have enough experience.

But neither woman had long to reflect upon the matter. Before they had agreed on their course of inaction, they looked up, and there he was, coming towards them. There was nothing hang-dog in his approach. He lifted the arm of his well-cut suit and waved exuberantly. His forty-seven years had been gentle to him. He had not thickened or coarsened. The grey of his thick hair actually enhanced his beauty.

'Thinking of buying the place, Monica, or just looking?'

Normally, both women, when they met Simon, kissed him. This afternoon they hung back awkwardly; and this one omission was more eloquent than any words. Filling the embarrassing silence, he continued. 'What a glorious day. I've sold just about enough sand to the Frogs – done rather well, actually.'

'I didn't even know you were in Paris,' said Monica, 'I assume it *is* in Paris that you have been selling sand, and not in Fontainebleau.'

'Do you remember telling us in Oakmoor Road that you had sold sand to the Egyptians?' asked Belinda. And, while they all attempted a formulaic laugh, she added, 'No chance of a nice reunion dinner, I suppose – tonight?'

'It would hardly be the same without Richeldis,' said Monica – 'or is she with you?'

'I'd love to join you,' he said. 'I'm taking a couple of French colleagues out – you know how it is.'

'Flying visit?' pressed Monica.

'I shall be back in England tomorrow.'

'Well in that case you must travel back to Paris on our 'bus. It is the very least you can do for us.'

'Oh, but Monica,' exclaimed Belinda. 'We have specially booked seats.'

'There were plenty of seats,' said Monica authoritatively.

She had begun to smile.

'I'm afraid I'd better not join you,' Simon was floundering. 'I'd better go in search of . . .'

'Oh, so your colleagues are with you?' Monica asked.

'No, no,' he said hastily.

'Well then, you've no excuse. You must come with us.'

'It's just that I thought I'd have one last look at the inside of the palace.'

'Lovely idea,' said Monica. 'We'd love that, wouldn't we, Belinda.'

A joke was a joke, but Lady Mason was coming to pity Simon in his predicament. Obviously, he had told his girlfriend that he would 'deal with' these tiresome friends from England and rejoin her later inside. Monica, having agreed to allow the whole matter to pass, had suddenly become aggressive.

'Perhaps Simon would like to be alone,' said Belinda, trying to give her a look.

'Oh, surely not. You don't want to be alone, do you, Simon?'

'I thought I just might buy a post-card or two,' he said.

'You don't need to be alone for that.'

He laughed. That was because, for twenty years, he had always laughed at things which Monica Cunningham said. That was the way their relationship – if they had one – had been conducted. There had been a tacit agreement between them, never quite explained, that everything Monica uttered was tinged with irony. The joke, if that is what it was, had never been examined and explained. That was why he had laughed. But today he simply laughed out of nervousness.

'Monica,' said Belinda, 'don't be cruel. If Simon wants to have a little time on his own, let him.'

'Nonsense,' said Monica, 'we don't see each other nearly often enough. I'm not going to let him spend his remaining *quart d'heure* at Fontainebleau without us.'

'Quarter of an hour?' His voice rose to a shriek. 'I really must.'

'That's when our 'bus goes. In fact, by the time we have walked there, we shall be just about ready to depart. If there are any minutes to spare we can look for post-cards in the café and drink *thé au citron*.'

'I feel as if I'm being kidnapped,' said Simon, with one last despairing glance back in the direction of the palace.

'I want to hear all your news,' said Monica. 'How are the children? How's darling Richeldis?'

2

At about the moment that Simon Longworth was getting on the 'bus at Fontainebleau, his brother Bartle was waking up in the suburb of south-west London known as Putney. Bartle lived with Simon's mother-in-law, Madge Cruden. The main reason for this was that she had asked him. He had nowhere else in the world to live, being what Madge termed a 'hopeless' character.

Bartle's main trouble, actually, was not an absence of hope. The crucially important fact in his life was that, until he was about forty, he had never cleaned his teeth properly. The importance of this truth no one recognised, least of all Bartle himself. For the first twenty or thirty years of his life, his carelessness with the toothbrush had mattered very little, but, by the time he had entered his fourth decade, there was any amount of decay and filth in his mouth, and it had started to become malodorous. He was married to a rather heartless, plain woman called Vera, who had never been in love with him. 'Vera is such a nice person,' he got used to saying, until he believed it. Everyone believed it; she believed it herself. She was much too nice to judge a man by the smell of his breath. The fact that it caused her discomfort to come within five yards of her husband must be explained in loftier terms. She had begun to tell herself, with bitter regret, that her marriage was dying. Her relationship with Bartle was suffering from an irrecoverable breakdown. She would not admit that the main trouble was the halitosis. She knew that Bartle was quite a nice chap, but this came to irritate her: surely a sign that theirs had not been a proper marriage in the first place. She began to lose her temper with him and blame him for everything. Things got worse. Then she fell in love with a physics master at the Middle School where she taught piano part-time. Some five years before this story starts, Vera left Bartle. He only learnt that she had divorced him, and married Keith, from some very impersonal solicitors' letters. Since then, Bartle has not seen Vera, and she hardly plays any more part in our story.

Vera's departure had been, at first, a surprise; then, a humiliation; and cumulatively a cause of crushing sadness. Bartle tried to struggle on with his job, but it was difficult in his line of work if a wife left you, though more and more clergy-marriages were, these days, busting up. Bartle was a vicar in a suburb of North London. Gradually, the depressions got worse, and he started to drink rather too heavily. Then, one day, he developed the most violent toothache, and it occurred to him that he had not been to a dentist since he was ordained. It wasn't pure cowardice. He had just never got round to it. W. *Greenhalgh, Dental Surgeon* were words which he had often read on the brass plate next door to the vicarage, but he had never thought of becoming one of Mr. Greenhalgh's patients. It was simple agony which drove him to Mr. Greenhalgh's chair. He assumed that he would be given gas, that the offending canine would be wrenched from his gums, and that the agony would thus be averted. Not a bit of it. Things have changed since 1959. The dentist took one peep at the inside of Bartle's mouth and said he refused to treat the tooth until Bartle had undergone a course of dental hygiene. What was that? Bartle had gone down the blue-carpeted stairs to the basement, little knowing that Destiny followed him each step of the way. It was there, among her tropical fish and her esoteric equipment, that he met Stephanie Moss, the hygienist. She prodded and poked and lectured. She told him about the dangers of plaque building up on the surface of the teeth. She told him about the really astonishing amounts of filth which accumulated between the teeth. She told him what it meant when he had bleeding gums. She was good at explaining things, Stephanie. She gave him some special pills to put in his mouth. When he sucked them they turned his whole mouth bright blue, and it showed how, even after quite thorough brushing, there is still much destructive plaque on teeth and gums.

Bartle became fanatically keen on brushing his teeth. It was decreed that he should have a course of treatment with Stephanie, ten sessions in all. He longed to get his gums clear. He longed to remove all the little bits of rotten bacon from his molars, and all the stinking plaque from his canines. After three or four sessions, he realised why he longed to be a success with tooth-pick, brush and floss. It was for Stephanie's sake, that he rose up in the morning and peered in the glass at those bright blue stains. It was for Stephanie that he rushed from meal-tables to the wash-basin, floss to the ready.

Stephanie was a beautiful girl with tight curls of dark red hair. She had small white hands and delicate fingers. Her pale cheeks were lightly freckled. He knew that his feelings about her were inappropriate in a clergyman approaching the age of fifty. When he told her of his love, on the eighth of their sessions, she did not laugh at him, as he had feared she would. She had been mysterious, but she seemed pleased. By the time the course of hygiene was complete, his toothache had disappeared, his halitosis was a thing of the past, and he faced the crisis of his life.

Bartle had always tried to be a faithful parish priest, though he had never much enjoyed the work. He was awkward with people, and the failure of his marriage made it even more difficult to operate 'pastorally'. He knew that his drinking, and his nervous troubles, made him an ineffectual administrator. Paperwork and parish work never got done. He failed to raise enough money for the parish 'quota', and guilt made it impossible to answer the irate letters from his area bishop. The introduction of Stephanie Moss into this muddled situation did not make things any better. Bartle's became a crisis of faith.

He still believed in God, but he felt distant from Him. He began to wonder what he meant by saying that he loved God. Then he realised that he did not love God as much as he loved Stephanie. He tried to explain this to her over a delicious noodle dish at the Dear Friends Chinese Restaurant, which they had taken to frequenting. She had only smiled and stroked his hand. Why *should* she understand? Stephanie was Jewish, ethnically, though not a believer in anything much except human kindness and trying to be happy. A precarious faith, hers.

There was not exactly a scandal. Bartle's life was too muddled to contain anything so clear-cut as a scandal. One of his churchwardens, an admirable fellow in his way, wrote a letter to the Bishop outlining his failings as a parish priest. Bartle was surprised that there were quite so many failings, but he fully admitted them. An inability to raise the quota. Forgetting a wedding. Cutting a meeting of the parochial church council and being seen, that very evening, at a Chinese restaurant with a young woman. Drifting absent-mindedly into prayers from evensong when he was meant to be saying Mass. 'Lighten our darkness' at ten o'clock in the morning. Yes, when the Bishop had it out with him, Bartle admitted that he was useless. VAGUE VICAR TO QUIT said the local paper.

It so happened that, at the very moment all this was going on, Madge Cruden was suddenly getting older. Ageing is not a gradual process. We continue in long ageless stretches to be more or less unaffected by the passage of time. Then we suddenly swoop or cascade or splat on to the next stage. A young woman all at once finds that her hair has coarsened and that she has a double chin. By a similarly cruel alchemy, a middle-aged woman of bustling vigour and strength falls ill, and, when she emerges from the illness, she is old.

This had happened to Richeldis's mother, who was a distinguished London publisher. For many years she was a director of a small firm in Bloomsbury. She was friends with all 'her' authors, who included several famous names. She was a powerful, even formidable, personality. Like most distinguished companies, Rosen and Starmer lost money hand over fist. Madge had no interest in modern business methods. Her interest was in the books, and to hear her talk in those days you would think she had written them all herself. Her favourite authors were the ones who let themselves be mercilessly edited. 'I really taught him how to write a book, d'you see,' she would say triumphantly of some moderately successful novelist. The firm was all in all to her, and she had almost no life outside it. Her authors, her colleagues, and her friends were all one and the same. Her house in Putney, in those days, was little more than an annex of the office. Sunday luncheons turned into editorial conferences at which she harangued younger members of the staff. And then there were Madge's famous parties, when with the cigarette in one hand, and the glass of scotch in the other, she talked compulsively about the latest literary news, while agents, authors, publishers and journalists milled about and took advantage of her liberality. Madge was a woman who attracted feelings of violent antagonism and deep loyalty. But none of this paid the bills. She resisted with all her strength, but 'her' firm was eventually taken over, becoming part of a large publishing 'group'. Silas Rosen, her mild old boss, retired and went to live in Kent. She stayed on, having ceaseless rows with the new managing director put in by the parent company. 'Her' authors, those who survived, began to be driven out by younger, more commercially attractive writers whom she did *not* invite to her parties.

'I'm in publishing to produce good, readable books. Books which intelligent persons might actually want to read. This notion that you can simply import a lot of whizz-kids and give them huge advances for writing porn will be the death of literature, do you see.'

After a few years of it, she had a violent heart attack and, when they sent her home from hospital, it was obvious that she would never return to work.

Richeldis was shocked by her mother's diminution. Madge had become all the things she had never been before: vulnerable, dependent, pathetic. It transpired that the great majority of her friends were not friends at all. Once she stopped giving parties or taking authors to luncheon in restaurants, her circle dwindled. No one from her former life came to see her, once the immediate crisis of her illness was over.

She had been so uncosy, so undomestic, that everyone had associated her purely with work. Moreover she was one of those unfortunate people whom the world designates 'formidable', which gives the world an excuse to neglect them in their misfortunes.

Richeldis was in awe of her mother. There had always been something so definite, confident and clearly-drawn about her. The father had been killed in the war not long after Richeldis was born. She found it hard to imagine her mother as a married woman; references to her father were not usually personal so much as literary and anecdotal – things he'd done with Ronald Bottrall or Michael Ayrton; the night he punched Roy Campbell on the nose. That sort of thing. Hitler's war was rather the era of Anglicanism. Charles Williams (a friend of Madge) enjoyed a vogue. Christopher Fry and the Reverend Hugh Ross Williamson and John Betjeman all came to Madge's war-time parties. Mr. Eliot, as well as being a fellow-publisher, once contributed a foreword to a book by one of 'her authors'. 'Dear Tom, I'm so fond of him.' Madge had never been exactly *croyante*, but her pregnancy had coincided with the period of her most devoted churchiness. (Lilian Baylis was another friend.) There was much talk at the time of Walsingham, and the revival of the shrine there by the redoubtable Father Hope Patten. Her attitude to it was frankly sceptical, that of her friends mixed. There were stories of the late King, George V, driving over to Walsingham and staring in astonishment at the Black Madonna, the hanging lamps, the votive candles, and asking, 'Is this my church?' This delighted Madge's High Church friends whose attitude to everything blended faintly camp irony with an underlying mystic seriousness. The original Saxon shrine of Our Lady of Walsingham had been built by a lady called Richeldis, who had reconstructed the Holy House of Nazareth from direct specifications supplied by The Virgin Mary. During her pregnancy, as a sort of joke, Madge took to exclaiming 'Holy Mother of God' in an Irish accent. One day when she did so in the office a group of them began to talk about Our Lady and the Church of England. It is a strange fact that, while many RCs call their children Bernadette, very few Anglicans christen their daughters Richeldis, even though it is such a beautiful name.

'If it's a girl I shall call my child Richeldis!' asserted Madge.

'You're joking!' someone retorted.

'Certainly not.'

So Richeldis got her name. Her mother's habits of piety faded after the war, though Richeldis could remember being taken to Nashdom for the Corpus Christi procession in Rose Macaulay's notorious green car. They hardly ever went to Church. Richeldis herself was a definite non-believer. Madge couldn't stomach all the modern translations of Bible and liturgy. For all that, there was a sort of appropriateness that Madge should have ended up, if ended up she had, in the company of a parson, albeit a parson like Bartle.

He woke, as we have indicated, shortly after twenty to four that afternoon. His body seemed to need more and more sleep. The couple of hours after luncheon, when Madge had her rest, were ones which he always tried to devote to reading or to the performance of some unavoidable household task. But after only a few pages of the *Lyttelton–Hart-Davis Letters*, he had snoozed off, and the book rested reproachfully on his chest, like some trophy on an entombed effigy.

To look at, there was not much of the Crusader about Bartle Longworth: undarned nylon socks; a bit of white ankle; grey flannels which looked like school uniform (Sherlock Holmes would have noticed that stains of oil on the right calf proclaimed the absent-minded bicyclist, too lazy to wear clips); a patch of white belly peeping through the string vest; Littlewood's shirt. The tie was Brigade of Guards, but having lifted it from a parish jumble sale Bartle did not know that. Above the poorly shaven chin (batteries running low in the electric razor) there was a thin serious face not unlike that of Dante Alighieri. High cheek bones, thin lips and a receding brow. Hair still dark, though thin and unkempt.

'Bartle!' The raucous voice had entered his sleep. 'Bartle!'

'Coming!'

The versicle and response were automatic. How many dozens of times they had been exchanged. Equally automatic was his habit, when swinging the legs off his bed and feeling with uncut toenails for his shoes, of making the sign of the cross.

'I could be dead for all you care,' said the chesty voice before shunting into an appalling cough.

'Coming.'

'Where were you?'

He shuffled along the landing, the laces still untied in the brown brogues. 'Dreaming,' he confessed.

'I called and called. I thought you had gone out.'

'What about a nice cup of tea?'

'Don't I get any lunch?'

'We've had lunch.'

'Really, you are a fool.'

'Yes,' said Bartle. 'I think I am.'

'That's what I said.'

'But we have had lunch. We had shepherd's pie and frozen peas . . .'

'I don't want to hear what you ate. Where's Richeldis?'

'At home, I expect.'

'She said she'd be here.'

'No, Madge. You've made a mistake.'

'Oh, why will you never listen? I don't make mistakes. It's all this thing of saying one thing and doing another, do you see, like Mr. Bagley.'

'Brandon.'

'Bagley.'

'The chiropodist's called Brandon.'

'Bampton, then. I don't care what he's called. But he said he'd come on Tuesday, and then expected me to be ready a day early.'

'I think we got the day wrong.'

'Don't include me in your fatuities. What is the point of making arrangements if you aren't going to stick to them? And another thing. I'm running out of paper handkerchiefs. Did you hear the play?'

'I dropped off.'

'On the *radio*.' Her cross tone implied he had contradicted her. 'The whizz-kids have been allowed to take over the BBC as well. Old persons listening to a nice play in the afternoon simply don't want this ceaseless concentration on our erotic functions. Have some whisky.'

He accepted a little swig from the bottle she kept by the bed. Then he said, 'I'll go and boil a kettle.'

This did not involve much of a journey. There was a sordid little arrangement of Bartle's devising on the landing just outside Madge's room: an electric kettle on a tray, a box of teabags, a slightly cheesey carton of milk. Sometimes they had tea downstairs in the drawing room, but more often, of late, they had taken to sitting in her large bedroom, staring over the leaftops to Putney Heath and supplementing their refreshments with regular recourse to the whisky.

'We could go up the road after tea and buy the paper handkerchiefs,' he shouted through the door, as the kettle began to hiss noisily at his feet.

'Well we could but Richeldis is coming, and I honestly don't want to walk very far because my feet still aren't right, in spite of Mr. . . . No, I always remember those poor little people in the Free French that Eric was so kind to.'

Eric was the name of Madge's husband. Bartle did not exactly listen to her conversation any more. The sound passed into his ears, he was aware that it was going on, but he no more concentrated on it than he paid attention to the noise of the kettle coming to the boil.

When he brought in the tea, he said, 'I've been reading the Lyttelton Hart-Davis book. Fascinating.'

'And there's far too much about the Royal Family,' she said. 'We don't really want to hear what the Princess is wearing every day, do you see? That's her business like the time Richeldis made a complete ass of herself by getting that ridiculous hat to go to the . . . no, of course, you wouldn't remember.'

'When was that?' It was vexing that she wouldn't respond in any way to his remark about the book. In another mood she would have spoken for half an hour about how much she liked Sir Rupert Hart-Davis with whom she had sat on the committee of the London Library.

'Bourne and *Hollingsworth*,' her laugh implied that Bartle was a total idiot. 'She went off to Bourne and Hollingsworth to buy herself a hat when they all said Tatty Coram was getting married. To old Professor Whatshisname. Well, do you see, the whole notion was ridiculous. I knew that my darling Tatty Coram would never marry him. Allison. Professor Allison. But the notion that a man and a woman might be very fond of one another and not be indulging in these activities so much favoured by the whizz-kids is something which we can't, as a society, any longer absorb. And I do think this has spoilt friendship between the sexes. An awful lot of my best friends have been men, but the idea that I might have been cohabiting with dear old Jonathan Cape, do you see, or any other publisher . . .'

'Rupert Hart-Davis?' prompted Bartle.

'And I think it's very much the same with the Princess of Wales, this constant pressure to have babies, and all these very smutty implications in *Private Eye* and other periodicals that she doesn't have a fulfilled and happy sexual life. It's all very much like what Rose Macaulay used to say . . . I mean you don't need all this perpetual sex, even if you do insist on persons having one baby after another.'

She sat bolt upright in bed to deliver this opinion. She talked very rapidly, almost desperately, as though, if there were silence for one moment, chaos would come again. It did not seem to matter what the nonsense was, so long as she was talking. She was still, in appearance, very fine. An abundance of white hair wound round her head in a bun was rigidly pinned to the very top of her head. Her dark beady eyes were still gleaming behind the spectacles.

'Here's your tea. I'll put it on the bedside table.'

'*Thank* you,' the effusiveness was heartfelt. 'You are good to me.'

'I don't think I am.'

'But now it's nothing but sex, sex, sex on the . . .'

'Television.'

'Don't you ever listen to what I say?'

'Wireless.'

'Radio, then. But as I was saying I can remember those people coming to London. Eric was very fond of them, the Communist ones. We met de Gaulle on a number of occasions.'

'I shouldn't think *he* was very keen on sex,' said Bartle.

'This tea is very weak. Did you put any sugar in it?'

'Two heaped spoonsful. And stirred them.'

'Let's put a little whisky in to make it nicer.'

Bartle poured some whisky into Madge's tea and added some to his own. The combination of tea and whisky is a delicious one. Soon his whole body felt warm and comfortable. The world which half an hour before had been harsh, jarring and cruel had become benign and tolerant of him. Madge prattled on. Her monologues had a polyphonic quality, several themes being pursued at once: the Princess of Wales, current sexual *mores* with particular reference to broadcasting and publishing, General de Gaulle and the Free French.

'And do you see, although I think many of Mrs. Whitehouse's utterances deplorably philistine I do in a way think she is right . . .'

The door bell rang.

'That will be Richeldis,' said Madge.

'I'll go and see who it is.'

Another feature of Madge's general decline was that she muddled the simplest arrangements, such as her appointment with the chiropodist, and sometimes imagined that appointments had been made when they hadn't. Bartle was sure that, were Richeldis coming to tea, he would have been informed.

Opening the front door he was confronted by Richeldis and her strangely solemn little child, Marcus. The boy was only six but the stoop of his head made him seem almost elderly, a bit like a judge or a cabinet minister.

'Hallo, that man,' said Marcus. Thus he habitually addressed his uncle.

'Hallo, that boy!' he replied. 'We weren't expecting you.'

'Hallo, that man,' said Richeldis, and kissed him on the cheek. 'You look as if you'd just got out of bed.'

'Hallo, that boy! Your granny said you were coming but I didn't believe her, I'm afraid. We haven't laid a table or anything.'

'Don't worry, Bartle, really,' said Richeldis.

The three of them went upstairs, Marcus continuing in a slow throaty prattle, 'We are going to see granny, we are going to see granny, aren't we, mummy. We are going to see granny and that man, aren't we?'

Madge came out onto the landing to greet them and only the bedroom slippers detracted from her air of grandeur.

'Who is this, who is *this*, coming to *see* me!' she exclaimed in exuberant, theatrical tones, and with a beautiful smile on her face as she held out her arms to her grandson.

'We are coming to tea with you, granny.'

'I know. Bartle and I have been having a little refreshing pot of tea upstairs before our *real* tea because we are both very old.'

Richeldis kissed her mother who showed no interest in seeing her, but who hand in hand with Marcus and one stair at a time was slowly descending.

'Granny is going to have to be very careful and Marcus is going to be very kind and hold granny's hand.'

'Does that man sometimes hold granny's hand?'

'Yes, he does. He is extremely kind to granny.'

'Is that man married to you, granny?'

'No, no, he isn't.'

'My daddy is married to my mummy but my daddy does not hold my mummy's hand.'

'Marcus, that's silly,' said Richeldis, following. To shut the child up she said, 'Mother, did you hear the afternoon play – I listened on the car radio, all about this cockney girl in the war who falls in love with a French resistance leader . . .'

'I know, dear, I was trying to tell Bartle about it, but he wanted to prattle about Sir Rupert Hart-Davis and other such persons.'

Tea of a sort was reconstructed downstairs. The remains of an old ginger cake were found in a tin. Richeldis made a fresh pot of Earl Grey, and felt depressed by the mess everywhere, and by her mother's decline.

'Bartle said you weren't coming, but I said, do you see, this is absolute nonsense. It's all this business of saying one thing and doing another.'

Richeldis listened to a rehearsal of the plot of the play which she had just said she had heard, interlaced with the saga of the chiropodist, and memories of the past. Each sentence was unfinished or merged imperceptibly into a quite different topic. After only a few minutes Richeldis felt her head spinning.

'. . . which isn't to say that the reprisals taken against the collaborationists at the end of the war were not regrettable and what was the man's name?'

'Pétain.'

'My chiropodist?'

'Mr. Bampton,' said Bartle.

'Bagnall, then. What have you done with Simon?' she asked with sudden sharpness.

'He's in Paris,' said Richeldis.

'With another woman?' Madge laughed knowingly.

'Mother! Really!' In the old days, Richeldis had quarrelled with the old woman if she was rude about Simon. Now things had changed. Madge had become merely pitiable. Her words were muddled and wild. The very idea of Simon in Paris with another woman made Richeldis smile.

'What's he doing in Paris? Seeing Tatty Coram? What *are* we to do about that girl?'

'I don't think he'll have time to see Monica,' said Richeldis, 'it's a business trip.'

'There is far too much travelling in the world today. No wonder they have so much skylarking . . .'

'Hijacking.'

'Precisely, other frightful crimes of this sort. Simon doesn't *need* to go to Paris.'

'It's very important to keep alive business contacts,' Richeldis parroted what her husband often said about these trips. 'Especially in these days of a highly competitive market.'

'Such rubbish, do you see; there's hardly any business which could not be done simply by writing a letter. His French customers aren't going to buy any more sand from Simon just because they've met him.'

'The chiropodist came then, did he?' asked Richeldis tenderly as she hugged her child. Marcus struggled to be free. He was clutching a plastic pencil case in the shape of a fish, an amusing enough weapon with which to strike Bartle on the head.

3

Ruth Jolly waited for nearly an hour in Napoleon's throne room. She watched the coming and going of several guided tours and heard the weight of the chandelier variously assessed in several tongues. Her mood drifted from boredom to terror (*what* had gone wrong? Something violent?); from terror back into boredom and then to seething fury. What in hell did Simon think he was playing at? Ruth did not budge from their appointed rendezvous. That, as she perhaps hyperbolically imagined, would be fatal. There would certainly be small chance of Simon finding her in any other part of the palace or grounds if she forsook her spot by the window. Attendants had approached her and asked her to move on. Not understanding French she had shrugged and disobeyed them. She couldn't tell who she hated more – Simon or the French.

Her anger and grief were made worse by the fact that, until an hour ago, they were having such a really wonderful time. Hitherto, her liaisons with Simon, who was her boss, had been hurried and secretive. In Dunstable, all eyes would surely be upon them. Even in London, it was hardly safe. They had 'used' Simon's flat in Bayswater a couple of times, but she could tell that it made him nervous. Their longest spells together had been those trysts in the local motel.

His bold idea of taking her to Paris for a purely fictional business trip seemed at first little better than dangerous madness. But they had got away with it! The hotel, which was modern and luxurious, more wonderful than anything Ruth had seen in her life, had accepted their arrival without a murmur. Since they had to show their passports there was no point in pretending that they were married. They had simply booked a room as Miss Jolly and Mr. Longworth. *Vive la France!* With what abandon their love had been celebrated over the next forty-eight hours, and punctuated with what meals. Ruth had been to Paris a number of times before, but never had the city been to her what it ought to have been: a backdrop to Romance. Never, that was, until now.

They were there on a package holiday. Hotel and air fare were all included, and with the tickets they had been given a number of vouchers, which entitled them to free entry to the Pompidou Centre, and one free trip, either to Versailles or to Fontainebleau. She had already seen Versailles, so they had gone for novelty. The drive was a bit boring, but it was so lovely to be *out* with her lover, to be able to hold his hand and stroke him and kiss him without minding about whether anyone saw. And then, just as they had come into Napoleon's throne room, Simon had gone white as a sheet and sworn under his breath.

Apparently, he had just seen two very close friends of his wife. Ruth felt a little timorous when he told her, but also a little bit of relief. 'At last, our love, which we have had to hide for seven delicious weeks, can be out in the open.' That was the sort of feeling. She was pleased that, at last, the lies and the concealment could stop.

But this was not how Simon reacted. It was incredible. He really panicked. He said he was pretty sure that the women hadn't seen them. Well, what if they had? He'd invent some lie. Say Ruth was a member of the Swedish board of trade.

'Don't move. Don't move. I'll be back in ten minutes,' he had said. And then, like an *idiot*, he had gone running after the two women. Back in ten minutes! That had been an hour ago. The time was fast approaching when their own 'bus would be returning to Paris. With reluctant steps, Ruth made her way back to the 'bus, straining her eyes at every turn to see if, by some silly chance, Simon had decided to wait for her somewhere else. He wasn't to be seen. She felt very near to tears on the 'bus and, when it started up and she knew that she was going back to Paris without him, she did in fact start to cry.

She knew it was a mug's game, having an affair with a married man. She wasn't stupid. She did not even approve of her own actions. She had a rather strict code of conduct where 'relationships' were concerned. It was simply that, when Mr. Longworth had taken her out to that pub lunch and declared that he was in love with her, she had been bowled over! She had noticed how he fancied her, and she thought he was very handsome. She was twenty-six and liked an older man. It happened to be some months since the conclusion of her previous affair. She had not been his secretary very long – just a few weeks before the pub luncheon. He was her boss!

Now, as she sat on the 'bus and thought about it all, she felt she had been conned. She felt filthy, exploited. He had used her. He had just wanted her as his sex kitten. He had told her that she was saving his life, that he was unhappily married, that there had never been any love between himself and his wife, that they slept in separate bedrooms and his wife would hardly speak to him. And yet, at the mere sight of two friends of the wife who meant so little to him, he had been reduced to a gibbering wreck. He had just run off and abandoned her.

When she had stopped crying, she wondered whether she could face spending the night on her own in the hotel, and whether she would be able, instead, to pack her bags and fly straight back home. Everything was in ruins, the whole lovely holiday.

The hotel, though centrally situated, took a bit of finding without Simon to guide her from the bus stop. By the time she did eventually find it, after a lot of stopping, and squinting at a street map, she was not merely hot and miserable and tired; she was also frightened. She had never been alone before when abroad, and, all of a sudden, everything seemed vaguely hostile. Figures whom she passed on the pavement, who would have seemed picturesque or amusing had she been accompanied, now seemed sinister and threatening.

She pushed her way through the heavy glass doors of the hotel and asked for her key at the desk.

'M'sieur has already gone upstairs, mademoiselle.'

In the lift, she was so dazed by this fact that she could not decide on a plan of action. She had so firmly decided that he had gone away for good, that his re-emergence was simply incredible.

When she got to her bedroom it was locked, and she hammered on the door.

'*Sorry*, darling.' He was smiling as he opened it. 'Thank God you came back at once. I knew you'd be sensible.'

'Sensible.' How dare he fucking comment on whether or not she was sensible? 'Simon, I waited over an *hour* for you.'

'God, if you knew the time I've had with those women.'

'What sort of time have *I* had, Simon?' She was crying again.

'Don't take on, for Christ's sake. I told you, those two women are my wife's oldest friends.'

Simon was always made angry by women crying.

'You didn't – have to – leave me,' she whimpered.

'Oh, don't be so stupid. You know quite well that it would be a disaster if my wife found out about any of this.'

'Why? Tell me.'

'If you're too stupid to realise . . .'

'No, Simon, I'm not stupid. And I'll tell you the only reason it would be a disaster. That is, you don't love me at all. Everything you've ever said to me has been a lie. You wouldn't have just left me there, else.'

Mere puzzlement was all that showed in his brow and eyes at this display of illogic.

'Don't put that expression on with me!'

'Ruth!'

'All I hear about is your fucking wife. Why would it matter if she did find out? She's frigid, isn't she? Won't let you make love to her? That's what you said.'

'I know. I know.'

'You want to deny it now.'

'I don't.'

She went into the bathroom and slammed the door. He sat down despondently on the edge of the bed. He wished he was at home and that he had never got involved in this ludicrous episode with Ruth. He wished, in more general terms, that he could master this whole difficult business of the chick getting fond of you just as you were getting bored with her. He had devoted an enormous amount of his life to thinking about the mystery but no answer provided itself. He assumed it was some evolutionary process to guarantee the survival of the species. Perhaps Nature's idea was that sexually potent males should spread their genes as far and as widely as possible, while fertile females 'settled down' and devoted themselves to the nurture of offspring? This explanation hardly answered the problem. Why was it, that the oftener a man went to bed with a girl, the more likely he was to get bored with her, while she, in that very frequency, grew fonder of him and started getting serious? He could understand why nature felt it ought to go on doing its best with the species, but, damn it, we aren't cave men. Nature might start sending off all kinds of false clues to the oft-bedded girl that she should keep her man, settle down, all that kind of thing. But the man himself in this case had been sending plenty of messages back to Mother Nature, and to Ruth Jolly, which could hardly be mistaken. The whole entanglement with Ruth – hardly even an affair – had been sandwiched around the demands of his family and of his work. He realised now that it had been silly to try the experiment of a visit to Paris. But surely she realised that the whole thing was a bit of fun, that she was just 'a bit on the side'? Mother Nature might be too thick to get the message, but surely the human brain could absorb it – even a human brain so thickly swathed in blonde hair, face-paint and mascara.

That sounds very cynical. Actually, Simon was not a thoroughgoing cynic, just upset. With one part of himself he was on Mother Nature's side. It was natural to settle down with one mate. He was not a convinced monogamist, but it was obviously natural to get fond of your sexual partner, to want children, to pitch your tent, to settle. With Richeldis, he recognised that, through sheer good luck, he had married someone who was an ideal partner in this respect. And in allowing himself to drift so far from his own ideal he had violated something of enormous value to him, something bigger, actually, than his relationship with his wife. Sad to say, she had come to bore him, quite a lot. That was a fact which he could not escape. But what mattered much more to him was that, at some stage of his married life, he had destroyed his ability to feel. He had become like a man whose palate is so coarsened by spirits and tobacco that he can no longer taste wine. There had been too many carnal couplings with too many people, too much love-making with girls he did not love; too much consequent self-dislike. He began to fear that he was incapable of love.

He used to feel, at the inception of each new adultery, that he might be about to discover True Love. He used to tell himself romantic lies which would justify deceiving his wife. He no longer 'loved' Richeldis but he did 'love' X or Y or Z. The trouble was, his 'love' never seemed to last very long and, in some tearful scene such as the present, it would all be brought messily to an end.

He was still just romantic enough to be troubled by this fear. It pained him to think that he might have grown incapable of loving any woman with anything like the wholeheartedness with which, say, he loved his children. It was the spiritual equivalent of impotence. But just supposing that SHE did really exist. Supposing that SHE came along, the One who would understand, the one he should have married all along.

Perhaps one day SHE would materialize. But he knew with that sickeningly familiar feeling that she was not the girl – red-eyed, sniffy, trying to be dignified – who was emerging now from the bathroom. With total contempt, he noticed what a very stupid face she had.

'Sorry,' she said quietly.

Oh hell, she was now trying to be conciliatory.

'I just panicked,' she added. 'I'm being ridiculous.'

'You are rather.'

She gave him a friendly little punch and he, with automatic ease, enfolded her in his arms.

'Did they see us?' she asked, about an hour later, when they were snuggled on the pillow.

'Couldn't tell.'

'Then I don't suppose they did.'

'I'm not sure.' He sighed, a stagey histrionic sigh, to indicate that he did not want to talk about the matter.

'You're such a wonderful lover,' she said. 'You're so gentle. You know how to please me. Oh, you do.'

Stifling a yawn, he asked, 'Have you got a cigarette?'

As she stretched to the bedside cabinet, he bit her arm.

'Do they live in Dunstable, these friends of yours?' she asked. 'Extraordinary coincidence when you think about it, their both deciding to go to Fontainebleau just when we did.'

'One of them lives in London and the other – ' his cigarette was alight, and smoke shot in straight rays from his nostrils, 'the other lives in Paris.'

'Very nice. What does she do here?'

'Nothing.'

'Oh, be like that.'

'No, she really does nothing. That's what she does. You know, in the way you're a secretary and I'm a managing director. Monica does nothing. Those two this afternoon shared a flat with my wife a long time ago. They've been friends ever since.'

'You like her, don't you.' Ruth's flirtatious finger prodded him to drive home the point that he was, in one of her phrases, 'a bit of a lad'.

Any reply to this question would have been untrue as well as ungallant. He smoked silently.

'So you've known them how long – Monica and this other one?'

'Twenty years.'

'Nearly as long as I've been alive.'

'Monica was always weird. Linda got married shortly after we did – a disaster of course. But Monica – somehow one knew she wouldn't.'

'Ah!' It was as though he had said that Monica had had both legs amputated. Getting a Man, in Ruth's view, was one of life's necessities. 'Not a dyke, is she? Not that I'm being rude.'

'I can't make out. The funny thing was that, all the time they were living together in Oakmoor Road, Monica was nursing this funny crush on one of the authors she edited – Old Professor Allison. We all used to joke about it a fair bit behind her back. Then he died and left her a small fortune. Oh, about fifteen years ago. She's lived in Paris ever since.'

'Dirty old man!'

'I never knew – and I don't know to this day whether he was or he wasn't. Monica never said anything about it. But one thing is certain. Her affection for the old man was obviously reciprocated.'

'And that's when she started to do nothing?'

'She left her job in publishing and came to live in Paris. Just like that. Never seemed to regret it.'

'And never had a bloke since.'

'Let's go and get something to eat.'

They found a nice restaurant near the hotel and were bold enough to eat a cassoulet. The tantrum had died down, the girl was in good humour, and he felt fond of her again. At various points of the meal, he thought of sentences beginning, 'Ruth, you know that this can't go on,' but it was too much trouble to say them. Why not let her enjoy her last evening in Paris without any more tears? He could always tell her in the plane going home, if she had not got the message.

Hand in hand, they retraced their steps to the hotel. Somewhat blearily, they made love again. Another cigarette, and then, after some routine murmurings of affection, she fell asleep in his arms. Sleep came less easily to him. He thought of Richeldis, and of her kind, placid, sensuous face. Sometimes, when half-asleep, he imagined her on the pillow beside him, and began some sentences about one of the children that would have been quite meaningless to his present companion. He thought of the children and silently blessed them one by one. He thought of poor little Marcus and realised that he should have been at Sandilands at that moment, helping Richeldis to look after him. He thought with a wild horrified regret of all the lies he was going to tell about his 'business conference'. He thought, too, with a mixture of pity, contempt and wonder (for goodness always excited in him a sort of wonder), of the complete belief that there would be on his wife's face when he told her those lies.

And then he thought of the days of their youth, and the three girls in Oakmoor Road. Funny little Monica.

And never had a bloke since?

Ruth's vulgar enquiry haunted him. One somehow did not think of Monica in those terms, not because she was not attractive (he had always been aware that she was) but because one had absolute confidence that she would get by on her own. She did not *need* a consort.

In his mind, he rehearsed Monica's extraordinary behaviour of the day before. It was obvious that Belinda did not particularly want him to come back with them to Paris on that 'bus. Why had Monica been so insistent about it? He had known that he was being teased. But she could hardly have *known* about Ruth? Had they – the paranoid idea floated more than once through the brain – had the two women actually followed him and Ruth to Fontainebleau? Was the encounter not one of chance but of design? It had all been highly uncomfortable. Belinda, on the 'bus, had kept up a merry flow of inane talk. She had a way of expecting you to remember all her old friends. So, there had been a lot of: 'Have you see Gerard and Alex?' 'Not for fifteen years.' 'My dear, you *must* have seen them more recently than that – you mean you haven't seen Gerard's beard? You'd die.' Every now and then Monica would penetrate Belinda's relaxing mini-sagas with her own sharp enquiries. 'When did you last take your poor wife on holiday?' and – more than once – 'Simon, are you *really* travelling alone?'

He had insisted that for the whole of the next morning he had business engagements. But she had got out of him the fact that his aeroplane did not leave until three o'clock from Charles de Gaulle. This left time for an early lunch, she said. 'Oh, but – ' No buts.

It was perfectly natural that two of his wife's oldest friends should want to see him, but nonetheless he felt hemmed in, threatened. In the morning, when Ruth was awake, Simon found himself oddly tongue-tied about confessing the day's arrangements. The morning could be spent together until half past ten. Unfortunately she would have to make her own arrangements about luncheon. It would probably be safer if she made her own way to the aeroplane.

'You didn't have to say you'd have *lunch* with them,' she wailed.

'I know I didn't have to, they somehow *made* me.'

'Made you! For Christ's sake, why couldn't you just say you were busy. This is meant to be a business trip you are on. You could have had a business lunch.'

'I just didn't.'

'So I go to the airport all on my own?'

'It would save you hanging about for me.' Then, taking a deep breath and feeling that this would be a good moment to declare that their association was at an end, he began. 'Ruth, Ruth, you know by now . . .'

The telephone rang. They looked at each other in fear. Who could want them? They had ordered no food.

'Hallo,' he answered.

'A call for Mademoiselle Jolly, monsieur,' said a voice from the reception desk.

Her face asked him who it was. He replied with a shrug. They both felt a sense of panic which in that moment drew them together.

'Hallo.'

Silence.

'Hallo.'

After a short pause she put down the receiver.

'It's gone dead,' she said, afraid now. 'But who can have known I was *here*?'

'You must have told someone,' he said crossly.

'Look, Simon, I told you, I didn't tell anyone. I told my mum I was going to London for a few days.'

'Someone heard you buying the tickets.'

'How could they? I got them from a travel agent in London, like you said.'

'Well, someone must know, or they wouldn't have rung the hotel. I'll speak to the exchange.'

He sat on the edge of the bed and dialled. She was pawing his back when he got through.

'Cut it out,' he snapped. 'No, no. Hallo. It is room 207 here. Yes, that's right, Monsieur Longworth. Look here, we had a call not long ago and we both got cut off. A telephone call. I was wondering whether . . . No. Longworth. Yes.' He turned to Ruth and whispered, 'They've got some cretin on the telephone exchange.'

'Try speaking his language.'

'Hallo, encore une fois. Oui, c'est Monsieur Longworth. Shut up, Ruth.'

The girl was giggling foolishly.

'Depuis cinq minutes nous avons reçu un coup de téléphon. Oui . . . Malheureusement nous étions . . . disconnected, vous comprenez? Christ! Ici on parle anglais, n'est-ce pas . . . Oui. Nous étions interrompu, sur le téléphon. Oui. C'est ça. Et je me demande qui, um . . .'

'Qui vous avait appelé, monsieur?' prompted the cretin.

'Exactement, ça.'

'C'est impossible à dire, monsieur. Je suis désolé.'

'Etait-il un homme ou un femme?'

'Un homme ou *une* femme, monsieur.'

'Oui, oui.'

'Une jeune femme, monsieur. Je crois.'

'Thanks,' he said. As soon as he replaced the receiver he said, 'It was one of your bloody friends. So much for your being able to keep a secret.'

4

When she had recovered from what she termed her hysterics, Lady
Mason began to think they had both behaved badly. Of course it was
all 'priceless'; 'killing'. But then, as the evening wore on, she decided it
was all too heartbreaking. Monica, she rather suggested, had been the
one who had behaved worse. Monica had got 'them' – didn't she mean
'him'? – into this mess. Monica must get 'them' out of it. In short,
overcome with shame, Lady Mason said she could not face seeing
Simon for luncheon tomorrow. There might be confessions, and she
was still sticking to her view that the least they knew about his real
reasons for being in Paris, the better.

'Poor *lad*,' was her concluding judgement over the toast and coffee
next morning.

'You have a peculiar system of values.' Monica removed a cherry
stone from her mouth. 'I don't see what is poor about Simon. He has
behaved abominably.'

They had devoted about an hour and a half the previous evening to
hooting over how well they had handled the Fontainebleau episode,
before they had fallen to wondering whatever had happened to the girl
with long yellow hair. If they had been her, they both agreed, they
would have returned at once to England in a huff. Monica, however,
was not satisfied with speculation. She thought they might be able to
discover who the girl was.

Belinda was quietly appalled by the obsessive skills of her friend's
detective work. So, it was as easy as this to uncover adultery.

'Think,' said Monica, recognising that in Lady Mason's case this
was a tall order. 'Simon is a moderately busy man. He has a wife and
family and a business to run. Where would he find the time to go out
and meet girls.'

'Men will always find the time.'

'Even so, the field is limited. She's not the woman who looks after
Marcus.'

'Mrs. Turbot is about sixty. Oh, he could have found her anywhere.
You can get girls with long blonde hair just by ringing up numbers in

49

the *Evening Standard.*'

'But you don't take them on outings. No, I bet it's his secretary.'

'His new secretary is called Miss Merry. Richeldis told me all about her when we last had lunch. Said she wasn't a bit merry, moaned about not having a golf ball, whined for luncheon vouchers. Simon is said to find her an absolute pain in the neck and very inefficient.'

'Well, it still could be Merry. Worth a try.'

'He's never really had a decent secretary since Maggie left him seven years ago. Richeldis keeps a close eye on them . . .'

But Monica was already dialling a number. How foolish he had been to tell them where he was staying. There was an air of triumph in her faultless high-pitched French, an actual edge to her voice when she asked if there were *un homme d'affaires* staying in the hotel called Longworth.

'Et son assistante, une Mademoiselle Merry?'

'. . . Ah, oui, Mademoiselle Jolly, c'est ça.' She scowled at Belinda, who got everything slightly wrong. 'Oui, puis-je parler avec Mademoiselle Jolly? Merci . . .'

It was all in a good cause, but Belinda did not like to see Monica doing it. At first she wondered whether it wasn't just the instinctive dread of a diehard adulteress seeing the doughty defendant of matrimony at work. But it wasn't just that. Monica was going to work with zeal. It was not quite nice to watch. Was she, Richeldis and Belinda had often wondered together – was she not becoming just a shade crabby, spinsterish?

Not long after breakfast, Belinda took herself off to queue for another lot of pictures. Monica smiled at her friend's appearance; although still striking, she was starting to look every inch the middle-aged divorcée – the large sun-glasses hovering on top of the swept-back platinum blonde hair; the moist lamp-induced bronze; the pink lipstick which was so unbecomingly juvenile; the red dress from Harvey Nichols.

Her friend's departure gave Monica an hour and a half for revising numerals. Since Russian is an inflected language there was more to it than simply learning one, two, three, four, five. You needed different words to say *five* dogs, *of five* soldiers, *about five* windows, *with five hundred* sausages. But as she tried to master the declensions she found that the dogs and the soldiers and the sausages had a great tendency to float out of the windows. And then she found that they had all been replaced by businessmen. Of five businessmen, with three business-men, with one businessman. The Russian for businessman was *biznismyen.*

She smiled at her own folly, and went to the glass to brush her springy light brown hair. She peered at her pure white skin. No blemishes. Were her pearly teeth quite clean? They were. Were her eyes clear, her pores well sponged, her lips free of cracks, dryness, lipstick? How strange to care! Why should it matter? She was only having lunch with Simon. She peered at her face, allowing her very bright green eyes to meet those in the looking-glass. It was no source of shame that she loved her own face. She loved its good taste. She loved the very subdued colours, the infinite faintness of her very pale pink lips, the marbliness of her white Ingres cheeks, and then, in the midst of it all, those eyes! Why, though, was she bothering what she looked like? All that mattered was that her appearance was pleasing to *herself*. Surely that was all that she looked for in the glass that morning? The usual check to see that there were no smudges on her clean, unmade-up face? Of course! She laughed at herself, and tried to return to her cerebral exercises. We fought with five hundred soldiers, we were talking about five hundred soldiers, we were talking about one businessman, we were thinking about one businessman, all night long I was thinking about one businessman.

The appointed hour came soon enough. When the doorbell rang she cast a final glance at the mirror and wondered whether she did not regret the relentless twin-set, the good tweed skirt.

'Monica!' He was standing there with some freesias, too awkward to kiss her. She recognised them, as having come from the stall on the corner of the street. She fluttered about in the kitchen, filling a vase with water, while he, in the other room, exclaimed about the beauty of the garden. When planning it all with Belinda, the lines she was going to speak had been so clear. Now, he was actually here, and it all seemed so much more difficult. Anything said might be really dangerous: for poor Richeldis that is. Would it not be simpler to let him off the hook, take him out to a nice meal, talk to him in the teasing, slightly silly way that she had been talking to Simon Longworth for twenty years? Oh, it was obviously safer to say nothing. And if, when she returned after her cowardly solitary salad, Belinda heard that nothing had been said about the floozy, wouldn't she be pleased? For her own sake? For Richeldis's sake? For all their sakes?

'I thought we'd go to the Deux Magots because you liked it the last time,' she said, coming back into the room with water in the vase. 'These really are lovely, Simon. I always remember your coming to Oakmoor Road with those chrysanths for Richeldis.'

'I don't remember that.'

'The first evening you took her out. You went off to the Cypriot

Kebab House and I thought how exotic it sounded, never having eaten a kebab.'

This morning he looked exceptionally smart. The white of his collar and the dark blue of his pinstripe and the gleam of his black brogues were all impeccable. His thick hair (how grey these days) was immaculately washed and combed from his perfect forehead. But today there was an obvious vulnerability in his beauty.

'I'm afraid I don't keep drink in the flat,' said Monica. 'We could go to a bar, or straight to the restaurant.'

'I'll survive without a drink,' he said, unconvincingly.

He was peering at her, to see if she knew. Just for a moment, Monica forgot Belinda and Richeldis. She forgot being kind to Simon. She felt his look as a reproach. Either he was looking at her under the genuine misapprehension that she was stupid, or he was silently pleading with her not to mention what she had seen yesterday. She felt cross, and this emboldened her.

'I hoped Miss Jolly might lunch with us,' she said, 'but perhaps she has other arrangements.'

'I don't know what you mean.'

'Of course you do.'

He turned away from her and looked out into the garden. He wanted to be very very angry. In fact, he felt only a dart of grief. There were tears in his eyes and he did not know why. It was worse, somehow, to be confronted with his sins by Monica than by Richeldis. His wife, he vainly felt, would be able to forgive. His wife, surely, had long ago *guessed* that he was not one hundred percent loyal. But Monica was so remote from life, so detached, so nunnish, so prim, so innocent.

'I don't think there's anything to discuss, Monica. I think it would be better if . . . This sounds awfully rude, but I really *do* think you should mind your own business.'

'Let's go and have that drink,' she said with some authority.

Hang-dog, he followed.

They walked through the familiar streets, grey stone splashed with violent sunlight, and found the table they had booked, and the waiter who bowed at Monica's arrival. Without asking Simon what he wanted to drink, she commanded two large whiskies to be brought with the menu.

'They obviously know you well here.'

He was genuinely impressed.

For the duration of their walk they had been completely silent. It was in fact a surprise to her that he had bothered to come with her to the restaurant rather than cut and run. Of course, with her blackmailer's knowledge, she had the whip-hand. But what to do with it? She felt a little tainted!

'You see,' she began, 'Belinda and I now both *know*. So things can never be quite the same, can they?'

'How do you mean?'

'I assume that Richeldis doesn't know that you are in Paris with Miss Jolly.'

It was his last chance. His large watery brown eyes met her fierce green ones. He could try a bluff. He could pretend that he was here for a business conference and that Richeldis knew that he was bringing his secretary. But to do so would run the risk of Monica talking openly about Miss Jolly the next time she came to Sandilands.

'Look,' he said, sipping his whisky slowly, 'perhaps we could have a little private agreement to forget all this. We don't want people to get hurt.'

'People have been hurt.'

'How do you mean?'

'Do you realise that for the last twenty years I have regarded you and Richeldis as a sort of ideal couple? Belinda's life has fallen into a mess. Everyone else's is a mess.'

'Rather sweeping.'

'And I haven't wanted that for myself. But you and Richeldis appeared to be able to live without that sort of mess.'

'All this is sheer fantasy. I'm hardly answerable if you have been entertaining some ludicrous picture of the lives of your friends . . . Sorry, that sounds rude.'

'It does,' she said. 'Isn't it a fantasy that Richeldis shares?'

He did not answer that.

'I don't feel like eating,' she said, 'but perhaps we should.'

'Something light.'

In the event everything looked and smelt so beguiling, as it wafted past to other tables, that appetite returned. She had a delicate salmon mousse, and he ate artichoke hearts. Then they both had *civet de lièvre* with her ever-beloved *purée de pommes de terre*.

'If there were no other reason for living in Paris, I would stay here for the mashed potatoes,' she confessed. 'You choose the wine, it means little to me.'

An expensive Burgundy was ordered.

'Oh, it's childish of me, and selfish,' she said. 'I had just idealised you both. That's all.'

'It doesn't matter.'

'Of course it matters. I know it's none of my business, but does

Richeldis have love affairs, too?'

He mopped up some vinaigrette and took a great interest in his bread. She wasn't persuaded by his mumbled, 'Expect so.' This was the moment of greatest significance in the conversation. She should have challenged him. Those one and a half syllables said by a mouthful of bread were a calumny, and she should have said, 'You know perfectly well that Richeldis has always been a faithful, good and devoted wife. You have no *right* to justify your cheap little adulteries by pretending that she behaves in this sordid way. You know she doesn't. As well as being a philanderer, you are a liar and a cad. Richeldis is my oldest friend. She is, quite simply, the very best person in the world. She is also the daughter of my dear old employer: no easy thing to be. She is a devoted mother to *your* children. You know that she has never been unfaithful to you in thought, word or deed.' That was the speech she should have made. She sipped some wine, and all she said was: 'If you're unmarried it's hard to understand the way married people behave. It's none of my business.'

'You think I'm behaving very badly, don't you?'

'I did.'

'You did yesterday, but you don't now? How come?'

'Simon, it's so much to take in. I thought I *knew* you and Richeldis, better than anyone. Now I don't, and I'm going to have to go back to Oakmoor Road and start from scratch.'

'You left Oakmoor Road twenty years ago. Or perhaps you hadn't noticed.'

'It's easy for you probably. You probably feel that you know about a hundred and fifty people reasonably well. But I find people difficult as others find languages difficult. It takes me an age to learn even one. And when I discover that I have been so completely wrong . . .'

'Don't you think you're making a bit of a fuss? I can assure you that I don't do this sort of thing often. It's just the sort of selfish silly thing married men do, when they've been married twenty years.'

'You're not telling me that this is the first time you ever committed adultery . . . ?'

'You make it sound so *serious*. It's the first time I ever took a girl away, if you must know.'

'So Miss Jolly is important to you? You are in love with her?'

'Of course not.'

What right had she to ask? What reason had he to reply? What could explain the sensation of pure relief which descended on the conversation after this confession?

'Where is she now?'

'I'm afraid Ruth has gone home in a bit of a bate.'

'You mean she's left already?'

'She's at the airport. I suppose we'll sit together on the plane. I can't imagine we shall have much to talk about.'

'Poor Miss Jolly. Poor you.'

For the first time in the course of the meal Monica smiled. It was a smile of pure solicitude. She knew that Simon should not be allowed to get away with this, but by now she wanted him to! She wanted Miss Jolly out of the way.

'Simon, do you mind me asking you just one more important question?'

'Depends what it is.' He looked at her uneasily.

'Are you going to have the chocolate mousse or the apple soufflé?'

Perhaps they had had a little too much to drink, for there was truly nothing in this exchange to justify such spluttering explosions of mirth. They both had apple soufflé, with which they drank Beaumes de Venise.

'One more question, though.'

'Oh, all *right*.'

'If you're not in love with her, why did you bring Miss Jolly to Paris? Was it just because she had pretty hair and a passable body?'

'I suppose so.'

'No other reason?'

'Cripes, Mona' – suddenly, the old Oakers diction – 'Why else do you think I took my secretary to Paris?'

'I thought perhaps you did it because you were unhappy.'

'With Richeldis you mean?'

'Unhappy generally.'

'And you would say that I had no right to be unhappy. You would be correct. I am probably five times richer than the average member of the population. I have an easy job, a comfortable house, a kind wife, a nice family. What possible excuse do I have for unhappiness?'

'I didn't say any of that. I also have too much money. I have a beautiful flat, and I don't even have the burden of a large happy family. And still I'm not happy.'

'Not ever?'

'Not *happy* happy. I'm get-by happy. I never imagined I could be anything else. Somehow I always assumed that you were different. You know what sports stars say when they are successful. That they're over the moon.'

'No, I've never been over the moon,' he confessed.

Coffee came. Their glasses were refilled with the delicious Beaumes de Venise. It might, conceivably, have been possible to end the conversation there. To all appearances she was still prim and upright on the other side of the table.

'Then there's poor little Marcus,' he said. Monica shuffled in her chair. These were deep waters indeed, but she could no longer bear to restrain him. She wanted him to tell all, assuming there was an all to tell, about the twenty-year closed secret of his married life.

'It sounds terrible' – there were tears in his eyes – 'but I have always blamed Richeldis for the birth of that child.'

'Oh, but, Simon . . .'

'I never wanted it. One can't exactly wish that one's own child did not exist, of course, even a child . . .'

'He's a dear little chap.'

'That's just it, isn't it?' he said bitterly. 'You never used that tone to me about my other children. But Marcus is a dear little chap. Well, he may be a dear little chap, but he's also a bloody menace. He takes up so much *time*, Monica. If the others weren't at boarding school, I don't know what we'd do – even *with* Mrs. Turbot.'

'Richeldis couldn't help having a baby. You, presumably, had something to do with the matter?'

'Oh, I'm not being rational. She wasn't really to blame, but I blamed her. We had *had* three children. We had talked about it. I thought we agreed that we didn't want any more. She just took herself off the Pill without telling me.'

'You mean, *not* a mistake?'

'The child should never have been born. I shouldn't be telling you this, I know.'

'It doesn't matter. Tell me.'

'I have never felt the same about Richeldis since Marcus was born. I started to wonder if I had ever been in love with her.'

'You wouldn't wonder that if you had *seen* yourself at Oakers.'

'Oh, bugger Oakers. You don't know what it felt like being me, then; you don't know what it feels like being me now.'

'I know I don't.'

He put down his coffee-spoon and said to her with passionate intensity. 'Do you think I *like* myself for what I am doing at the moment? Dirty mid-week breaks with Ruth Jolly? Do you think that is what I want to do with my life?'

'I imagined it had its compensations until you were found out.'

Inevitably he laughed. But he added, 'I just hate the whole sordid *mess* of it.'

'You can't blame your wife for the fact that you chose to commit adultery.'

'Why not?' he asked furiously.

That was the end of that phase of the conversation, because she did not wish to answer his question, nor to probe any more deeply, at that juncture, into his reasons for posing it. The luncheon had changed everything for ever; not merely her vision of Richeldis, but her friendship with Simon. The whole history of the last twenty years would have to be rewritten. Within the space of the hour, he had changed her entire picture of what 'Simon and Richeldis' were like. He had shattered one of the purest images in her heart, and she found that all her anger with him, and all her disapproval, had evaporated. More disturbingly, she no longer found Richeldis in the least a sympathetic figure to contemplate. The warmth of her maternal devotion seemed monstrously self-indulgent, in the light of the suffering which, almost knowingly, it had caused. Her famous devotion to her husband and her family began to seem, in Monica's eyes, slobbering, sentimental and demanding.

There was not much time for him to get his 'plane. In fact, she rather doubted whether he would get to the airport on time. She said goodbye outside the restaurant. 'Come back to Paris, Simon. Soon. We haven't really finished this conversation, have we?'

And, before he could kiss her or make reply, she had lost herself in the thick crowds on the pavement outside Saint-Germain-des-Prés.

5

About three weeks later, Richeldis awoke in the dark grey near-dawn and heard a solitary bird twittering outside the bedroom window. She concentrated upon it, unable to identify the sound, which was in fact a starling imitating a thrush. The swallows had gone south already, but it made her happy that there was still some sort of dawn chorus. She stretched across and felt her curled-up sleeping lover, and kissed his naked shoulder before tucking it more warmly beneath the duvet. Gradually, as she fixed her attention on the bird song, she left all drowsiness behind her, and recovered full consciousness.

The early mornings were very precious to her. The rest of the family all had difficulty in waking up. It was in the precious hours before seven a.m. that Richeldis was able to luxuriate in the knowledge that she was alone, safe from the intrusions and demands of the others. She recognised that these demands were her life blood. She wanted the dependence of Marcus; she thrived on the demandingness of the man who lay beside her. The drudgery of life as a wife and mother was something which she felt well-equipped to manage. She was an efficient person, and she had enough money to pay for adequate machinery and domestic help. Marcus's screams when he lost his little trainers, or Simon's disgruntlement because he believed (always wrongly) that there were no clean shirts in the airing cupboard, were merely the boring manifestations of their need-love, which in all the caresses and soothing words, the happy meals, the delicious times together, it gave her such joy to satisfy. But even someone as happy as she needed to rouse herself in silence to get strength in solitude for the coming day.

Rising naked, she enjoyed the very cold air of the bedroom. (Simon hated warm bedrooms, and they both enjoyed the challenge of pretending that they were much too poor to have the central heating switched on before November.) There was a pink mohair jumper on the back of the sofa at the end of the bed and she slipped this one over her head. Then, for extra warmth, she put on Simon's towelling dressing gown, it reached her feet – before drifting noiselessly from the room.

It was rare if there was ever total silence at Sandilands. The gas water-heater in the utility room could nearly always be heard, ticking or revving itself up or, as Richeldis sometimes said, talking to itself. The downstairs lavatory had an automatic fan which whirred for five minutes after you had switched the light off. And for most hours of the day the kitchen would be a-murmur with machines. The gentle swish and stir of the Zanussi washing up the previous meal; or the violent, apoplectic shakings and throbbings as the Hotpoint Automatic moved into spin dry. Just for the moment, however, at this early hour, none of these sounds had started up, and all that mighty heart was lying still. It was a full household. Emma and Thomas were home from school for half-term, and of course Simon and Marcus were there. In the spare bedroom, Belinda Mason was lying with her latest. Jules. Richeldis could not help smiling to think of him, the previous evening. But now, with conscious effort, she disengaged her mind and gave herself up simply to an appreciation of the light gradually returning to the garden at Sandilands; the blue cedars, first an ink-blue smudge of darkness, gradually sharpened their black silhouettes against a watery pink sky.

Savouring the silence, she held off the moment when the electric kettle would begin to purr, and reached into the deep freeze: a hunk of lamb, an onion quiche, made the previous Friday. Some of this year's raspberries from the garden, hard, formless, unappetizing. She clonked them down on to the fitted unit and wondered if one freezer-bag full of the frosty little red bullets would be enough. Deciding it wouldn't, she got out another bag. There would be nine for lunch, a real family affair: three children and their parents; Belinda; Jules; and Bartle was bringing Madge for the meal.

The frosty cellophane bags having been got out, she felt the luncheon was 'under way'. The kettle was now switched on for the pot of tea. She thought of Bartle's sad intelligent face, so recognisably that of Simon's brother, and yet so unlike Simon in all its hesitancy and mysticism, so oblique in its humour. Poor Bartle, was the automatic phrase. In fact she almost thought Poorbartle was his name so invariably did she apply the epithet to his name. She watched the garden emerge under a red sky – the dewy lawns, the Virginia creeper scarlet on the opposite wall, the fading Michaelmas daisies and chrysanthemums, the trellises where a few late roses bravely flowered. She often wished that she could, like Bartle, put feelings into beliefs and beliefs into words. Then she could say, or sing, what she felt about such moments of mystery as the present. For she did not merely love her husband, family, garden, house. She loved Life Itself. For her, consciousness itself was the deepest mystery. Here, on the first Sunday in October, a miracle was being enacted for her – the sky, the cedars, the lawn – merely because she had two round moist lumps the size of grapes connected by tenuous sinews to the nervous system.

These infinitely fragile things, eyes, which a single blow, a punch, a knife could obliterate, brought before her the whole visual universe and all its beauty. Likewise – sound, smell, taste and touch were, for Richeldis, the causes of increasing wonder, awe and delight. Life brought with it the realisation that nothing could be taken for granted, nothing. This consciousness produced in her a profound inner thankfulness which she would have liked to be able to express. THANKS BE! She longed to cry it out, to sing it. She knew that she was so lucky. But thanks be to whom or to what, she did not know. Perhaps, had there been some little animist shrine in Dunstable or Leighton Buzzard, she would have gone there to pour thankful libations or offer sacrifices of her first fruits. The bullet-hard raspberries in their freezer-bag. Such rites would have satisfied in her the sense that she should, in thanksgiving to Great Nature, return something of Itself to Itself. Sometimes she had gone to church with Bartle in this spirit, but the religion of church made absolutely no sense to her. One reason was that Christianity insisted on a (to her) wholly artificial vision of human depravity. She knew that there were evil people in the world, but she did not believe herself to be one of them. It made no sense to be told that she had been condemned, even before she was created (St. Paul's view) or that she was guilty of the sin of Adam. It made even less sense to think that this primeval curse could only be blotted out by the shedding of Christ's innocent blood. Bartle said there was no need to think of Sin and Atonement *in this sense*, but she did not want to think of it in any sense. She did not really want to think of God, not the Christian God, anyway. She could not think of the Great Nature before whom she felt such awe being endowed with the personal characteristics of the Christian Deity. The idea of God's anger shocked her by its silliness and by its particularity. Why should individual sexual activities – Belinda upstairs with Jules, say – make God angry? It did not make Richeldis angry. Why should we suppose that God was so petty, so simply gossipy, as to mind what went on in bed? Yet there were thousands of Christians in the world who appeared to have no difficulty in worshipping a God who, while doing nothing to prevent plagues and earthquakes, was said to be made angry by two people innocently enjoying themselves in the spare bedroom.

Still staring out of the window at the garden, she remembered Bartle, on his last visit, quoting to her:

I kiss my hand
To the stars, lovely-asunder
Starlight, wafting him out of it; and
Glow, glory in thunder;
Kiss my hand to the dappled-with-damson west:
Since, tho' he is under the world's splendour and wonder,
His mystery must be instressed, stressed;
For I greet him the days I meet him, and bless when I understand.

Well, she had always loved the lines. Hopkins had been one of Madge's favourite poets. And in a way, yes, she would have gone 'as far as that'. It was the way the clergy spoke, as though they were coaxing you along with tempting little morsels of nature-worship until suddenly the mousetrap snapped over you. But Richeldis had said that if you had to have mysteries, such as the mystery of Outer Space, explained to you (which she didn't) she wanted a rather better explanation than the poet's

It dates from day
Of his going in Galilee;

Bartle, though, thought the day of his going in Galilee was absolutely central, the most important thing there was, and, even though he was hopeless at explaining things, she could tell from his screwed-up eyes and tolerant smile that it really mattered to him as much as anything. Richeldis tried to say, without being offensive or trampling on Bartle's faith, that 'it' couldn't date from anything or be tied up in one person, let alone one human being. 'Without him was not anything made that was made.' Did Bartle really believe that the Galilean had been responsible for bringing into being the sky, the weather and the trees? The idea that a man *was* God, even such a man, just did not make sense. And Bartle had said, well, no, of course he did not find it easy to hold on to the faith with his mind, but that it would not leave him alone. Wasn't she really the same? And she had agreed that these questions were fascinating to her even though she and Bartle always came to differing conclusions. And then Simon had implored them to stop 'quarrelling about religion' and said it was an embarrassing subject, as well as boring. But they weren't quarrelling. They were trying to see if any of their chaotic perceptions of the Truth overlapped, which isn't the same. And then Bartle had really been very interesting, while he helped her to wash up the roasting pan and other vessels too large for the Zanussi, about the Trinity, how it was a myth, but a truthful myth, which proclaimed that God's infinite power consisted in powerlessness, that the Creator of all, and the Lord the indwelling Spirit, were in complete union with a naked man dying on a public gallows.

While Richeldis made the tea and laid breakfast in the kitchen, and thought of these things, Simon slept. When, some minutes later, he awoke, he experienced an immediate realisation of pain, quite as vivid as if someone were goading him with a dagger or lighting a flame under his feet. The shock, however, was purely spiritual, and it differed from physical torture in being shot through with holy joy. For the first time in his life Simon Longworth thought he might know what Bartle had been going on about, all those years before, when he had blahed on about his 'vocation'. (Look at what had happened to that!) Simon had only been a teenager when Bartle, in his early twenties, had announced to the family his intention of becoming a priest. In four generations of Longworths, Bartle was the first eldest son not to go into the family business. And he had annoyed them all very considerably by his claim that he would have been much happier *not* to be a priest. Well, then, why do it? Because he sort of had to, was the answer. Because, even if it were all a disaster, he would never be happy with himself unless he took this miserable step. These were the ludicrous answers Bartle had assembled, and to the younger brother they had always sounded like the purest hogwash. Until now. Simon lay there and remembered all Bartle's 'arguments', and how hurt and angry they had made the Old Man. Now, his own feelings were remarkably similar. They had accused Bartle of hating them all, of despising the house, the firm, the family tradition. Similar accusations would be levelled against Simon. They would accuse him of wanting to smash everything up. Nothing could be further from the truth. He loved Sandilands, he loved his family; in a prosaic sort of way he still loved his wife. The whole comforting establishment had, hitherto, provided him with a reason for existence. The fact that he occasionally enjoyed himself with a girl made not a halfpenny worth of difference to his steadfast loyalty, his love of the place, his feeling for the firm, the quarries, the family, the house. He was a Longworth. He had been born at Sandilands. And, though the firm was no longer technically his, he was still 'Mr. Simon' to the older men.

And now he was assailed with a feeling that he would be willing – more than willing, compelled – to leave all this behind him. It couldn't be true! Let it just be a dream, a silly fantasy, some sort of brainstorm from which he would recover or nightmare from which he might awake. Let it be! Let it be! These were his waking thoughts. He did not want his security shattered. Although everyone supposed Simon to be a much tougher character than his brother, he had never had Bartle's courage, or desire, to cut the cord which bound him to Sandilands and Longworth & Sons. The whole of his life, he now realised, had revolved around this house, those quarries, that firm. Even his love for Richeldis had quickly developed into an expansion programme to produce more Longworths. If somebody had told him that all along he had *really* been looking out for True Love, he would have dismissed the suggestion as sentimental twaddle. But he *had* been nursing such a hope. Songs such as 'Some Enchanted Evening' always brought a lump to his throat because he thought it possible that one *might* one day meet a stranger and *know* . . . know what exactly, he had never specified. But each day when he woke up now he groaned because he realised It had happened to him. He had met the stranger. He had known the Stranger for Twenty Years, and now she was offering him True Love.

He sat up resting on his elbows and looked about the room. It had been his parents' bedroom. Perhaps he had been conceived there. Now, somewhat to his dismay, it reflected what he thought of as Richeldis's 'folksy' taste. Simon never really took any notice of other people's houses. The recovery of William Morris, of Liberty patterns, above all the rise of Laura Ashley, were not things that he had noticed as generalised social phenomena. As far as he was concerned, they represented a purely private fad of Richeldis who, as he thought, wanted to 'prettify' his mother's perfectly nice arrangements. He rather missed the quilted headboards and repro-Georgian bedside cabinets which had been there in his parents' day. Gone, too, were the bell-shaped pink lampshades, with their silk tassels; gone the semi-circular glass-topped dressing table, gone the heavy wardrobe in whose mirrored door he had watched his mother squeezing herself into whale-bone corsets and pink suspender belts. Now as he lay beneath the duvet on a brass affair bought at And So to Bed he saw only one thing in his room which recalled his childhood. It was a large water colour of St. Mark's Square in Venice, hanging, glazed and gilded, by the bedroom door. It had caught his mother's fancy on her honeymoon in 1928. It had no artistic merit, but he loved it all the more as being the last surviving object in that room which his mother would have recognised. It was ten years now since the wardrobe had been replaced with fitted cupboards. They had been put in at the same time as the additional bathroom *en suite*. The stately-home-style blinds were gathered in inappropriate festoons against the low-leaded 1920s windows. The Chesterfield was not, as it happened, Laura Ashley, but Peter Jones. The dressing table was Habitat, so were the bedside lamps – pseudo brass things. The wobbly bedside tables had been bought at something called an Antiques Fair held monthly at a hotel in Leighton Buzzard. Across the expanse of floor, where Turkey carpet had once covered the dark-stained boards, was fitted, from skirting board to skirting board, a sea of pale-blue foam-backed Axminster. Across this carpet Simon watched the advance of his son, waving a plastic fish.

'Emma says it's really early,' said Marcus gravely.

'It is rather, old boy.'

'Thomas was asleep, until I showed him my fish.' This was funny for some reason.

'Come and sit on the bed.' The father hugged his little boy guiltily, wishing that he had never, in Paris, given voice to disloyal thoughts about him. The child's innocent announcement of his morning routines, the crashing about in every bedroom in the house, brought them all vividly to mind, with their assumption that dad would always be there. He thought of his oldest boy, Daniel, in Canada. A great guy. Was he going to return to England and find his father gone?

'And I did go to Belinda's room too, and she said she was asleep, but if she was asleep she wouldn't have said so, would she?' More laughter. 'Jules was giving her a little cuddle.'

'Was he, old man?'

'Why does Jules wear ear-rings?'

'Dunno.'

'Mummy wears ear-rings.'

'Sometimes.'

'Do mainly ladies wear ear-rings and sometimes men or . . .' Uncontrollable laughter before Marcus produced his Socratic conclusion.

'What?'

'Is Jules a lady?'

'Not really.'

'Just listen!' said Richeldis, bringing the tray into the room and putting it on the dressing table. In spite of the cold of the morning she flung open the casement window. A full change pealed across the evergreens calling the faithful to Holy Communion.

*   *   *

Bartle emerged from the early service in Putney wishing that he could spend the day with Stephanie Moss. There were Sundays when she was mysterious about her movements, and he was much too jealous and too timid to be able to 'ask'. On other Sundays, often at quite short notice, she would become available, and either Bartle would traipse to West Hampstead or she would come down to Putney, usually for a walk on the Heath after lunch. This week, she had been free. She had rung and herself suggested a meeting, but it had not turned out to be possible. Bartle had already agreed to give Madge a lift to Sandilands this Sunday. Not seeing Stephanie, as well as being acutely disappointing in itself, brought with it the hateful possibility that she might take offence. Then he might not see her for weeks, months even. Once she disappeared from his life for two months and he thought he had been 'dropped'. She came back in the end. Today, well, there was no point in dreaming how today might have been spent if he didn't have to look after Madge.

It was a cold day. He had been glad of his donkey-jacket during the HC and afterwards he drank his breakfast-coffee in eager gulps.

'I thought you'd never get back from . . .' Mrs. Cruden searched for the word. She seemed contemptuously amused, rather than worried, by what she took to be his lateness. In his absence she had waddled about, dressing-gown-clad, slightly terrible with her hair hanging loose in a plait, and warmed rolls, put on water for an egg.

'Service,' he prompted.

'Aye, aye, sir. Oi do me best,' she said in a mock cockney.

'You haven't forgotten we're lunching with Richeldis?'

'Midnight mass!' The word had at last come back. The fact that it was the wrong word did not diminish her evident sense of triumph. 'No, of course I haven't forgotten, which is why I was so amused by your cutting it so fine.'

'It is now ten to nine.'

'So?'

'It takes about an hour to get to Sandilands. If we left here at eleven we would be in plenty of time.'

'Oh, if you *want* to be difficult'.

She lit a cigarette as she drank her coffee and it slightly spoilt his enjoyment of the boiled egg.

'I don't like Sandilands,' she said. 'I never have liked it. I'm *not* John Betjeman.'

It was the house where Bartle had been brought up and he had never liked it either. In fact there had been periods when he actively hated Sandilands, and his father and everything about his family, so vehemently that he thought the only way to keep himself from crime against them was to emigrate. The Bahamas he had thought of in more fervent days. Was it the pressure to conform? Or had it been the everlasting oedipal battle with the Old Man? Whatever caused it, dissension had dominated life at Sandilands as soon as Bartle emerged from puberty. At first he had not been conscious of hating all which that house embodied: the pride in the commercial achievements of Longworth & Sons; the idea which the Old Man put about that there was something virtuous in having made a lot of money out of sand, and about having done so for several generations; the pretentious boarding schools which they thought this entitled them to send their sons to; the Jaguars, the gin, the golf-clubs. No difficulty now in seeing why he reacted against it. He had thought of politics. He was naturally a man of the Left. But, looking back, he now thought there was a kind of genius, on the part of his subconscious, in having lighted upon the church. A parson as managing director of Longworth & Sons? It was unthinkable! At the first signs of grief and disappointment in the parents he had pressed yet further; or, rather, he had been led on further – he was innocent of any desire to wound them. He had a vocation! That justified everything. There were even moments when he felt he had such a strong vocation that he might have to become a monk. As it was, he had merely gone to Ely Theological College; but it was enough to end any idea of his following in the Old Man's footsteps.

At the time, he had not considered his motives. It had seemed *then* so clearly the will of God. With the gradual departure of innocence over the years, Bartle had become more, not less, wary of Sandilands. The parents had died. Simon effortlessly stepped into the Old Man's shoes, as Bartle always knew he would. The mysterious 1960s, a decade which changed everything, even money. Inflation, was it? Bartle knew nothing of such matters. It somehow became more 'feasible' – that was one of the words – for small firms to get absorbed into groups and conglomerates. Longworth & Sons became simply Longworth. He had enough pity for the Old Man to be glad that he had died before the takeover. He always suspected that Simon had diddled him in the matter, but he didn't really care. In those days £25,000 was an enormous sum of money. This was what Simon gave to Bartle as his share of the family fortune.

It all had a mysteriously corrupting effect on Vera. He did not blame her for leaving; it had not been much of a marriage. He had never felt about her as he now felt about Stephanie. He did not blame the takeover of Longworth & Sons for the breakdown of the marriage but the one thing was a direct consequence of the other. It was funny to think of now. By the strict standards of his younger self, everything was a terrible *mess*. The young ordinand who had considered becoming a monk of Mirfield would have thought it almost sinful to speak to a clergyman whose marriage had gone hay-wire. Now he *was* one. It had been miserable, sure enough. But Vera would have *had* to stick it out without the money. They had used the £25,000 to buy a house – a bolt-hole from the parish. Vera had no sooner got it furnished and ready than she announced she was going to live there with Keith – well, you couldn't blame her. So Bartle thought.

Preparing to return to Sandilands brought all these things flooding back. Curious that if it had not happened like that he would not now be living in Putney and looking after Madge. By now she was on her third cigarette of the day and was still sipping the very strong coffee. She had woken thinking about Lilian Baylis, and had started to move through her experiences of the theatre. She was in mid-flight about Sir Anton Dolin. '. . . just to see him was glorious. And so funny. There was one evening when I was taken to see *The Nutcracker* which was for me one of the most moving experiences I ever had at the ballet, and afterwards there was a party, with lovely things to eat, d'you see, and Dolin was there, and Sir Fred, oh, and Gielgud, and I went up to him and said we had never been introduced but that I had admired him since his days with Miss Baylis at the Old Vic – "Never been introduced," he said (Mrs. Cruden's imitation of Gielgud was rather good), "but, dear lady, your name is a byword." Well, of course, it turned out that he had known Eric frightfully well in the 1930s and he talked to me at great and very entertaining length about Miss Baylis, who as you know had this curious twisted mouth . . .'

Madge comically contorted her own features and did her Lilian Baylis voice – 'You get on wiv this scene, dear – acts itself, 'Amlet – I'm orf to Mass.'

On some days Madge spouted near nonsense. On other days, she relived high spots and glories of the past. Bartle rather liked the recitations of the high spots, but he knew by now that she would rehearse them without cessation until she fell asleep that night. After her bath and her laborious dressing she said again, 'One of the most moving experiences I have ever had at the ballet was . . . What was it? . . .'

'*The Nutcracker.*'

'No,' she said automatically. Then, 'That's right,' as if grateful that the gramophone had been wound up once more and made to function. 'Just to see him move was *glorious* . . .'

They had it driving through central London, and again on the motorway. Like many a repetitive tune which you can't get out of your head, Madge's monologues were not unpleasing. The second or third time round they were not even particularly boring. Bartle, at the wheel of her nasty little Fiesta, was no longer listening. He was watching the expanse of cold grey sky grow larger and larger as, off the motorway now, they drove 'home'. He was watching the earth grow flatter and browner. He was noting the familiar landmarks, the stretches of abandoned railway line, the surreal sight of overgrown railway bridges in the middle of meadows, connecting nothing with nothing. There were the ominous mounds of sand, and the quarries. And then, on the outskirts of what they whimsically called a village, plush gardens, houses called 'The Paddocks' and 'The Laurels'; dark coniferous lanes; half-timbered gables jutting out from the shrubbery; large lawns heavy with pine needles; a 'private road', neither town nor country.

'No,' said Madge, as though the late Poet Laureate were sitting with them in the Fiesta, 'no, John Betjeman, I do *not* like Sandilands.'

'It's not just us,' said Bartle gloomily, pointing a gloved finger towards the unfamiliar black Porsche scrunched up at an angle on the gravel.

*   *   *

After luncheon, Emma and Thomas helped their father to sweep up leaves in the garden. There had been several quarrels in the course of the morning, and Emma was in tears because she thought Marcus had bust her computer game. Bartle stayed indoors with the little chap, lethargically playing with his Lego, occasionally accepting Marcus's suggestions of how the garishly coloured pieces of plastic should be assembled. Madge nodded to sleep over *The Pickwick Papers*. Jules retired upstairs, exhausted by her conversation at the table, and sank into profound slumber. The washing-up was whirring in the Zanussi and tea was a good hour away. Belinda and Richeldis, with much mock-condemnation of the other lazy-bones members of the party, announced that they were game for a walk. In fact they wanted to be alone together. There was always a moment on Belinda's visits when she wanted simply to be with Richeldis.

Today was the first time the two friends had been together since Belinda's return from France. The initial shock of discovering that Simon was just like all the other men she had ever known had worn off. Belinda had absorbed it almost cheerfully into her vision of the Longworths. The visit to Sandilands, from this point of view, had been deeply reassuring. The fact that he sometimes had 'a bit on the side' (she cocknified the phrase to make it seem more acceptable) did nothing to diminish her regard for 'old Simon', as he had mysteriously become. Here he was, obviously perfectly fond of Richeldis in the way that men were fond of their wives, doing the garden, carving the Sunday joint. We should not idealise our friends and then be cross when they step down from the pedestals we have built for them. Or so she silently reflected.

But, when she was alone with Richeldis, the shock of Fontainebleau did return. Belinda always forgot how very, very fond she was of Richeldis, how much she revered her and wanted her happiness.

'A real family Sunday,' said Richeldis, sniffing the cold misty air. She wore a navy blue, rather silly woollen hat with a pair of matching gloves, and a camel-coloured Windsmoor. From beneath the blue hat peeped two arrowheads of hair, one on either side of her pink, happy face. 'I always think that poor Simon needs this one day of rest. He takes too much *on*.'

'I love coming this way,' said Belinda, feeling she knew too much about what old Simon took on. They were walking down the footpath behind the tall yew hedge at the end of the kitchen garden. At the path's end, there was a stile, and once across it they were in the large brown field, newly sown with next year's barley, known as Bunyan's Field. The visionary was said to have preached there in the seventeenth century. Whether or not he had, it was easy to imagine the crazed tinker asleep under one of these Bedfordshire hedges, dreaming of the Slough of Despond or the Delectable Mountains. The huge clay expanse undulated slightly, like a vast sea of strong cocoa. Above, larks trilled in an immense grey sky. When they got to the further edges of the field, the two women could see the town, and the chimneys of the brick works, and, in the further dingle, the excavators and diggers of the sand quarry on which Simon's fortune was founded. To their left, England stretched with infinite dullness into the East Midland flats, the landscape broken by a long row of chimneys which seemed to move as they walked along.

'It would be better in so many ways if he had cut loose from the firm at the time of the takeover.' Richeldis really never stopped talking about Simon. 'Naturally he was flattered when they asked him to stay on as joint-managing director, and he does have a sentimental interest in the family business. But it *is* a commitment on top of his work in the City. And this last couple of weeks he has even had to do his own correspondence. He says there are some letters you just can't send down to the typing pool, and ever since he got back from Paris he's been without a secretary.'

'Really? Poor man.'

'Yes. Goodbye, Ruth Jolly. Would you *believe* it, she insisted on taking her holiday just when he went away and then, blow me, when he got back she gave in her notice. He said it was good riddance to bad rubbish because she was a hopeless secretary. I often tried to get Simon on the telephone in the afternoons and just found she'd switched on an answering machine. I mean what do you *pay* secretaries for?'

'Certainly not that.'

'He thinks she spent the afternoons having her hair done. Wasn't it funny you were in Paris at the same time as Simon? Sorry you couldn't have a meal with him on his last day. You know, I think he finds poor Monica rather hard going.'

'Surely not.'

The two women were about to move into the conversation they Always Had about Monica.

'She seems perfectly happy. I don't think she wants any of the complexities of ordinary life.'

'It depends what you mean by happy,' said Richeldis. 'She can't possibly be fulfilled. It's obvious, for instance, when she comes here that she *adores* children.'

'I can't imagine a child in that flat.'

'I remember it as rather inhuman. But, Belinda, she can't go on living like that *forever*.'

'She seems to want to.'

'It gives me the creeps, rather,' said Richeldis. 'I'd hate to say so to Monica herself but I think there's something absolutely *awful* about it. Every time one sees her, she seems narrower, *weirder*. It isn't good not to see people. What does she do with herself all day, for heaven's sake?'

'There's this Russian.'

'You're not serious? A bloke?'

'No, no, she's learning Russian.'

'I thought for a moment she'd found some gloomy Slavic lover. It would rather suit Mona actually. Do you think she's a spy or something?'

'As we've often said, she's a happy nun.'

'Belinda, you don't think . . .'

The possibility that Monica might be a virgin was often glanced at by the two others, but they could never quite bring themselves to discuss it. Had she turned out to be a coprophiliac, a trans-sexual, a sadist, it could almost have been absorbed into the area of discourse. Virginity was shocking, unmentionable.

'Monica's just a perfectly contained, sensible sort of person. A bit like you, Richeldis, but *totally* different from me.'

'I just think it's sad – well, that she hadn't got a man.'

'Honestly, my dear, I'm surprised at you. Do you honestly think sex matters that much?'

'Of course I do!' Richeldis laughed. 'It's terribly important. It's good for you, like eating the right food.'

Richeldis could not understand the pained expression which passed over her friend's face. Lady Mason, for her part, *was* shocked. She had begun to tell herself that 'old Simon's' failings could be put down to a cooling off in the marital sack. This celebration of connubial affection by Richeldis could have been bluff, but that is not what it seemed like.

'You look as though I've said something frightfully improper,' Richeldis turned and said.

'No, no!' the whoop of hilarity was noticeably forced. 'I'm unshockable! I'm just surprised you attach such importance to it. I mean, most people we know aren't getting it, whether they want it or not.'

'And most people we know aren't happy.'

'You can't honestly think it would make so much difference if they just started banging around. Richeldis, it's all less simple than that.'

'Is it?'

'You *know* it is. Some people are natural celibates. Monica is one, I'm sure.'

'Well, I should start to worry the day Simon didn't want his oats,' said Richeldis, and she strode ahead where the path narrowed.

Lady Mason followed the blue woollen head, which bobbed up and down in front of her, ducking the twiggy overhanging hawthorns and briars. Every now and then it turned, and Richeldis smiled to make sure that her friend was keeping up with her. 'But I'm just lucky,' she added, 'just incredibly, incredibly lucky.'

*   *   *

Bartok on the turntable filled the drawing room at Sandilands with sounds of the purest melancholy, which suited the crushing sorrow of Sunday evening. What was it about that hour of the week? Partly, it would be the thought of the coming Monday with all its nagging demands that once more we should be serious grown-ups, the sort who have to wear suits and ties and go to offices. Simon had on his lap an auditors' report which he should have mastered since Friday. Somehow, its plastic cover and the perfection of its electronically-typed columns were rebarbative. He could not concentrate on sales figures and this fact created a sense of anxiety mingled with as-yet undirected anger. If only he had managed to seize half an hour out of the previous weekend! But the house had been so full of people and noise and activity. Instead of concentrating on profits for the previous quarter, he calculated that there had been fifty-one hours since Friday in which he could have read the documents on his lap. Was it really the case that out of these fifty-one hours he had not been able to find so much as thirty minutes to himself? As soon as he had got back from London on Friday afternoon, it had been time to drive over to Bletchley and pick up the children from the station. There had been their supper and catching up on all their news. And then, next day, Belinda and – mon dieu! – Jules had arrived. In spite of the present chill, Simon kept the drawing room window wide open, hoping to banish the pong which Jules had left behind: tipped Gitanes and some pungent Cologne which really 'got' to your sinuses. And how that bloody woman could talk. Belinda had gone on and on and *on* about Oakers and about the various acquaintances she and Richeldis still had in common from those days. Not exactly interesting. Then, the following day, Simon had to catch up with a few essential jobs in the garden. And bloody Bartle had come, bringing the Mother-in-law. Actually, in spite of her general decline, Simon rather enjoyed Madge's conversation. He preferred hearing about the Old Vic in the old days to listening to Richeldis and Belinda jabber about their nonentities. Madge seemed the only person capable of shutting them up. Emma and Thomas started giggling when the old bat repeated herself, and their father wished he had managed to have more time with them on his own. They had been so *silly*, amongst themselves, and hurtfully uncommunicative. The simplest questions about how they were getting on at school had provoked either incomprehensible laughter or churlish silence. The fact that they had hurt him by this behaviour made it worse when, at six o'clock, he had driven them to the station, *en route* for their boarding schools. As he kissed Emma and Thomas his sense of parting was disproportionate to the occasion. He might have been seeing them off to the Western Front in 1916 rather than bidding them farewell for – what? six weeks? It was this parting which created such particular gloom as he sat in the drawing room, only one lamp lit, the auditors' report on his knee, the glass of whisky and water on the table beside him, Bartok's plaintive misery filling the room. Back to school. However many years one grew away from it, nothing could diminish its horror. It was not Thomas's return to school that he was mourning. It was his own Sunday evenings brought back, all those grief-stricken moments of parting at the school gate, and hurrying back in time for chapel. Why did he feel them so intensely today? Was it because he was himself about to depart for the Western Front? Was it because he feared that, when

Emma and Thomas returned in six weeks' time, he would not be there to meet them?

His thoughts were interrupted by a violent crash upstairs. He immediately thought of Marcus. Another reason for Simon's total exhaustion was that Marcus had been awake and active for what felt like a whole week-end; shouting, laughing, banging, running up and down, interrupting conversations, piddling on the lavatory floor. He had done his best to play with the child, talk with him, allowed him to wreck his quiet hours of gardening ('Bartle and I have made a Cathedral'). He had hoped by now he was asleep. The noise of glass shattering made him leap from his chair and call up the stairs: 'What's happened?'

'All right!' called Richeldis.

What sort of answer was that? He pounded upstairs. Everything sounded far from all right. She was standing in the bedroom at the ironing-board. It was a mystery to him why she sometimes chose to do ironing in there since there was a perfectly good laundry room next to the kitchen. She was ironing one of his shirts, and the radio was on.

'Your music's loud,' she said, 'Elgar or whatever it is.'

'What on earth happened?'

Then he saw that the large water-colour of Venice bought by his parents not long after they were married had fallen off the wall and smashed its glass. There was nothing of value in the picture. Richeldis had more than once hinted that she did not much like it. For Simon, it was a link with the past which he treasured. There she stood at the ironing-board, having lifted not a finger to pick the picture up. *Thump* went the iron, hiss, rub up and down, *thump*. How noisily she did it. He felt the thumps 'going right through him', as his mother would have said.

'I thought something had happened to Marcus,' he said.

'It would be a change if you noticed.'

'What?'

'Oh, *sorry!*' she tried to smile off her tired snappy little sarcasm.

'I should like you to repeat what you have just said.'

'I didn't mean it.'

'A funny thing to say if you didn't mean it. I've done almost nothing all weekend except look after Marcus while you nattered to that silly bitch.'

'Simon, you will *not* speak of Belinda in that way.'

'Why not? It's what she is.'

'Oh, *look*,' Richeldis did not want to quarrel. 'This is silly.'

'I suppose I am meant to clear up this mess?' He waved despondently over the shattered glass, the broken frame.

'I'm in the middle of ironing. I'm trying to get one of your shirts ready for the morning.'

'If you insist on thumping so loudly it is hardly surprising if the pictures bounce off the walls.'

'Simon, *darling*.'

'You are pleased, aren't you? You never liked that picture. The Old Man gave it to mummy on their honeymoon.'

'Well, you sweep up the mess, then.'

'You smashed it, I sweep it up. I see.'

'I did *not* smash it. How can you say such a thing? Oh, blither you,' she said tearfully, throwing down the crumpled shirt. 'Here am I, worn out after a really tiring week-end, ironing one of your rotten shirts, and all you can do is be beastly.'

'I never asked you to iron my shirt. It is a job you do conspicuously badly.'

'Oh, stop it, Simon, stop it.' She was crying like a child now.

'There's a perfectly good pile of shirts in the airing cupboard, ironed properly by Mrs. Turbot. Why pay a woman to do a job and then fart about . . .'

'I'll get the dustpan and brush,' she said woodenly. She tried to walk through the door without catching his eye. He stood there despondently, his anger increased tenfold by the fact that she made him feel, and indeed behave, like a total shit. When he heard her lugging the vacuum cleaner up the stairs he went and hid himself in the lavatory. But each tinkle of glass made him wince. As well as feeling furious with himself for his outburst he also felt convinced that Richeldis was a complete incompetent. After the clink of glass into wastepaper baskets and the scraping with dustpan and brush, there was the greedy roar of the vacuum cleaner. And in the middle of that he heard the following colloquy.

'What are you doing, mummy?'

'Cleaning up some glass. A picture fell off the wall, darling. Now, go back to bed.'

'Why did the picture fall off the wall, mummy?'

'I think the cord was rather old, darling, the string which it was hanging from.'

'Why are you crying, mummy?'

'I'm not crying, darling.'

'You are.'

'Marcus, will you *go* back to *bed*.'

The sudden change of tone produced shocked wails of lamentation from the child, which her return to cooing maternal affection did little to assuage.

'Come on, little man, come *on*. Back to beddy-byes with mummy. Someone I know is very, *very* tired.'

'Waaaaaaaaaaaaaaaagh!'

'Poor old Marcus! There! But mummy's very tired too.'

'Waaaaaaaaaaaaaaaaaaaaaaaaagh!'

It was an ear-piercing, heart-rending shout, louder than anything, louder to his father's ears than gunfire or thunder. While Richeldis was settling the boy Simon slinked downstairs and helped himself to another slug of whisky. He sat in his chair absorbing it, aware neither of the passage of time, nor of any particular thoughts passing through his brain. Rather than any consecutive thoughts, he felt a whole cluster of raw, scarcely endurable sensations. He felt deep self-hatred. He was appalled at the way he had just behaved. At the same time he felt bubbling, almost murderous anger with Richeldis for having provoked this bad behaviour. He felt a generalised aching sense of sorrow which was detached from his anger. He felt a strong self-protective need to get away from the whole dreadful set-up. At some point during this concatenation of disagreeable sensations, his wife came into the room. She was wearing a simple brushed cotton nightgown tied at the lace collar with a bow. She had been rubbing her face with a wet flannel, and she had combed her hair which looked lifeless and greasy. Her appearance was a sort of reproach. To prevent himself pitying her he noted with ungoverned revulsion how much she had lost her looks. The face was puckered and blotchy. Bags under the eyes. Ineradicable lines round the mouth. If she now made any suggestion that he drank too much, he would not be answerable for his own actions. He sipped his whisky and looked at her, almost taunting her to speak.

'We're all tired. Why don't you come to bed.'

He did not reply.

She advanced, and sat on the arm of his chair. She was about to stroke his forehead when he said, 'Oh, leave me *alone*.'

'Simon, what on earth's the *matter* with you?'

Silence.

'Have I done something wrong? I've never seen you like this.'

'You have never seen me like anything,' he said carefully. 'You never looked.'

'What?'

'Do I have to spell everything out, or are you so stupid?'

She started to cry again at this mysterious remark. He felt annoying gushes of pity welling up at the sight of her tears, but he was *determined* not to be influenced by them. The alcohol gave him a sort of freedom. So, strangely, did the lateness of the hour and the darkness of the room. It was as though for a moment they were cut off from time and space in the little golden oasis surrounding the chair and the lamp. He could have spoken his mind if in truth there had been anything on his *mind*. The Great Thing, which he could have confessed, remained unmentionable.

'Please don't be horrid to me,' she whimpered.

'Don't you see, we're just prisoners of – this whole horrid situation?'

'What situation?'

'This farce.'

Richeldis did not quite know what he meant. The idea that anyone, still less Simon, could regard her marriage as a farce was not conceivable.

'Has something gone wrong?' she asked.

'Oh, come *on*,' he said roughly. 'It makes it worse keeping up this horrible pretence.'

She peered at him through her tears, quite baffled.

'I know you loved that picture, darling. We'll have it mended. I'll take it into town tomorrow.'

'You manage to spoil everything, don't you?' he said. He rose, and tried to shake her off, but she clung to him.

'Simon, Simon.'

'Don't you see that I simply want to be on my own.'

'Oh, please!'

She had sunk to the floor now and was grovelling round his ankles, crying and crying. The ridiculous exhibition sobered him up and made him feel stony, remote.

'Go to bed,' he ordered.

'And,' her words hardly came, 'will you come too . . . please . . . my darling . . .'

'What we both need is a good night's sleep,' he said, with clinical detachment.

He was not to be granted this himself. For the first half of the night he tried to settle down in the spare bedroom but the stench of Jules on the pillows made it unendurable. As quietly as he could, he padded along to one of the children's rooms and lay beneath the quilt immeasurably disturbed in spirits, and unsettled by the unfamiliarity of the mattress. It felt almost incestuous to be lying on Emma's pillow, surrounded by all her teenage clutter of unfolded clothes, cassettes, photograph albums. Whether Richeldis slept at all, Simon was not sure. Sometimes he tried to reassure himself that she was snoring. At other moments in the night he could not fail to make out that the murmuring from his bedroom was the sound of his wife moaning and sobbing into her pillows.

6

To need, *nuzhdat'sa*; to confess to, *soznavat'sa*, to doubt . . . to doubt . . . Monica Cunningham hesitated. She had forgotten the word to doubt.

That was probably enough verbs for one morning. She had already learnt, in half an hour, how to decide, how to insist, to believe in, to turn into (two words for that) to grumble and to produce an impression. This was surely a sufficiently impressive range of accomplishments, without adding the capacity to doubt. But – *somnevat'sa*, capriciously, it came to her.

Would she ever be the mistress of this extraordinary language in which, as far as she could make out, there were seventy-five different words for *go*? On some days she returned from Agafya Mikhailovna almost in tears at her own inadequacy. Perhaps she was just too old to be learning declensions. Spanish and Italian had come easily enough; the grammar was rudimentary, the vocabulary entirely predictable for someone of her education. But with every new Russian lesson she was swimming into strange waters, dark and cold. There was simply so much to remember! This was its charm as well as its challenge. It was, or demanded to be, a full-time occupation. She did little else these days except pore over grammar-books and stare out of the large French window into the little garden.

In the afternoons, she struggled through *Kapitanskaya Dochka*, ferreting through the dictionary for every other word and making vocabulary-lists in a notebook.

She laid down her grammar and as she stared at the lawn and the scrubs of earth from which all traces of life were being frozen out – silver grass, dead leaves like little scrolls of cigar paper littered hither and thither. The elegant cast-iron seat at the foot of the old plane – her fingers once more felt for the bundle of envelopes which she had been using as a marker.

Both Belinda and Richeldis were faithful correspondents but of the two Lady Mason was the more frequent and copious. Her round-bottomed words cascaded from bulging blue envelopes a good once a week, a great source of delight to Monica:

My dear, I wish you could meet Jules. Of course, it can't last, but at the moment I simply can't believe my luck. The whole thing has been most wonderfully rejuvenating apart from anything else and how one needs that at our age!! I took him to Sandilands last weekend, and since in your last you said you would be interested in how this went I am happy to tell you that it was a *triumph*. Jules was *sweet* with the children as I knew he would be – I don't think they'd ever met anyone like him!! – and Madge Cruden (who I haven't met for yonks) came over for Sunday lunch and she was obviously very taken with him. They swopped all sorts of theatrical stories and had us all in fits. The sort of conversation when I wish I kept a diary. Apparently she knows John Gielgud really well and will put in a good word for Jules when they next meet. He *does* need a break, poor lad. The work he is doing now is frankly demeaning. Altogether I wish you'd been there, though completely *entre nous* I began to see what you meant about Richeldis having become just the teeniest bit of a dullette (hilarious word Jules introduced me to!). It's sweet that she loves her children, but one doesn't want to hear about their every exam result, tooth extraction, etc. It wouldn't surprise me if Daniel doesn't stay over in Canada when his year there is up.

  Richeldis says Simon is coming over again for another business trip soon. Can this be true? Please keep me informed. I assume he will be alone, or has he found a new flame? Richeldis tells me that Ruth Merry has been sacked. Quite honestly, Monica, Richeldis was being such a dullette I began to feel very differently about poor old Simon and the whole Fontainebleau 'Experience'. I don't really blame him. I'm afraid I can't take your high moral stand much as I admire it. Probably a bit of my old feeling for Simon lingers on. (Don't worry, I'm not going to elope with him, but I think we were all a bit smitten with him in Oakers. Do you remember saying he was like Omar Sharif, standing in the Snow?) One slightly feels that old Simon needs a slightly jollier time than poor Richeldis is giving him. Must sign off – the telephone's ringing, and Jules was at an audition this morning so I'm on tenterhooks. It's only a part in panto but there's a chance, if this particular theatre likes him, that he might land a part in an Ayckbourn farce there early next year. Much much love. P.S. He got the part!! In the panto, that is. But he has only just broken it to me that the theatre is in Swindon, of all places.

It was impossible not to love Belinda. The picture of Jules which her letter gave off was, sadly, not entirely inconsistent with the less favourable verdicts of Richeldis, whose letters had a flavour all their own. An influential schoolmistress had once told Richeldis that no lady ever used the first person pronoun more than three times in the course of a letter, however long that communication might be. In consequence of this dire advice, Richeldis had developed an extraordinary epistolary style in which the word *I* never appeared at all. A funny sort of telegraphese had evolved over the years, liberally laced with clichés, and with epithets which would have sounded obsolete forty years since.

> . . . My mother as you know likes strong stories, but! Didn't myself think sex lives of actors at all suitable topic in front of children. Afraid whole visit disaster! Know it sounds v. intolerant but the sooner she drops Jules the better. Felt sure he was on drugs and v. short hair, black leather and ear-rings all just sinister. He obviously thought Sandilands fearfully yawn-making and also v. insensitively stayed up too late. Rather selfish of B. to bring him when myself had hoped it would be quiet family gathering. Thomas has mock O's before Christmas and Emma having grown so v. fast needed rest. She was v. excited that Jules had been on TV, but, my dear – CROSSROADS, a v. minor rôle at that, and one B.O. advert.
>
> This letter really to beg as special favour that you will look after Simon when he redescends on Gay Paris. He seems really vague about whether he would look you up. Never myself twig what goes on at these business things but think they work him too hard. Last time he came back exhausted. Hotel was crumby. This time he's trying old world elegance of Hotel Scandinavia where perhaps you'll leave a message if he fails to get in touch with you. Much envy him seeing Paris – and you. Come and stay with us again. Much love R.
>
> P.S. Do you remember 'horrible Edward'? You'll never guess where he's raised his ugly head – as headmaster of Daniel's old school!! Many happy memories of his trying to persuade one of us to wash his shirts!!!

These were the letters Monica had received in the previous few days. She had read and re-read them a few times. One of the many delights of her present way of life was the opportunity it presented for the nearly-vanished pleasure of letter-writing. She had been corresponding with Belinda and Richeldis ever since she had lived in France. For the first time in all that period, the letters made her uneasy. So, now, did everything. Her Russian was in chaos, her tapestry full of mistakes. She was anxious and off her food. She found it hard to be still. Her little strolls were no longer pleasing recreations. She walked because she needed the outlet of nervous movement. She strode, rather than ambled, in the Luxembourg Gardens that afternoon. Her anxiety was visible in every gesture of her trim little figure, now in its brown winter-coat.

Standing in the middle of the park, she opened her handbag. She could not resist re-reading the two much-perused post-cards she found there. One of them was of the Luxembourg, a photograph of seventy years before, a Proustian scene, of bowler-hatted men with waxed moustaches, and little Gilbertes beating hoops with sticks. On the back:

You let me off very lightly. I am truly grateful! It was very funny, but during our conversation I felt we were getting to know one another for the first time. You said, to get in touch when next in Paris. As it happens I shall be there in ten days' time. Any chance dinner Thur. 6 Nov? S.

The other card was of flowers, an interior by Vanessa Bell from some English provincial gallery. Three days' steady examination had not yielded any definite 'message' in the flowers themselves, but on the back was written:

It was such a surprise – needless to say a nice one! – to hear your voice on the other end of a telephone. And at the office, too, where normally I only have dull conversations. I promise to try Proust. Before that I hugely look forward to seeing you. Your flat at 6 Thurs. S.

'Oh, *pardon!*' she said to a jogger, who almost collided with her as she stood there. Then she put the cards back in her bag and continued on her way, the wild winds of November blowing her hair, and hurling about her, like confetti, a rain of orange leaves.

7

'That was a perfect meal,' said Simon Longworth, as they sat back over their coffee. An extremely ingenious thing resembling a Swiss Roll, composed of turbot and salmon with sauce Nantua, had been followed by a partridge, puréed carrots and endives. She had warned him off mange-tout: '*Tout le monde les mange.*' A beautifully mature camembert had been eaten with the salad, and it had been followed by *tarte aux poires*. They had drunk, hitherto, only Vichy water, and their heads were happy and clear. But with the *tarte* they allowed themselves a glass each of Beaumes de Venise, so fruity and delicate that it really did feel, as you drank it, as if you were standing in a sunshiny vineyard at harvest time.

'Isn't it funny — I felt really shy before this meal — really frightened!'

'Why?'

'Oh, fear that it would go all wrong. Fear that we'd sit staring at one another without having anything to say.'

'I didn't mean, *Why did you fear?* I mean, *Why is it funny?* We have everything to fear, you and I.'

For the first time that evening in three and a half hours, they fell silent. They had tired the sun with talking and sent him down the sky! They had talked of books, music, of Parisians and the French, of Monica's Russian lessons, and of whether Agafya Mikhailovna was a spy. For someone who had deliberately elected to have 'nothing' in her life, Monica Cunningham appeared to have a lot to say, a lot to talk about. Only of Richeldis and Belinda did they say nothing. They looked at one another throughout the meal. The waiters were particularly smiling, kindly, deferential, as though they discerned what was happening between the two. This complicity made them both pleased. They were on the edge; they both knew it. They had not yet plunged over. There was still the chance that they could enjoy this delightful meal, and part as friends. Both would know, without having to declare it, that the other was no longer *quite* safe. But, with each second that passed, the situation became less ambiguous, and each discerned in the other's face a longing to tell, to talk, to confess. The very silence which had fallen was tantamount to an admission that Things, those mysterious Things of Love, that Things had gone too far. Then, with a gulp, he heard himself plunged over the edge.

'Why do you say we have everything to fear?'

'Perhaps we are talking at cross purposes. But,' she added, 'I don't think so. We haven't been talking at cross purposes all evening. Why should we start now?'

'Because we are in love,' he said simply, and he reached out for her hand which was fiddling nervously with the candle-holder in the centre of the table.

'Why do you say that?' she asked.

'Because it's true.'

'How do you know it's true for me as well as for you?'

He surveyed her face. Normally, it was a prim, slightly alarming face on the very verge of being plain. Richeldis had once pointed out how it resembled Cassandra's sketch of Jane Austen. It had, normally, an ageless superiority, a quick-wittedness, and an intimidating sharpness. Now, those satirical green eyes were dancing with a wild and silly trustfulness, and her smile was almost heartbreakingly happy. And he knew that he looked the same; he knew that all trace of world-weariness and cynicism had been removed from his face too, and that they were looking at each other with the happy innocence of Adam and Eve in Paradise.

'Well, I don't *know*,' he said. 'In fact I was only joking. And I think you're just teasing me.'

Momentarily, a look of terrible pain passed over her face. It was not the look of a woman being teased. It was the look of someone being flayed alive. And then, when she was conscious of being teased, the radiant look returned, but she withdrew her hand.

'We were fools to have this meal,' she said, 'and *gosh*, I'm glad we did.'

'I don't think we were fools.'

'Oh, Simon, you know we are. One can't go around falling in love with the husband of one's best friend. And he shouldn't *let* me be in love with him. *Mon dieu*, we're old enough to be grandparents.'

'What's that got to do with it?'

'Simon what would Richeldis say if she saw us now? Just think, Simon, think.'

'She'd say, there's Simon having dinner with Monica. How nice for them.'

'And if she knew – what we know?'

'Then she would refuse to believe it.'

'I think I refuse to believe it,' said the oldest friend of Richeldis.

Simon sipped his wine and then, after a silence, he spoke 'Do you ever think about death?'

'Yes, I do.'

'I never have done, until the last fortnight. Since our first conversation, our first *real* conversation, after Fontainebleau, I've begun to think of what I shall have to look back upon when I come to die. Many people, looking at my life from the outside, would think that I could die tomorrow and feel my life had been some sort of success. I have four children. I have continued to make money. I live in what many people would think was a nice house. I have a devoted wife. My work isn't all boring and, besides, I don't really have to do very much these days.'

'Except attend non-existent business meetings in Paris.'

'But in fact, I have nothing to look back upon but a steadying corruption, a steadying emotional deadness. In unreasonable moods, I've blamed Richeldis and sometimes I've blamed myself. But I don't blame anyone now. I realise I have been trying to live without love, Monica.'

'Isn't having a wife and children love?'

'I'm not pretending I was never in love with Richeldis. Anyway, I thought I was in love. But if our love had been – well *real*, for want of a better word – why all the other women?' He saw her flinch but he continued, 'I must mention them, Monica. Given the circumstances of our last meeting, I can hardly avoid doing so. At first I did it because it was so easy. It gratified my vanity, I suppose. It was fun, of course. Then the discovery that so many women were available – willing – simply bowled me over. I think when I was a very young man I always assumed that there was only one thing a woman wanted – to settle down, and have a family. The discovery that there were plenty of girls who actually enjoyed . . .'

'I get the general idea without your going into details.'

'Well, what started as an exciting revelation and turned into a sort of addiction quickly became a decidedly mixed blessing. It *spoilt* everything. I'm not saying it wasn't my fault. I'm not trying to escape the blame, but blame isn't the point. Do you understand? Yes, of course you do because you understand everything: that is why I'm risking *saying* all this to you. A lot of promiscuous people justify themselves by saying, 'Oh, but it doesn't *mean* anything to me.' They made love to ten people last week but it doesn't matter because it doesn't *mean* anything. That's what became the trouble for me. It meant nothing. And, after a while, nothing *meant* anything either, not my work, not my family . . . Children grow up, however parents behave or misbehave. My grown-up life has not been dominated by my parents. Why should I suppose that my children's lives will be dominated by me? They're just waiting to shake free of me altogether. What about *my* life? I don't mean me at home or me at work, I mean *me*? Life hurtles on, I'm not talking about physical decay. It's not just a matter of getting my leg over as often as possible before the first coronary thrombosis. It's a matter of what I've allowed myself to turn into. You know that poem about a tomb . . . ?'

'What will survive of us is love?'

'Yes. Knew you'd know it. Well, I may be like a girl in a Mills and Boom Romance but I've started to feel that the whole of existence is completely *crazy* unless I am free, and able, to love. I'm no longer satisfied with a cosy centrally-heated house and the pleasantness of chaps at the golf club and the niceness of my family – I need something else.'

'And why do you think you will get it by sitting in expensive restaurants with middle-aged ladies who aren't your wife?'

'Be serious, Monica.'

'I can't help being serious.'

'Maybe you don't share my idea. I admit it sounds crazy. Love!'

He reached out for her hand, but it firmly withdrew and clasped itself round her glass.

'Let me tell you something,' she said. 'It's a little story. Long ago, there were three girls living together in a flat. And one was wild and beautiful, and the other was pretty, and the third was a plain little mouse. And the beautiful one and the pretty one went in search of young lovers, but the plain little mouse . . .'

'You were never plain, and it's ridiculous to say you were ever like a mouse . . .'

'This is a good story. Don't interrupt.'

She touched his lips for a moment with her long cool index.

'The plain Jane did not go out in search of lovers because she had a secret lover. He was an Elizabethan historian and she had first met him because it was her job to edit his books . . .'

'Do you mean that you and old Professor Allison were . . .'

'And this historian, who was much older than she, loved her very much. As for her, she wasn't sure. She had let it happen at first because she was flattered by his attentions. And then she let it continue because she was frightened of it stopping. Pity made her frightened. She knew that he really loved her, and that, if she broke it all off, he would be a broken man. So she stayed "with him", though at that stage she wouldn't live with him, and she tried to make him happy, and she had no idea what to do. And then, at that stage, the girl she had been sharing a flat with got married, and Madge, her employer, asked if there was room at Oakers for her pretty daughter, and Miss Beautiful came too, about the same time. Beautiful worked for a glossy magazine and was tremendous fun and had lots of merry love affairs, and Plain Jane did not envy her in the least. Pretty Daughter, though, was different. For one day she got herself a marvellous lover. He was rich, and handsome. He was the sort of man you could imagine having as a friend as well as the sort of man you would *pine* for. And whenever Plain Jane saw him she went weak at the knees . . .'

'You're making this up?'

'Plain Jane knew he would never look at her. Besides, she had to go on looking after Professor Allison. When Pretty Daughter married Marvellous Lover, Plain Jane pretended to be thrilled for them both, even though she thought it would break her heart . . .'

'But why didn't you *say*?'

'And, when the year in Oakers ended, I moved in with John and we lived together for four years. But I never officially moved in, if you see what I mean. I always kept a bedsit as my notional residence near the office. It never even occurred to me that he was rich. I'd seen his royalty statements often enough and they were nothing to boast about. And then he died, at the age of sixty-two, and left me everything. And there I suddenly was with lots of money, and a very great uncertainty in my mind about this business of love. You see, the more I thought about it, the more I realised that I did not just envy Richeldis in a generalised way. That is, I did not want just a nice, clever, beautiful husband a bit like hers. I actually wanted hers. But I couldn't have hers. For one thing she was my best friend. And, for another, she and her husband were blissfully, idyllically in love. They had discovered the secret of happiness. Spoiling that happiness would have been a desecration, a blasphemy: even if I had the faintest chance of attracting the NCBH. So, I decided to get right away, to come and live in Paris.'

'But not just because of me?'

'Everyone thought I'd be lonely, but I wasn't. Madge was furious with me for giving up my job, but she was another reason for my being glad to get out of London. She was so overpowering. I decided to see how life went if I remained completely alone. You can fill a day perfectly happily with reading, walks, nice food. Belinda comes and stays quite often. Colleagues from publishing sometimes take me out for a meal. But I have never felt lonely. I was happier to live in this way until I'd sorted out the love business in my mind. It isn't that I don't like sex. It is that I don't want the nightmare of being entangled with someone whom I don't genuinely love.'

'And was that what happened with old Allison?'

'Darling John. I've made him sound like a sugar daddy. We were *deeply* fond of each other. I was just too young for all that overwhelming adoration. Why did people in those days want to gobble me up? Madge did too in a different way. I couldn't ever hope to inspire such feelings in anyone else ever again . . .'

'Oh, but . . .'

'There's no need to make gallant speeches. I am speaking the straightforward historical truth. At that particular moment, when I came to Paris first, I thought there was no hope of repeating my life with John Allison. I didn't want to. I grieved for him a lot. I still do. I adored him. But I wasn't in love. I don't want to flatter you by suggesting that I spent my whole life here in Paris pining for you, Simon Longworth! Funnily enough, the danger period passed, as far as all that was concerned, a long time ago. When you make up your mind that something is completely impossible, that is what it becomes. I was confident in knowing *you* were impossible, because I knew that you were the most faithful and magnificent husband to the nicest woman in the world. And then I went to Fontainebleau.'

A waiter hovered for payment.

They both instinctively wanted to be outside. The blue-black sky above the Boulevard Saint-Michel was full of bright stars. She thrust her hands deep into the pockets of her sensible blue tweed coat (her English nanny's coat, Belinda had once called it) and Simon knew that he was not meant to take her arm. Neither of them was in the least intoxicated but they both felt in a daze as she pursued her talk.

'You see, at first, I just had the simple feeling of envy all over again, when I saw you with that girl. And then I dismissed it as absurd because I knew that you couldn't possibly want me.'

'Oh, but I do want you.'

'Simon, you say you want me, but I *can't* just be like all the others.'

'Didn't you *listen* to what I was saying to you just now?'

He did take her arm now, turning her around so that she was forced to look at him.

'I am in love with you, Monica.'

'I know, I know.'

'I am in love with you as I have never been in love with anyone else before.'

'You have been in love with me for a fortnight. I have been in love with you for twenty years. I think that entitles me to ask for a bit of time. Let us be candid. Let us be completely truthful with each other, in so far as human beings *can* tell the truth about the way they feel about one another. I could not possibly just have an affair with you. I could not see you for week-ends and odd days. It just wouldn't be possible for me. Besides, there would be no *point* in that. In almost no time at all we should settle down into some degrading and dishonest arrangement. It would be unworthy of both of us.'

'I do not want an affair either, Monica. You must understand me. I *was* trying to tell you the truth. I couldn't want anything degrading or dishonest with you. You have it in your power to give me back my innocence.'

"Ah, my dear,' she took his arm gently. 'That's a delusion. We are neither of us innocent, and nothing we ever do can restore us to a condition we never had in the first place. But, but – it's simply that . . .'

'What?'

'If you went away tonight and I never saw you again, I think I could more or less endure it. People *do* endure such things. Men have died and worms have eaten them, but not for love. I would go on with my life, and you would go on with your wife. And we'd *survive*. And we'd avoid causing so much pain. *So much pain*, my darling Simon.'

As she spoke, in her slow, sensible voice, tears had begun to trickle down her round, pretty cheeks.

'Three weeks ago we were all right, weren't we? Not so happy that we wanted to jump for joy, but happy *enough*. Weren't we? Why should a few stupid conversations and a few post-cards and one telephone call and a couple of meals make so much difference?'

'Because they do,' he said.

'No, they *don't*. We could stop now. We could *stop* this happening to us.'

'This? Do you know what *this* is?' He swung an arm upward and pointed to the sky: 'The love that moves the sun and other stars! We weren't *meant* to grub about this earth simply being all right, and making money, and eating and crapping and getting wrinkled and dying. We were meant for something else! And what I feel for you is too big to neglect . . .'

'Meant by whom? You are talking like a child. You have a wife, Simon. You have a job, you have children. However much we may be in love with each other, those are *facts*. They are things we can't escape. And, whatever else we do or feel, they will continue to be the facts. You must realise that.'

'But I've told you what I *feel*.'

'And I am trying to say what I feel. But I am less good at analysing my feelings than you are. I have fewer of them I suppose. But what I think I feel is this. If we part tonight and never see each other again, I think I could *just* bear it. But, if we became lovers, I could not answer for the strength of my feelings. And, however much pain it causes us or anyone else, I could never release you. It sounds so selfish, so demanding. But, you see, I either want you entirely, Simon, or I don't want you at all.'

They had reached the Pont Saint-Michel and she was trying to look away from him as she spoke. But her speech had awoken tears in him, tears from the very depth of his heart, and they stood on the bridge crying like children in the cold autumn air.

8

Bartle awoke in the darkness of the small hours. His throat was very dry and sweat was pouring from his brow. It felt like the onset of very severe 'flu. He felt a crushing sense of disappointment, for today he was meant to be having dinner with Stephanie at the Dear Friends. It was ten days since they met. Perhaps he could struggle to Highbury, even with 'flu? But what if she caught it?

Some hours later he woke again and, apart from feeling bitterly cold, he did not think he was ill at all. He made the sign of the cross and stood beside the bed. By this stage of the year, Bartle no longer undressed, much, to sleep. Under his pyjamas he was still wearing the high-throated long-sleeved thermal vest, long johns, nylon socks (one blue, one black) and, he noted, a tie. Must have forgotten to take his shirt off when preparing for bed the night before.

Padding along the landing to pee, he could still hear Madge snoring, a reassuring regular sound. After using the lavatory he peered at himself in the glass: an unshaven wreck, as he would have conceded to all comers, but no worse than usual. Left eye rather bloodshot, but it always was, for some reason. Tongue no more than usually coated. Glands – he felt behind the ears – not swollen in the least. The fever must have been a freak thing. He brushed his teeth, flossed between each one, brushed again, and then gargled with some mouthwash. Then he came out, switched on the electric kettle on the landing and went back to bed until it boiled. On the small transistor radio by the bed, he heard *Thought for the Day*. It was a non-conformist minister talking about an aircrash. Nothing religious in it at all. The only person Bartle liked on *Thought for the Day* was a Rabbi, who made rather good jokes. Smiling at the thought of this man, but even more at the knowledge that his evening with Stephanie was not to be cancelled, Bartle repeated to himself the collect which thanked God for bringing us to the beginning of this day – praying that we fall into no sin, neither run into any kind of danger. By the time he had finished this prayer, Bartle could hear that the kettle had boiled, and he went to make Madge's tea.

Later, shivering in pullovers and cardigans over their sardine breakfast, they discussed the day.

'I hope that you will be all right, Madge. Tonight is when I'm going to Highbury.'

'I shall be perfectly all right if I don't die of pneumonia in this freezing house. I must own that I made a great mistake having all these radiators put in. Do you see, this notion that you can get heat out of water rather than fire . . . I mean we had quite *nice* gas fires . . .'

'It is cold, isn't it?'

'And you could simply switch on your gas fire when you felt cold instead of waiting on these heating persons whom we really must *implore* to . . .'

'The engineers?'

'I know what they're called,' said Madge crossly. 'No, you go to Huyton. I'm expecting a visit from Tatty Coram and we can either stay here and open a tin or there's that really nice Italian place . . . How one needs this on a morning like this.'

She topped up her breakfast cup with whisky. Bartle did not say no when she offered him a nip.

'Who's Tatty Coram?'

From time to time, prompted by guilt or nostalgia, old friends or colleagues from Madge's publishing past descended for drinks or meals. Everything was so muddly these days in her conversation that Bartle could never remember who they were. Confusion was increased by her life-long habit of giving people nicknames. Sometimes even the nicknames themselves got distorted or forgotten. The postman who had begun life as the Noble Moor was now the Noble Whatsit.

'Yes, little Tatty Coram will take me out for supper and we'll have a lovely bottle of Valpolicella.'

They shivered their way through the morning. Against the possible advent of Tatty Coram, they took a 'bus down to the shops and bought some made dishes at a supermarket – a lasagne which looked very tempting in the picture, and quite manageable with false teeth, a fish pie and an apple tart. Since they were planning to eat more than usual in the evening they went to a pub for a snack lunch: a few packets of crisps and more whisky. Anyone seeing them out together could have taken them for man and wife. Mrs. Cruden still looked magnificent in a dark green coat trimmed with black velvet and a little fur hat. She looked much sprucer than Bartle whose sandals, donkey jacket and dandruffy polo-neck gave off a decidedly collapsed air. In the corner of the pub, with the music of WHAM! blaring from the juke box, they shared a single helping of scampi in the basket.

'Most delicious. You see, Tatty Coram was one of the last to go before the arrival of the whizz-kids.'

'Oh yes,' said Bartle.

During the afternoon, back in Rockingham Crescent, they slept off the lunchtime whisky, and when he woke Bartle was once more suffering from a terrible, sweaty, fever. In fact, during his brief doze, he had sweated so much that he needed a bath – always rather an event in his calendar. Having swilled about in the tub, he scrummaged in the airing cupboard for a clean shirt. There wasn't one, but when he returned to his bedroom he found a striped thing which, with shaking out, was *wearable*.

'I think I'm starting 'flu,' said Madge, as they had their tea. 'It's the Putney drip, constant catarrh and cold sweats. Everyone was sweating like a pig in that pub at lunch. The rank sweat of an enseamed bed. Do you see, it's like what that frightfully amusing clergyman was saying about air travel this morning. I thought he was fundamentally right. In the old days people hardly strayed from their own village and this is still common in Russia. I know people criticised Eric for being a communist, but he always used to say that it was very sensible of Stalin to forbid people to travel within the Soviet Union. It only spreads these frightful diseases, travelling about. Look at Christopher Columbus.'

'It was hot, certainly,' said Bartle. 'And I never rang the heating engineer. I'll do it after tea.' But he forgot. He got into a sort of dreamy haze as soon as he had taken the tray downstairs. He began to wonder whether Madge was all right to be left on her own. But – she was right. We *did* all travel too much. Travelling to Highbury he read a Ruth Rendell, which was so exciting that he overshot his station and arrived at the Dear Friends a quarter of an hour late.

Conversation between Bartle and Stephanie was never exactly about anything. It was not Boswell and Dr. Johnson. It was low-key, good-humoured, restfully uninteresting without being (to Bartle) in the least boring. They ordered, and consumed Deep Fried Wan Ton, Sizzling Beef with Special Fried Rice and a side-bowl of Noodles Cantonese Style, followed by toffee bananas. They drank weak tea throughout the meal. Stephanie was not much of a drinker and, when he was with her, Bartle felt no need to swig spirits.

She looked, was, kindness itself, her placid white face fringed with tight red curls. While they ate, she sometimes allowed Bartle to hold her hand while she recited what had been happening since their last encounter. By happening, Stephanie meant happening at work or in the family. She never spilt any beans about her 'private life'. This reticence about her other evenings caused Bartle agonies of tormented jealousy, but there was nothing he could do about it. He did not dare to pry. He did not dare to say, 'Where were you this time yesterday evening?' for fear that the answer might be, 'I was with my lover.' He knew that there must *be* a lover; perhaps several. But he preferred not to torture himself with the specific knowledge of who they were or when they saw Stephanie. Better the meetings they had than no meetings at all. Better Dear Friends than Severed Lovers.

'That's enough about me,' she said. In fact she had said nothing about her. It had all been colleagues at work and where they had been, or were going, for their holiday. A girl called Sandra had been to Lanzarote and came back as brown as anything. But who cared about Sandra?

'How about you?' Stephanie asked.

'The usual. Madge has some good days – then she seems in a muddle about everything.'

'Shame.'

'We went out to lunch with my brother's family the Sunday before last.'

'That must have been nice.'

'I don't know that it was.'

She laughed: 'You are a funny one.'

'What was funny about that?'

'Oh, *nothing*.' She often said that.

'The terrible truth is that I don't like my brother.'

'Bar-tle!'

'Just jealousy, I expect. He's good at all the things I'm bad at. I suppose he despises me quite a lot.'

'Bartle! Never!'

'It's quite a relief to admit it to myself, actually. For years I was very awkward in my brother's company. It's easier now.'

'Is he like you?'

'Not in the least.'

They were silent for a moment, lost to the absolute deliciousness of the sizzling beef. It was so good that, even though they had eaten quite a lot already, both of them quite slavered at the chops as each mouthful approached them.

'Perhaps I'm just lucky,' she said. 'I don't dislike anyone.'

'You're blessed with a nicer disposition than mine,' said Bartle.

'I think you're nice.'

'You know what I mean.'

'I don't.'

'Some people find it easy to be good. Richeldis does – my brother's wife, Madge's daughter.'

'Do you fancy her?'

Stephanie often had a bit of a giggle over the question of Bartle's amorous propensities. She obviously thought it would flatter him to pretend that he was in love with all the girls. He had told her several times that she was the only girl he loved, but she did not seem to take this seriously.

'Fancy Richeldis? She's my sister-in-law.'

'You could still fancy her. It would turn some men on.'

'She's quite pretty, I suppose.'

'You're blushing,' she exclaimed.

'I'm not.'

'Honestly, Bartle, you are.'

Stephanie was giggling uncontrollably. The laughter hurt, even though he knew she wasn't exactly laughing *at* him.

'I was going to say that Richeldis is a naturally nice person whereas her mother, say, is not.'

'Poor old *soul*. She can't help . . .'

'I wasn't saying anything nasty about her, Stephanie. I just recognise Madge as someone much more like myself, someone who finds it hard to be good. It is probably a matter of the physical metabolism as much as anything else. And,' he smirked with schoolboy weakness, 'sexual frustration probably comes into it.'

'I think you and your brother are probably *both* very nice,' she said briskly, directing the subject away from herself. 'People in families aren't always compatible. Take my gran; and then Aunty Ray tries to shut her up and Uncle Lenny . . .'

There was not even a main verb in this utterance, still less a 'point', but mention of Uncle Lenny's name was always a cue for laughter. Stephanie had lost both her parents in a car crash in early infancy and she had been brought up by her uncle, a Leonard Bernstein, who drove a taxi.

'Anyway,' she said, as they scraped the little wooden serving dish clean and ate the last grains of rice with the sizzling beef sauce, 'what's Madge doing this evening, then? Richeldis with her?'

'No, she's having dinner with some old publisher, Tatty Coram she calls her.' He wondered whether to explain about Madge's erratic use of nicknames, or whether to explain that Tatty Coram was a character in Dickens. It was possible that Stephanie had not read, or heard of, Dickens.

'Weird name.'

He smiled back. 'There's an Italian restaurant nearish,' he said, as if this was an explanation.

'Don't much fancy Italian food,' said Stephanie, 'not the way I like Chinese, anyway.'

'You've taught me to like Chinese,' he said, aware that his face had assumed its Adoring look.

'Too many tomatoes, know what I mean. Aren't these toffee bananas super?'

'I shouldn't think they'd do our teeth much good,' said Bartle, with impish daring.

'Won't do you any harm if you brush them when you get home,' she said with sudden seriousness as she popped one of the delectably sticky little brown spheres into crimson-stained wet-look lips.

On the way home, he was disturbed by her inquiries. Did he actually 'fancy' Richeldis? He thought with a new tenderness of these so-called religious arguments which he had so much enjoyed over the years with his sister-in-law. He thought of her round serious eyes, while she confessed to doubts about religion which he had often entertained himself. But in conversation with her he always took the line of simple orthodoxy. Why? Could it be that he wished to beat down her vague, woolly, 'female' arguments with his hard, male 'reason'? The schoolboy thought (of the sexual thing) produced a bold smile on Bartle's ravaged features. Fellow passengers on the District Line that evening saw only a silly ass grin. It looked like a smile produced by one half pint too many of ginger-beer shandy. Inside, it felt like a smile of triumphant lust. It was clear to him now why Simon was always so off-hand. He feared that Bartle was deeply attractive to Richeldis. In his reverie, part D. H. Lawrence, part Book of Genesis, they were all young again, and Richeldis had better teeth and longer hair.

When he got back, having walked from East Putney station, Madge was still sitting up, smoking cigarettes. Her chuckle when he appeared in the sitting room immediately alerted him to the fact that she was 'high'.

'Here comes Mr. Dick!' she cried. This was a new one. 'You've missed Tatty Coram, but we've had an absolutely glorious . . . Have a little night cap with me, dear *boy*. No, she took me to the . . .'

'The Venezia?'

'No, the Italian place.'

'The Venezia is Italian.'

'That's right. I need some more, too,' she waved an empty glass at him stagily. He gave her a refill and himself a generous slug of Claymore. 'We talked about everything under the . . .'

'Sun.'

'Don't interrupt, dear boy. And she entirely agrees with me about these regrettable whizz kids on the dear old Rosen list, even if they do win the Booker Prize and other things of this sort, and she told me about . . . oh, where she lives?'

'Paris?'

'No.'

'You said Paris before.'

'That was Eric and de Gaulle, and the other thing, do you see, is the boiler. You remember the day I told you about Mr. Bardell?'

'The chiropodist.'

'Yup.' Her bossy nod while she lit up another Peter Stuyvesant suggested that with patient training Bartle might, once and again, get things right. 'Chiropodist, General de Gaulle, where were we? Yes, not Bardell, that's a character in . . .'

'*Pickwick Papers.*'

'*Martin Chuzzlewit.* Bodkins. Well *you* said,' again the contemptuous laugh, 'that we needed to get the . . . oh, for the *boiler.* You know.'

'An engineer?'

'That's what I said, isn't it?'

'I believe one ought to get these central heating boilers serviced every now and then.'

'Well, it isn't the boilers at all, do you see, it's the . . .'

'Radiators?'

'No. Thermostat.' It was as though she knew this sudden accuracy was surprising. She looked at him darkly as if to say, 'You didn't expect me to remember that word, did you?' She continued, 'Thermostat. Completely wrong. Now Tatty Coram, who is an absolute genius, said, "Bit cold in here, isn't it, Madge?" "Cold?" I said – "it's absolutely *arctic*," which she thought frightfully amusing. But then she went and looked at the thing in the hall . . .'

'The thermostat?'

'Exactly, and she said, "No wonder you're so cold." "Why is that?" I said. "Your heating is timed to come on for a few hours during the night and an hour after lunch, otherwise it's off for the rest of the time . . . I suppose someone had been fiddling with it." '

Bartle thought there were few more boring subjects than central heating. While they drank their refills of Claymore he remembered an evening when Richeldis had been unable to stop talking about the central heating at Sandilands. He felt penitent about his lustful day-dream, so disloyal by silent implication to Stephanie. When he had helped Madge upstairs and clambered into his own little truckle at one a.m., it was of Stephanie that he dreamt.

9

She waited in the library of the University Women's Club, trying to absorb herself in last week's *Times Literary Supplement* and casting envious glances at an old woman in the corner, chuckling over *Private Eye*. The old woman — white hair, horn-rimmed specs — had a leathery ageless quality. She could have been any age between seventy and a hundred and ten. Monica guessed she was the retired fellow of some Oxford college: older, certainly, than poor Madge, but in a hundred ways more alert and alive. What had *happened* to Richeldis's mother? Monica had not seen Madge for six months. The last time they had had dinner together in this very club and the old girl had been her usual self; loud, bossy, self-assertive when the drink had flown, a little high, but completely in control. They had deplored, as usual, the present condition of British publishing, they had rehearsed some old gossip and — as always — Madge had poured forth a stream of fascinating books she had been enjoying — Anthony Hecht, Bulgakov, a new biography of Ivy Compton-Burnett, the *Mémoires*, again, of Saint-Simon. But last night! Monica felt her head spinning from it. There was no subject which they managed to hold on to for more than a few sentences. The jumble of nonsense was exhausting: Dickens, de Gaulle, sexual ethics. At least she had managed to put the timing switch right on the central heating. Perhaps she should have stayed to tidy the place up. She was so appalled by the squalor that she had left early.

Why had she gone? She always did call on Madge when in London, but there had been something special about this visit. She had asked Madge not to *say* that she had been, but in her present condition it was hard to know what the old girl took in. Discretion had never been her strong point. But Monica deeply wanted to see them all in their English setting: Madge, Belinda . . . and, if she was brave enough, Simon — to see how it affected her judgement of the situation.

Since she parted from Simon on the Pont Saint-Michel she had been completely certain that it was her destiny to throw in her lot with him, to live with him and be his love, whatever anyone else thought or said or did. But she had held back. There had been some telephone calls (one of them lasting two hours). And there was no doubt that they were both in love. But this was not going to be an affair. Apart from the fact that they were both too serious for anything of the kind, they were both too old. There wasn't time. She desperately wanted – though they had not discussed this yet – his child. All these thoughts, desires and possibilities had suddenly flooded into her life, like sunshine bursting into a dusty lumber-room locked for nearly a quarter of a century. She blinked at the light and did not know quite what to do. But one thing she could do was to see them. She had half-envisaged actually discussing the matter with Madge, who would not necessarily have taken Richeldis's 'part' just because she was her mother. In the old days, Madge never tired of saying how *idiotic* the king had been to marry Mrs. Simpson, how crazy such and such a girl had been to marry this publishing colleague. Doubtless marriage was a very mad step, Madge's included. But, even if she had not confessed the situation to Madge, Monica wanted to be with her, and imagine her receiving the news. How would she *take* it? The question was prompted by one deeper one. Given that she was in love with Simon, could Monica bring herself to inflict the pain on her friends which was the inevitable consequence of that love?

Judged by this strict questioning, last night had been difficult. Madge might mind *terribly* if poor Richeldis was betrayed by little Tatty Coram. On the other hand, the old girl was so capricious that it was equally probable to imagine her saying – 'I must own, I never thought Richeldis should have married Simon Longworth in the first place . . .'

Who could guess whether her love for Simon would break hearts in Putney or elsewhere? It wasn't even as rational as that, her slightly sly desire to see them all before the news broke. It was to satisfy a need within herself. It was a little like pinching herself to make sure she was awake. In Paris, she knew no one, and the only thing which was real was what was happening inside her own head. Perhaps that *was* all that was happening? She did not know any more.

Lady Mason was no great expert on morality, but she would be more difficult to face. She would have to be told, and Monica had written a difficult letter asking for her presence at the club. When she did arrive, still, in November, wearing sunglasses and tinkling with bangles and necklaces, Belinda exclaimed, 'My dear, this is too exciting, I can't wait to know what's up. It's like something in a spy film.'

Monica cast an apologetic glance across the library towards the crone with *Private Eye*, but she had gone, taking the magazine with her. Belinda and Monica were left alone in that brown comfortable room. Belinda always maintained that it was 'the end' that Monica belonged to this institution. But she looked perfectly at home there. Her sensible shoes, her skin-coloured tights, her kilt and crimson cardie did less to shock the room's understated spinsterish tones than Lady Mason's splash of geranium-coloured boiler suit. Likewise, Miss Cunningham's clean well-cut hair and unmade-up features were more in keeping with the club's general ambience than Belinda's newly streaked and highlighted platinum blonde.

'Can we get a drink in this place?'

'You mean alcohol? I know you think it's weird but, if one is no longer English, it is nice to have a club – somewhere to stay in London which is a shade less impersonal and half the price of an hotel.'

'I'll have a vodka and tonic if you're having one.'

A maid in a black dress and starched apron, looking as though she had stepped from a farce by Ben Travers, received this order. Monica asked for a little dry sherry to keep Belinda company.

'I spent the morning looking at Bond Street galleries,' she said. 'In one, there was a charming little Vuillard which I could almost afford. It is years since I was tempted to buy anything. But I haven't broken my rule.'

'All that nonsense about not having anything which you couldn't slip into a suitcase.'

'The Vuillard could be slipped into a suitcase.'

'What about your curtains?'

'I'd leave them behind if ever I sold the flat.'

'Darling, you didn't come over to London in order to discuss your curtains.'

'Not exactly. I'm not sure I'm up to discussing anything.' She was silent a space. Then she added, 'Don't press me, Linda, dear. I might tell you, and I might not quite have the courage.'

'You're going to get married.'

'Not exactly.'

'Oh, this is exciting.' She gleamed toothily and the ice-lumps clonked about in her glass as she slurped her vod.

'A bit too exciting, in a way. You know me. I'm not used to this sort of thing. I just don't reckon on it happening to me.'

'But I *was* right. Someone in your life?'

'Your tone implies "at last". I assure you that I was adequately happy for fifteen years without – this.'

'There are complications? Yes?'

'That's where you come in.'

'Darling,' said Lady Mason with sudden earnestness, leaning

forward and touching Miss Cunningham's wrist. 'It isn't Jules? I'm sorry, but I just couldn't bear it . . .'

'Jules? Who is Jules?'

'I wrote to you about him.'

'I'm sorry. I've been so . . .'

'Phew-eroo. You know for the most awful moment I thought the only possible explanation for your wanting to see me in this strangely formal way was that you wanted to tell me you'd stolen Jules. And I'm sorry, Monica' – mock gravity overtook her voice – 'but it would have been a serious no-speaks situation. One thing a girl does *not* do is pinch her best friend's man.'

'Oh.'

After a very long silence Belinda said, 'Well? What's the problem?'

'I have.'

It was awful at such a serious moment, in a way such a tragic moment, but a smile of triumph crept irresistibly to Monica's lips as she spoke.

'But you just said you hadn't.'

'I've never met Jules, Linda. It's not Jules that we are talking about.'

'Well, who then?'

More silence. Then Monica said, 'It's silly, but I can't say his name. I just cannot say his name to you. Oh Lord, Linda, I'm sorry.'

It looked horribly as if the demure Miss Cunningham was on the verge of tears.

'You're having an affair with a guy, right?'

'No! It isn't *like* that!'

'Not with a woman!'

'No!'

In spite of themselves they giggled.

'Oh, Belinda, I'm sorry.'

She rose. At first Belinda thought that Monica was going to walk out of the room and leave her sitting with the remains of the mingiest glass of vodka ever offered to a fellow human-being. Then she thought Monica was simply crying, as she stood by the window. She walked about the room, however, and stood a long way behind Belinda, and, when they could no longer look at each other, she was able to speak.

'You probably think I've been the most awful cold fish all these years. Your life has gone on its excited course and I haven't really had a life.'

'My dear, you've been a *tower* of strength whenever I get into one of my awful scrapes – though, for once, this time I really think I've landed on my feet. Jules is so *sweet* and I'm simply longing for you to meet him. I'm only sorry he's down in wretched Swindon of all places for this panto – such fun!'

'It's not that I have not wanted to love,' continued her friend, 'it is that I'm slow. I can't get over it so bravely as you seem to. There was something years ago – never mind about that now – and then there has been this.'

'This guy we are talking about.'

'Yes. I think I always was in love with him. But it has become suddenly different, because he's . . .'

'Oh – my – God!' exclaimed Lady Mason. 'You're talking about Simon, aren't you?'

Monica's voice continued in its same calm tone. 'He's in love with me, you see. That's what makes it different.'

'You don't think,' said Belinda, scrummaging for Falstaffs in her bag, 'that I could have another glass of vodka.'

'I'm *so* sorry, was the first glass not nice? You should have said.'

'It was fine, but I drank it.'

'Of course.'

Once more, the disapproving re-entrance and exit of the farcical maid.

'Are you lovers?' asked Belinda.

'I've just said.'

'And you were even before we went to Fontainebleau – that's why you were so shocked.'

'No, no. This has happened since.'

'You've been to bed with Simon in the last three weeks!'

'No. Does that matter?'

'Of course. You mean this is just something you've *spoken* of, the pair of you?'

'We *will* be,' Monica said. 'Lovers, I mean. We are in love. Oh Lord, Linda, what *are* we going to do?'

'When did it *happen*? I just don't believe it! Do you mean you've planned to make love and it just hasn't happened? On the telephone or something? It's so *weird*!'

Then Monica said, 'Do you mind? Are you cross?'

'Funny question.'

'I don't mean it would alter things in any way, whether you were cross or not. But I am interested whether you mind.'

'Darling.'

'No, please say.'

'I just think poor you – poor Simon – poor everyone.'

'So you *do* mind. Everyone in life is entitled to be happy except me, apparently.'

'What a very un-Monica-ish remark.'

'I'm feeling un-Monica-ish.' With a gritty little smile she added, 'Bloody un-Monica-ish. Let's go and have something to eat!'

10

The next day at breakfast, Richeldis said, 'I thought of asking Monica here for Christmas.'

Simon just managed to avoid spitting out a mouthful of coffee in his astonishment. This was *typical* of Richeldis. It was just what she bloody well *would* do. Someone or another tells her that her husband has been seeing Monica (How? Some shit at work must have overheard his tender conversations to Paris on the office telephone). Any other woman would scream or throw things or threaten to ring up her lawyer. Richeldis decides to be nice and talks about having Monica to stay for Christmas.

'No, darling, finish what you've got,' she said to Marcus who was baying for Sugar Puffs.

'I like Sugar Puffs.'

'Yes, darling, but finish what you've got.'

The same coo-ing, sweet, even-tempered voice. As he listened to it Simon revised his panicky judgement. She could not possibly know anything about him and Monica because there was nothing to know. He said nothing.

'Not if you really couldn't bear it, darling. Only mother will be coming, and Bartle.'

'Oh, Christ!'

'And you know how impossible mother is.'

'I like granny very much.'

'Yes, darling. Monica is always so good with mother. Well, they've lots of things in common and they worked together.'

'Rather a houseful you're planning.'

'We could stretch it. I mean, Daniel won't be here, and Marcus could come in with us . . .'

'You have it all worked out.'

'No, darling.'

She looked at Simon, who had been so crosspatch lately. Already that month he had called Belinda 'that bitch'. Richeldis could not bear it if he started to attack Monica. But, it was *true*. Monica *was* good with mother.

'I'm awfully worried about mother, actually,' she said, as she spread Flora on to her toasted M & S whole-wheat sliced bread. 'Yesterday she was so *muddled*.'

Simon rustled the *Daily Telegraph*, and peered rather despondently at the financial pages. Coffee, in which he had speculated a certain amount lately, was easing.

'This coffee's vile,' he said, pushing away his cup.

'It's the same as we always have.'

'The two statements aren't necessarily incompatible.'

Oh, she didn't *want* to score points in this way. She loved him. She wanted everyone at home, all being happy together. Why was he suddenly so bloody?

'Tastes awful to me.'

'Home for supper, darling?'

'No.'

'*What?*'

'Thought I'd go up to London for the night. There's a meeting in the morning.'

'You could take an early train. I'd drive you to the station, my darling.'

'That's what I was afraid of.'

This was his valediction. She followed him out into the hall.

'What's the matter with you, Simon?'

'Nothing.'

'We've got to talk. It isn't right . . .'

'So, at last, you've noticed.'

'What have I done? What *have* I done?'

'Why are you crying, mummy?'

'I'm not crying, darling.'

'Well, goodbye both of you.'

Simon was in his coat. He had his bag all ready, then. Richeldis had not been aware of his preparations to spend another night away from home. He always seemed to be going away these days. She looked at him, hoping for some explanation or some glimmer of affection in his face, but he seemed like a stranger.

'Don't go, Simon. Not just like that.'

'I shall be late.'

He leaned over and kissed his son's head. As he closed the door he could hear the boy saying. 'You *are* crying, mummy. I can see that you are crying.'

Simon stomped out towards the garage. He could watch his heart thumping beneath greatcoat, jacket, jersey and Viyella shirt. It was as though something were being kept prisoner in his chest and was battling to be let out. His whole body shook. He had come out in a sweat and he was feeling terrible. He was panicking, and longed to escape. He felt so uncertain, so crazy. He hated himself. He loathed behaving like a shit. Particularly he loathed being horrible to Richeldis. And yet he was guiltily aware that adultery somehow felt more justifiable if you were getting on badly with your wife. This being horrible was a sign that the marriage was a failure.

He wrestled with the cold-dewy handle of the garage door. There had been a frost that morning, now melted. The garden was heartlessly beautiful in its dead way. Dew hung on everything – the last umbered roses, the few scrubs of Michaelmas daisy, the silvery expanses of lawn.

He got the garage open, flung his case on the back seat of the Rover and started the thing up. But, as he reversed out of the garage, there was Richeldis standing on the gravel in bare feet and nightdress. Scarlet faced, her features ugly with agony, she stretched out her arms in imploring gestures. He had to stop the car, for fear of running her down, and this increased his irrational fury to apoplectic levels.

'What is this?' he asked through the closed car window.

She was clawing the glass. 'Darling, darling.'

'Well?'

'Please don't go, my darling. Please. Please.'

She was hysterical, as though even she had sensed that something absolute and terrible had befallen them. There was obviously no point in trying to talk to someone in that condition.

'Go back indoors! What would Mrs. Turbot think if she arrives and finds you like this? Or the postman? Anyone would think you had gone mad.'

'Please,' the words came in dreadful jerks, '. . . tell . . . me . . . what . . . I've . . . done . . . wrong.'

'Go back indoors.'

'Say . . . you . . . forgive me . . .'

'There's nothing to forgive. Oh, for heaven's *sake*, Richeldis.'

In spite of himself he got out of the car. 'You must come back indoors.' He took her elbow and led her back to the porch.

'Sorry to be so silly.'

He handed her a handkerchief.

'You are crying, mummy, I *said* you were crying. Why are you crying, mummy?' said Marcus when they stood on the parquet of the hall.

His mother's tears made the child cry. The father too found himself close to tears. 'I have been very busy lately,' he said. 'Overwrought. I spoke harshly.'

'No, you didn't, my darling.'

She was holding him now; her hot moist face was on his shoulder. In that moment he felt nothing but revulsion and contempt, but he clutched her, and knew that she was interpreting his hug as a token of their old affection reviving. Pity entered in, then, and made him hug her more, just to stop her crying. She raised her face, salty and slobbering with grief. He kissed it.

'Sometimes you frighten me,' she said. They ignored the child. For the moment, it was just the two of them.

'Don't be frightened.'

'I love you too much.'

'Yes.'

'And you love me, too, don't you, my darling. You *do* love me?'

He put his face sideways with her and squeezed her more.

She said: 'Sometimes, when you get cross, I am so frightened. You look at me as if you wished I was dead and I just feel you don't love me at all.'

'Look,' he said, 'I've got to go. I'll stay at the flat tonight. I'll ring you up, see you tomorrow.'

'Thank you,' she whispered. Her tears were dry now. He did not look back. He could hear her picking up their child and murmuring to it.

In the car he was still shaking. He lost himself to music, by putting on a cassette of Saint-Saëns's organ symphony. Its familiar impassioned sounds mopped up his own raw feelings, made them manageable.

From the first, music had been one of the things which divided him from his wife. She seemed not to need it. On the very rare occasions when she put a record on the turntable it would be some pop song of yesteryear – 'Can't Help Falling in Love' was the one most frequently belted out – or some dreary medley of Gilbert and Sullivan. In early days he had tried taking her to concerts, but it was like taking a blind woman to a picture gallery. He could feel her, awkward and fidgeting beside him. The actual mystery of music itself simply failed to engage her. She 'joined in' with a rather toneless hum if she recognised a tune – Bizet's *L'Arlésienne*, say, or the second movement of the Pastoral Symphony. But she did not listen. If at home he put a record on himself she would invariably *talk* through it. For his part, the drug of music, particularly of romantic music, became increasingly necessary; he fed himself with it in larger and larger doses. He bought headphones, so that he could play Brahms to himself; at home Brahms, in particular, was the favourite. Actually, though, Simon found that almost anything composed between the era of Brahms and that of Elgar gave him pleasure as did a lot of twentieth-century music, especially Bartok. Poor Richeldis made a joke of not liking music. She thought it was a trivial thing, in the same order as not liking bread and butter pudding. For him, it revealed a fundamental crudity in her nature. One might quite *like* a person who saw no point in Brahms. But one could never respect them or take them seriously.

Saint-Saëns took him as far as the motorway, and then, fumbling in the aumbry where other cassettes were stored, he found Jacqueline du Pré playing Elgar's cello concerto, and crawled down the M1 into London in a bath of consolingly poignant sounds.

The business which occupied him in the City, for once, was quite genuine: foreign contracts, and discussion, with a commodity broker, about his own assets. Should he cut his losses in coffee futures and try something else? Sugar? Aluminium? Potatoes? They lunched at a heavy old-fashioned restaurant near the Mansion House and talked of money, a subject, which like music, consoled. Since the sale of the family business, he had quite a lot of the stuff, a fact which never ceased to preoccupy and interest him. He was not absurdly rich but he had enough to require the advice of experts to keep it all ticking over. Last year, he had made quite a killing in 'soft' commodities, having bought and sold futures in sugar at imaginative moments. This year things were doing less well.

Money almost more than anything makes differences between persons. For most of us, 'money worries' are about whether we can afford to pay bills without getting overdrawn, and whether we can afford a holiday. For Simon, money worries concerned such matters as whether he had made or lost ten thousand pounds as a result of the exchange of various bits of paper by certain City shysters. He was not so constituted as to feel guilt about such things, but nor was he insensitive to his privilege. He was very lucky – luckier even than his brother who hadn't got such a big whack of the Longworth fortune, because in Simon's view he had neither needed it nor worked for it. Bartle had been too stupid to query the settlement anyway.

The luncheon and business concluded, there was really no reason why he should not have gone home. It was the hour when businessmen go to massage parlours or take their secretaries to hotels. Simon longed only for Monica. His heart had suffered a great wound, that evening on the Pont Saint-Michel. It was not merely that his pride was damaged by her refusal to sleep with him. He was moved by the grandeur of her gesture. It was so serious. When she walked away from him and got into a taxi on the rank at the bottom of the Boulevard Saint-Michel, he had realised that she was to be like no other woman he had ever known. She was, in fact, the Woman in his life. He was humbled, broken, awestruck. Day and night, ever since, he had been haunted by her pale, intelligent features, so often smiling and satirical. He knew that she had complete power over him.

A loose perusal of the evening paper as he whizzed westwards from the Mansion House on the Central Line, revealed that his favourite Brahms string quartet was to be performed that evening at the Wigmore Hall, and, having no other plans, he decided to alight from his train four stations too soon and purchase a ticket. When he got to the hall, the booking clerk asked, 'How many?'

'What?'

'How many tickets?'

'Oh, two,' he said.

For some reason he felt shy of admitting to the girl behind the little window that he intended to go to the concert on his own. The tickets safely stowed away in pocket book, he returned to Petersburgh Place.

Shoes off, lolling on the bed, he had thought to have a quiet read, an early snack, and then to set out, refreshed, for the concert. But the luncheon subdued his resolve and, heavy with claret and roast potatoes, he was soon asleep. Oblivion was only interrupted by the telephone ringing.

'Did I wake you up, darling?'

'How did you know?'

'You sound sleepy.' Richeldis laughed gently.

'Well, what is it?'

'I'm sorry to disturb your nap, darling. And I'm sorry about this morning. We all get so tired, the three of us.'

'Three?'

'Marcus, you and me. It's a little lesson we must all teach each other, to be stiller and calmer, to respect each other more . . .'

His impatience with this gibberish was hard to restrain.

'Was there anything special?'

'Listen, darling, I know you're tired, and I know you're busy, but I am worried about mother.'

'You always are.'

'She's just rung and, darling, it did sound very confused. I'm sure Bartle is doing his best to cope.'

'A fat lot of good.'

'I wonder if she's been drinking a little bit too much. She sounded so agitated and, well, incoherent. Bartle has gone out to see a parishioner, or so she said.'

'He doesn't have a parish.'

'I didn't know whether to believe her or not. And she said she hadn't eaten for two days. And then as we were speaking – it was about ten o'clock this morning – I realised she thought it was late at night. I'd go myself but I can't, darling, not with Marcus, and I can't leave him with Mrs. Turbot – poor Mrs. Turbot, she's really very fluey. So, darling, if you could face it.'

'You want me to go to Putney?'

'Only if you have time. Just to keep an eye on things.'

'Richeldis, I'm very, very busy.'

'I know, darling.'

During a long silence, it occurred to him that she might be worried enough to come to London, bringing Marcus.

'I'll do my best to go,' he said.

'Thank you.'

'Goodbye, Richeldis.'

'Darling?'

'Yes.'

'I'll lie and kiss you tonight, my darling love, and wish you were with me.'

'Goodbye, Richeldis.'

'Goodbye.'

He looked at his watch. It was ten to four. With guilty awkwardness he realised that he should go to Putney. He quite liked his mother-in-law. He liked her definiteness. If Bartle really wasn't feeding her, this was intolerable. With extreme reluctance, Simon dragged himself off the bed and made the journey by train.

It was not quite five by the time he got there and he decided to stay twenty minutes. Approaching the house he noticed how lamentably it was all going to seed: the crumbling paintwork on doors and windows, the downstairs curtains half drawn, the dustbins still by the front door, neither of them with fitting lids. When he tried the bell he wasn't sure whether it had worked, and when he rang again it made a faint whirring noise like dottle being sucked through an old man's pipe. After an alarming pause, which gave him time to picture Madge unconscious at the foot of the stairs, she opened the door a crack. It was still on its chain.

'Are you completely nuts?' she asked.

'No.'

'What time do you think it is?'

'About five o'clock. Can I come in?'

'At least you admit it,' she cackled. She led the way through the sordid hall. Newspapers, books and clothes were piled up all over the place.

'I'm doing some work in the dining room,' she said, leading him into the front room whose curtains were half closed. It had been years since her last dinner party there. In those days it doubled as her study, and the walls were lined with shelves, stuffed with bound proofs and file copies of books which she had published herself. There were also melancholy heaps of books, their once shiny new jackets faded with sunlight, which had evidently been sent to her as complimentary copies, and which had never been read. There was dust everywhere. Cobwebs were festooned in thick grey lace from the stucco dado, from curtain rods, from shelves. The central table, draped with green baize, was littered with books and newspapers. There were several bottles out, and some dusty old glasses.

'Have some gin,' she suggested.

'No thanks.'

'Oh, Mr. Jaggers.' She sometimes called him this, sometimes Eric, sometimes his real name. 'Well, give me some.'

She held out a cobwebby glass at random. He poured in some gin. She coloured it with some old madeira.

'This is me lunch,' she said, very cockney, 'and that's me breakfast.' She indicated a grey fluffy glass which was balanced on *Crockford's Clerical Dictionary*.

'I've been looking up his nibs in *Crockford's*,' said she, resuming her normal tones. 'Very interesting because he isn't in it. So much for his parish visiting.'

'What name did you look him up under?'

'You are *clever*! So you know this business of names?'

'His name is Bartle Longworth.'

'I looked him up first as Mr. Dick. Then as Longworth. He isn't in this book under either name.'

It was a very old copy of the Clerical Directory, 1929. Several years before Bartle's birth.

'Bartle may be a bad clergyman, Madge, but he is real. I went to the service when the bishop, you know, made him into one.'

'They made him into a very bad one indeed. There is no Bartle Longworth in this book, but there is a Walter Kendall and a William Knight.'

'So?'

'W. K. Whizz-Kid. Now, over here' – she proudly tapped a pile of paperbacks – 'is my next bit of evidence. What is it he reads? Ruth Rendell – R.R. What does that make you think?'

'Not a lot.'

'Rogue Riderhood. Really, Eric, you are a fool. Rogue Riderhood is out in the parish. Now does it make sense? You see, he'd been to France. No, you were the one who went to France.'

'We've all been to France at some time or another.'

'Eric – that was my husband – helped the Free French. I said he was a fool, but in many ways he was right. De Gaulle and all those other patriots tacitly admitted, do you see, that, without the communists, they would never have beaten the Germans. So he goes out with a Ruth Rendell novel sticking out of his pocket.' She laughed once more, whether at 'his' folly or her own brilliance Simon could not tell.

'Don't you think you should be in bed, Madge?'

'Why the hell should I be in bed?'

'Bartle will be back soon.'

'He's been down to the river to look for bodies.'

'I expect he's just been down to the shops.'

At that point the front door opened and Bartle came in; he was wearing a greasy old cloth cap (bought at a Sue Ryder shop) and the usual grey flannels hoist several inches above the nylon-socked ankle. Over the whole, the tattered donkey jacket which Simon remembered giving to his brother for a jumble sale seventeen Michaelmases before.

'Hullo there,' said Bartle, 'I popped out for some milk.'

'Madge says you've been visiting parishioners.'

'Well, I did have lunch,' he said uneasily, 'with an old parishioner.'

Leaving the old woman in the dining room, Simon followed Bartle into the kitchen. A scene of unparalleled squalor was spread out. The eye caught only details – a pamphlet called LOOK AFTER YOUR TEETH!; a mountain of tea-leaves on an old copy of the *Church Times*; on the table, quite old to judge from its greenish perimeter, a fried egg.

'It's a bit of a mess, I'm afraid,' said Bartle. 'One can't keep abreast of everything. One does what one can.' Absently he picked up a small pile of underpants and transferred it to a pot on the stove. 'Oh,' he said, shaking the pants free of chicken-bone, 'bother.' And removing them from the stock pot he placed them in a neighbouring saucepan with Madge's 'whites'.

'Madge is drinking herself silly,' said Simon. 'You might at least give her proper meals.'

'At half past twelve I gave her lunch,' said Bartle with a flare of rage.

'I gave her fish fingers and baked beans which she seemed to like, and some ice cream. At four o'clock I gave her a cup cake and a pot of tea. You cook for her if you are so bloody sure I'm doing it all wrong.'

'Sorry.'

'I shall now start making her supper. Soup and some eggs. I miss *one* meal with her when I just happen to have lunch with a friend and you come round here and tell me I'm doing it all wrong.'

'Calm down, cool it.'

'She's *your* mother-in-law.'

'Yes,' said Madge, coming into the kitchen with a cigarette ablaze between her lips. 'She's your mother-in-law. That's right, talk about her behind her back.'

'We were only . . .' began Simon.

'Talking about me,' said Madge with all her old, formidable poise. 'A fine time to choose. Do you know the time?'

'I must be going,' said Simon.

'Do you know the time?'

'Twenty-five past five.'

'Exactly. Where does that leave the clock – the one in the hall?'

'The thermostat,' said Bartle.

Simon was surprised that Bartle should know such a word.

'You twiddle with it,' she said, 'I think it's been programmed all wrong. I can't get any heat out of it.'

'I really must be going,' Simon repeated. He was relieved, and surprised, that she appeared to be getting on with Bartle perfectly well in spite of her earlier fears that he was in the habit of picking up bodies from the River Thames.

She seemed, in fact, to rally. He wondered whether she was quite as muddled as had been made out.

'Of course you must go.'

'I'm going to a concert.'

'Of course you are.'

'A Brahms string quartet.'

He kissed her on the cheek and she stood by the front door smiling intelligently. As he walked away down the pavement she cried after him, 'Johannes Brahms. J.B. Joey Bagstock, J & B. Glass of whisky, have a drink!' Her face had all its old intellectual sharpness, but it was as if her vocal chords had been taken over by a demented parrot.

I I

The players at the Wigmore Hall were not distinguished, but Simon found it reposeful to be there and to allow, in the first half of the concert, various pleasantly minor pieces of music to waft over his head. There was something by Tchaikovsky, the Ravel string quartet. And they allowed him the reflection that a composer can labour to create a piece of music and end merely by the production of perfectly competent *sounds*. The great stuff came from a hidden depth and touched something within us; or so it seemed to him as this lesser tune-making washed over him. While they played he allowed his mind to switch off, which did not mean that he had no thoughts. Rather, thoughts swam in and out of his head in unarranged fashion. He felt keenly, for example, that something should be *done* about his mother-in-law. The scene which he had just witnessed at Rockingham Terrace was ugly. The unseemliness of it was somehow typical of Bartle with his sloppy inefficient ways. Simon at that moment held Bartle responsible for Madge's decline, rather than recalling that it was precisely because of her decline that Bartle was there at all. Then, Tchaikovsky being sweetly melodic, his mind halted, and the next time he was aware of a thought lodging there he found himself angry with his wife, for suggesting that he go to Putney in the first place, when he could have been more usefully employed. Why *should* he do Richeldis's drudgery for her? Madge was her mother. Marcus was no excuse. He now belonged to a playgroup, and there *was* always Mrs. Turbot. More music banished the thought of Bedfordshire, and then he found himself back in the past, recalling Madge in the days of her glory. There had been more than a touch of greatness in those days. The first time he had ever met her was at one of her celebrated parties, it had been an extraordinary experience for a young man born (as Madge always said) into 'the purple of commerce' to walk into a room and find himself standing next to household names: there were authors and actors, as well as the hard-core party fodder – Theo Gormann. Jonquil Yates.

'More hooch, Mr. Eliot.' Yes, there were giants in those days, and he remembered Madge filling the great man's glass – very frail, the poet was then, and rather silent.

And suddenly, in the midst of all this reverie, there came a dart of unendurable pain. His thoughts had involuntarily refashioned a fifty-five-year-old Madge, hair grey not white, cigarette and whisky glass in hand; and by her side he saw once more the timid, and yet amused, face of the woman he now so desperately loved.

The scene was the same – the offices of Rosen and Starmer – but they were no longer filled with people drinking, and smoking. He and Richeldis had called round to take Madge out to lunch. And there she stood, a terrible figure in a bate, waving a wodge of typescript as if it were an offensive weapon.

'Tatty Coram, you are absolutely *hopeless*!' Wham! the ream of paper, precariously held together with rubber bands, bounced on to Monica's desk. 'The *whole* of that needs to be done again. You've let him spell Montagu in no less than four different ways. You seem completely to have forgotten Hart's rules. If you think it is punctuated I would refer you to page 179 – it's really most amusing. But I find it hard to be amused that I have to read every bloody piece of paper which passes through this firm. Can't young people read? O generation of vipers!'

This was how Madge spoke to her staff, and, mysteriously, those who lasted more than a few days always appeared able to take it. That morning when Madge had been bawling her out, Monica had looked away and her eyes met his. The *look*, surveyed twenty years since, now seemed unmistakable. It was recalled to him with the freshness of yesterday. A young pregnant Richeldis was by his side. Madge was being a caricature of herself. And Monica had been indifferent to both. She had given him a look of unambiguous love. Had he not loved her, even then? It tortured him to acknowledge that he had not, on that morning more than twenty years ago, been in love with Monica. Yet now he was intolerably in love with her, and the fact made him view the whole past quite differently. It was not that he consciously wished to rewrite history. Rather, it seemed to rewrite itself, automatically, and to throw these hitherto forgotten scenes into sharp relief.

Another vignette, of Monica grinning like a happy child as Madge, in a very different mood, put an arm around her shoulders. It was after some evening they had all spent together in Putney.

'Tatty Coram, I *adore* you!' Madge had said – apropos of what, he did not recall. Tatty Coram looked then as though she could tolerate adoration.

The roar of applause for a really indifferent rendering of Ravel broke the chain of impressions, and he shuffled to the bar. The more recent memory of Madge downing her 'breakfast' and her 'dinner' from gin glasses produced in him an unwontedly anti-alcoholic shudder, and he drank orange juice. Being alone in a crowd usually produced in him a feeling of shyness, awkwardness. But, tonight, he was hardly aware of his company. He stared through the sea of unknown faces simply lost in the haze of his love, and wondering what he could possibly do about it. Unlike any devotion which he had ever formed in the past, this all depended on *her*. This was not going to be some cheap little affair in which he could seduce a woman by his charm or good looks. This was the grand, the destructive thing, it was as big as death. He could not pretend to be in control.

When the general shuffle began, and he followed the crowd back into the hall, he momentarily forgot his seat number, and feeling in his pocket he discovered the unused extra ticket which he had purchased. It made him feel vaguely ridiculous. He settled, surveyed his programme, and then the most extraordinary thing happened. That slight hush had fallen on the audience which signifies a collective knowledge that the musicians were about to appear. And then, just as the clapping began and they *did* appear, Monica came clambering along the row of seats and sat in the empty seat beside him.

Since he had supposed her in Paris, and told no one but Madge of his movements that evening, her appearance seemed little less than miraculous. He was about to speak. But she silenced him by placing a long white finger to his lips. The music had never worked on Simon so powerfully as it did this evening. First, the feeling of dread, of melancholy fear which the opening bars convey: tonight he felt not merely turned to gooseflesh but almost as if his hair were standing on end with shock. And then, when the rich Brahmsian melodies began, he wept openly. There was so much to this music: sadness transformed into energy; despair embraced, defeated, and cast aside in a triumphant abandonment to passion. And all the time that the music worked these beautiful effects upon him, for every second, he was fully aware of *her* presence beside him. It was as if she were an emanation of the music, or, more correctly, as if *it* emanated from *her*. They did not hold hands. They did not touch. Except for an occasional sidelong glance, they did not look at one another. But he could feel her there, the softness of her white cheeks, the wonderful thick clean hair, the clear bright eyes.

It was not a particularly good rendering of the string quartet. For him, though, the power of Brahms transcended the dullness of the playing, and communicated itself to the audience who were completely lost to the stillness of the last movement, rising to its violent crescendo. There was a pause of electric silence, and then a loud explosion of applause.

'Why are you *here*?' he tried to ask, through all the clapping.

'Come on, let's go,' she said. The audience were still crying 'Encore', and the indifferent 'cellist was grinning in sweaty triumph, as they wriggled their way out into Wigmore Street.

'I saw the blank seat beside you, and I thought I'd sit in it. That's all. I hope it wasn't presumptuous.'

'I thought you were in Paris.

'No, I was here.'

They laughed.

'Did Madge tell you I was here? I told no one else.'

'I didn't know you would be here. I came because I love Brahms. Simon, where do you *find* such musicians?'

So the magic had not worked for her. He felt more than a little crushed.

'Why have you come to London?' he asked.

'You know why.'

'I know nothing. After our last meeting, I knew less than nothing. Only what I felt.'

'And not what *I* felt. Oh, Simon.'

'It was more than feeling. I knew something had happened, but I did not know what you were going to do about it.'

They stood on the corner of Portman Square, gazing at one another, and now realising that there could be no turning back. He took her in his arms and kissed her. They had often pecked each other's cheeks in the past. Now he enjoyed, as if for the first time, the extreme softness of her lips against his own, the passionate firmness with which her little hands gripped his waist. When they broke apart, he saw a smile on her face which almost broke his heart, so intense was its joy. In the taxi, unable to speak, they nuzzled together. She put her head on his shoulder and he enfolded her in his greatcoated arms.

All that followed in the next few hours was inevitable. There was no 'shall we do this?' or 'would you like to do that?' They returned to the flat in Petersburgh Place, drew the curtains, removed their clothes and made love. Simon was overwhelmed by the transformation in her. Her sensible shoes had no sooner been unlaced than she abandoned her sensible manner. Her neat spinsterish manners were left folded on the chair with her neat spinsterish clothes. She became a wild, insatiable, intensely exciting animal presence. There was nothing cosy about what was going on. It was about as consoling as Niagara Falls or the Milky Way. It was vast, awesome, completely strange.

Many hours later, they were almost surprised to find themselves still in Bayswater, for it would seem quite appropriate to have opened their eyes and found themselves transported, in their rapture, to the Hanging Gardens of Babylon. They lay quietly now, gazing adoringly at each other's naked bodies, which had become, in the strange alchemy of the previous one hundred and fifty minutes, the most beautiful and fascinating things in the universe.

Monica put her face to his chest and whispered, 'Oh, my beloved man,' and he stroked her head and her neck and her shoulders.

'There has never been anything like that in my life before,' he murmured.

'Don't let's speak, don't let's analyse it,' she said. 'We both know what's happened. Oh, my *God*, I love you.'

About an hour after that, they found themselves on the floor. Then they stood up again and, hand in hand, they went to the window, drew back the curtain a little and looked at the sky. There was no knowing the time. It was not a matter of the slightest consequence or interest. But there was something important for both of them in being able to look out and see the sky, the tree tops, the dear old world. For, they had been to the Hanging Gardens of Somewhere, and returned, forever changed. That meant that the world itself was transformed for them and they looked upon it with new-born wonder.

'Was that lightning?'

'Let's count,' she said. Slowly, out loud, she counted up to eight before there was a rumble of thunder. 'Eight miles away.'

'More,' he said, 'You count slowly.'

Both of them, inside their heads, were counting the forty or so miles to Sandilands and wondering if Richeldis heard the storm. There was another lightning flash, and this time the thunderclap came sooner and louder.

'Here.' He came up behind her with a blanket, and draped it round her shoulders.

'Come in with me.' So he draped one corner round his own shoulder and they huddled there by the open curtain, staring at the storm with the excitement of little children. The next thunderclap was so loud that it might have been overhead. Bombs could not have been louder. London, the whole sprawling orange-lit rubbish of it, was involuntarily caught up in the violence of the natural order. The thunderclaps and the lightning came simultaneously now, lighting up the room and shaking it.

'I am safe with you,' she said. 'The lightning could kill us now and I would be happy.'

'I can't describe what you make me feel.'

'Don't try.'

'I want to try. Even though anything I say would sound like the words of any old philanderer with his arms round a woman.'

'That's what you are.'

'No. But, please.'

'Words won't do it.' Her tone was firm and tender and ironic all at once. A violent rumbling crack of thunder burst over their heads as soon as she had spoken. 'If words could do it, I would be able to say what it was like to discover, after all these years, that I was truly deeply in love with you. When I saw you being any old philanderer in Fontainebleau, that was the moment. If words could do anything I could describe the pain of that day, and yet the wonderful joy of discovering, on the next day, that you weren't in love with that girl.'

'Don't let's speak of that girl.'

'It's thanks to Miss Jolly that we are together. I don't mind talking about her. We are invulnerable now.' She stroked his chest inside the blanket, and she kissed his ear. 'After we parted in Paris, I was afraid you'd run away. I wouldn't have blamed you. I wanted to run away, too. Until this evening, I didn't exactly *want* this to happen.'

'Oh, Monica, if you knew how I have longed for you.'

She squeezed his hand, almost governessy.

'I didn't come to London to chase you, Simon Longworth. I came to test my own feelings. I wanted to see how it felt, being in England, knowing what you felt, what I was feeling . . .'

'A lot of feeling. How did it feel?'

'Simon, I've told Belinda.'

'Did you have to?'

'I had to tell someone in order to see if it was quite real. Do you understand that?'

'Oh, Jesus.'

'She won't tell . . . anyone. She may seem like a blabber-mouth but she is a good, loyal friend. She loves . . .' Monica hesitated, 'she loves us *all* too much to make mischief.'

'I don't mind who knows. Not now,' he said.

'I do. I dread the next bit so terribly.'

The storm said the rest for her: the noise, the light and now, against the window pane towards which they stared, a sharp spattering rain.

*   *   *

Bedfordshire, too, was swept with the storm. It woke Simon's son and terrified him. Marcus was terrified of bigness. He hated stories of giants and ogres. He even disliked big grown-ups, preferring small ones like granny. In his dream, a gigantic Jules, leather-clad and with hair like a brush, was twice life-size. He held mummy in one hand and he was crashing about the house. Marcus woke up in a state of uncontrollable, shrieking fear. Richeldis, wearing a pair of her husband's pyjamas, tried to comfort the boy in his own bedroom, but she could no more staunch his tears than she could still the storm. His screams, as always, caused her almost unendurable torment, so painful that she thought she might stop breathing. When the screams subsided into mere jerky sobs, and he tried to tell her of the dream which had so frightened him, she picked him up in her arms and carried him back to the warmth and softness of her own bed. At length, he lost consciousness and slept peacefully in her arms. She, however, could not sleep. The storm excited and disturbed her. She thought, as she lay there, of the garden and Bunyan's Field, and the country round about which she had grown to love so well. The trees writhed and whipped themselves. In their soughing rainsoaked branches, there were nests, and ruffled little birds. Richeldis thought of the water splattering on to the paths and on to the clayey fields; and she thought of the creatures in their holes, cowering from the noise, the wetness, the violence outside: voles, stoats, badgers, foxes, rabbits, some deep in the earth, some caught in the storm in the midst of their nocturnal peregrinations. For mile on mile the storm would be raging, on the human and animal world, on the rooftops of the dying, and on windows behind which newborn babies were coming into the world. And she and her beloved boy were safe from it; warm and snug beneath the quilt's soft lightness; warm in each other's love. It was an awful thing to be feeling, but she was rather glad that Simon wasn't here. Just lately, and for no apparent reason, he had been an absolute pig. His absence, like the raging of the storm outside, made the warmth of the little creature beside her all the more comforting and delightful.

*   *   *

It was the lightning which called Bartle from the depths of sleep. The sharp electric brightness filled his room for an instant. Then as he lay there in the dark, still half-possessed by dreams, the crash of thunder shook his whole bed, and he reacted to it as men have always reacted to thunder. He thought of God. Perhaps for the first time in his life, Bartle was really awestruck by the power of God. He knelt on his bed, with his elbows on the window-ledge, looking at the bleak, empty street, the shabby houses, the cars dingy in streetlight, the little trees and gardens, dreary as only South London can be, and all for a moment threatened by something infinitely bigger than the wildest air-raid. Creation itself was on the point of exploding. For a moment, so loud was the storm, that Bartle wondered whether this was not the great Armageddon which for more than half his life he had been wearing CND badges in order to obviate. But no. This was not a nuclear war. It was the thing we dread in a nuclear war, even more than the folly of politicians and the military. It was the naked, destructive power of nature itself. Bartle did not suppose that the Lord was *in* the thunder. A hundred times he had preached sermons about Elijah hovering on Mount Carmel and discovering the Lord not in the thunder or the fire or the storm but in the 'still small voice' which followed them. In extolling the still small voice above the thunder he was really suggesting that muddle was better than clarity, doubt more worthy than faith. His sermon was an unconscious celebration of wetness and vagueness. It was no wonder that he sometimes wondered whether he believed in God, since he had displaced the power of God in his mind, with this 'still small voice', and it really would not have made any difference whether this voice were audible or not. The voice of Bartle's imagination had nothing to do with the God of Abraham and Isaac and Jacob, who led Moses and Aaron and the children of Israel through the wilderness with the pillar of fire and a pillar of cloud; who drowned the Egyptian horsemen in the Red Sea and smote the great Kings of Canaan.

Crack! Crash!

'What manner of man is this,' said Bartle aloud, 'that even the winds and the sea obey him?'

He had missed the point, in all his 'still small voice' sermons, that the power of God is greater than the elements which He created. The still small voice was not a licence to be wet. It was the assurance that persons could hear, and converse with, a personal power infinitely greater than themselves, bigger than thunder, Bartle now felt it. For the first time in his life, he actually heard that still small voice for real. Awed, he received confidence that the apparently ungovernable power of nature was the creation of a Person. A Loving Being had called all this out of nothingness – these flashing lights, this rumbling storm. This Being was nothing but Love, for nothing but Love was powerful enough to move the sun and other stars. In the midst of an ecstatic sense of the presence of God in all His majestic and adorable power, Bartle smiled at his former self. As if outside his own body, he saw himself, in the old days, preaching a sermon on Christ stilling the storm.

'We all know, don't we, how our ancestors sought supernatural explanations for natural phenomena. And any of you who have been to the Middle East will know how storms suddenly erupt, and then vanish as if they had never been. Now isn't it all too likely that Jesus and his friends were caught up in just such a storm? And, when they returned to the shore, didn't one of those friends say, "It's funny the way you always feel safe in the Lord's presence"? And thus, when the teaching, the *Kerygma* of the early church came to be formulated, this story became a type, a paradigm of God's very real concern for people caught up in the natural order. And we too as Christians must reflect this concern in our attitude to parts of the world torn by storms. And there are storms worse than natural storms, aren't there? The storms of political unrest, and racial tension . . .'

Had he really preached this sort of thing? He had, he had! Bartle's thin body could feel itself shaken every time the thunder cracked, and he had to shut his eyes against the lightning, but still he shook with a sort of crazed, holy laughter at his former manner of expounding the story. The whole terribleness of that storm, its great otherness from himself, its bigness, came before Bartle. And someone had asked, in the middle of such a storm, *What manner of man is this that even the winds and the sea obey him?* They were not offering an explanation for natural phenomena. They were expanding the mystery. They could only ask the question because they thought Jesus stronger and more terrible than the storm itself. Bartle felt by the end of his sleepless and joyful night that he had never before understood *anything*. He felt that his desire to understand, to classify, to comment, was itself fatuous. But he knew that he had been given a revelation of God in his creation. Thunder and lightning died away northwards. There was only darkness, and rain falling on the window. Gradually the blackness of five a.m. became the greyness of six a.m. Dawn rose, and found Bartle still kneeling with his forehead against the window-pane, quite awake, more fully conscious than he had ever been in his life. He felt, after several hours of meditation, a wonderful release from the triviality of words; there was no need to express what he had seen and heard during the night.

*   *   *

A few yards along the corridor, Madge Cruden had slept through most of the night. She had not been surprised to hear the exploding bombs and the firing of heavy artillery. What terrified her were the sappers, who had got into the house and were now laying mines which would destroy not merely Rockingham Crescent, but the whole world.

Rumble, rumble, tap, bang. The noise came from the 'radiators' and it was only a matter of time before their radiation was activated. The computer was now installed. What a fool she had been to let Tatty Coram switch it on! It was a bitter grief that Tatty Coram had finally let herself be bought by the Whizz-Kids. The game was probably up. There was no point in rallying the troops – Jonathan Cape, Faber and Gwyer, Martin Secker, fresh from the sack of Constantinople, and all the special Constables from Constable . . . It was all too hopeless. The least she could do was to get out of the house and avoid contamination, for there could be no doubt that everything – water, fabrics, furniture – was by now completely contaminated. The problem was how to get out of bed without putting her foot on the carpet which, as well as being contaminated, was also scalding hot.

She was so busy, do you see. How *could* she go on heaving coal up and down stairs? It had seemed the obvious thing to install radiation. And she had *let* them do it! Oh, bitter, bitter. It was when she was at her busiest, and They had been through *every* room in the house, laying their network of radiation pipes under the very floor-boards. Now it was fully operational, and she could hear their throaty French voices singing through the radiator, *Marchons, citoyens!*

The room was terrifyingly alive, full of malign activity. So, they wanted her to put on the electric light. And get an electric shock herself? What did they think she was? A fool, like the rest of them? Everything would be all right if she could prevent the hopeless Eric coming up with a cup of 'tea'. That might really blow the world up. But to prevent such a calamity she would have to undergo ordeal by fire and walk across the carpet.

Sir Anton Dolin had joined the Whizz-Kids in the radiator and was making a speech about Madge which was of almost incredible malice. In fact if she had not heard it with her own ears she would have thought it was the invention of the Free French.

'She was never a proper communist. She always kept contaminated money in her knickers. *C'est vrai, citoyens*, she was a fascist whore. She sold her body to Himmler. The fall of her knickers was the fall of France . . .' Rapturous applause followed this calumny.

It was quite clear that They had got the house surrounded. Perhaps she could get down a drain-pipe. She realized that the *real* Anton Dolin had not made such a speech. He was an absolute darling. No, this was a fake Dolin, designed to intimidate her. Like the man in the last war . . . Oh, what was his name, who broadcast from Germany. Lord Hore-Belisha, that was right.

Her one hope was double-time. They might very well forget about adding five, and get there too late. Then she could at least be out of the window and making a *start*. The urge to get *started* was overpowering. It was all very important. First things first. Off with the contaminated clothes. She squatted on the bed and wriggled herself free of cardigan and nightdress. The belt she already had round her waist, and she left it there with a few state papers tucked into it. Now, what else? Oh, scissors.

The walk across the contaminated carpet was the bravest of her life. Her bedroom window opened on to a tiny balcony which overlooked the street. With trembling fingers, and a huge expenditure of effort, she threw up the sash window, creating an aperture large enough for her to wriggle through. She was only just in time. Below, in Rockingham Crescent, a Whizz-Kid in uniform, a sack of explosives over his shoulder, went from house to house posting dog shit through the letterboxes. It was too late to stop him, but not too late to shout her disapproval.

*   *   *

'Simon?'
'Yes.'
'Did you sleep?'
'Is that what you rang up to ask?'
Monica's head rested on his shoulder, and Richeldis's voice, grating as never before, came down the line into his ear. Bleary, he looked at his watch. Ten past eight, but these days it hardly ever got light.
'We've had a storm,' she said.
'So did we.'
'We?'
'We Londoners.'
'Oh. Darling are you still there? I thought the line had gone dead.'
'So did I.'
'Listen, Simon, did you see mother?'
'Yes.'
'How was she?'
'Rather drunk.'
'You see, Bartle's rung, and he wants me to go over there.'
'She's not dead?'
'No, but he says there's a bit of a crisis. Something about her shouting at the postman. I expect he's making a mountain out of a molehill, but the doctor is with her. They seem to think I ought to go.'
'Hell!'

'I know. Listen, Simon, Mrs. Turbot is coming to sleep in the house with Marcus and I'd better come and spend the night in London.'

'*Here?* In the *flat?*'

'Well, I might, or it might be better if I stayed with mother in Putney. We'll have to see. If she's really ill you'll have to come home and help Mrs. Turbot with Marcus.'

'I'm very busy.'

'This is a crisis, Simon. Anyway, see you soon. 'Bye, darling.'

There was a new briskness in his wife's tone which he did not like.

'You heard all that, I suppose.'

She kissed his chest.

'I wish it didn't hurt so much, hearing you talk to her.'

'There's been a crisis with Madge.'

'I heard.'

'It's Bartle's fault, by the sound of it. He's more trouble than she is. He's there to look *after* her . . .'

'If only I could go,' said Monica. 'I really *love* Madge, and now I can't – because of this, us.'

He kissed her forehead lightly.

'And at any minute,' she continued, 'your wife is going to drop in here on her way to Putney and find us in bed together.'

'In a way I wish she would.'

'No, you don't. Poor Richeldis has got enough on her plate without having to cope with us as well.'

'I wish you weren't going. I want to spend all day with you.'

'I want to spend all day with *you*.'

'I have to see the broker at ten. But I should be free by 11.30. Then if you like, we could . . .'

'Simon, we're going to be seen.' She sat up and hugged her knees, while he stroked her wonderful smooth rounded back, white and marbly. 'Somewhere in London we are going to be *seen*.'

'So? We've probably often been seen together in the last twenty years.'

'It's different now.'

'We know that, but other people won't.'

'Simon, people *always* know.'

He sighed, 'I know they do.'

'We've got time,' she said mysteriously. 'There's no need for us to do anything foolish. We have all the future – as long as we both shall live. One day poor Richeldis will have to be told, and we shall all have to work out what to do, the three of us. We can't do it kindly. It will be the cruellest thing we ever do. But at least let *us* be the ones to tell her.

Not some gossip who has seen us together. We mustn't touch each other in public. We mustn't even look at each other.'

'Aren't you being rather melodramatic?'

'No. Because, if we do it our way, we can at least tell Richeldis in our own way and at our own time.'

'Monica, don't let's delay. Let's just go, today. We'll fly back to Paris, and leave it all behind us. We'll explain in a letter.'

If he had said this before the telephone call from Richeldis she might have been wild enough to take him at his word. But, 'We can't,' she said, 'not yet, not with Madge as she is.'

12

For some time, Richeldis had been preparing herself for the death of her mother. She supposed that this was now about to take place. She was worried, upset, but a funny mood of excitement had taken hold of her, so it would not be strictly true to say that she felt unhappy. There was a crisis and she was now ready to be 'marvellous'. It was the man's role at such times to be 'hopeless'. Poorbartle and Simon-blither-him had in their different ways been most satisfactorily hopeless. Bartle had made no sense at all on the telephone. He had said it was impossible to talk, and begged, and begged her to come at once. Well, she jolly well would. She would muscle in and do what needed to be done. She was still cross with Simon-blither-him for making her so unhappy. But when she rang him that morning and heard his grumpiness she determined not to allow it to *get to her*. Let him sulk. She was just *not* going to care any more.

When she arrived at Rockingham Crescent it was only twenty to eleven. Not bad going, she considered. She had rung Simon-blither-him, organised Mrs. Turbot, bless her; taken Marcus to his playgroup; done a last-minute shop to make sure there were provisions for his high tea; and roared up the motorway in her little Renault.

'You took your time,' said Bartle, opening the front door.

'That's rather an abrupt greeting.'

'Come in, there's a doctor with her.'

'What happened?' she asked, adding reproachfully, 'Bartle, you could at least pick these up.'

The hall was ankle deep in newspapers.

'They're the ones that come free.'

'But you could pick them up. Where is mother?'

'Upstairs, there's a doctor with her.'

Richeldis opened her mother's bedroom door and was immediately shocked by the smell of urine. Hitherto, there had been none of that.

Madge shouted, 'Oh, why don't you go away!'

She was sitting upright on the bed in her dressing gown. Her hair hung loose in a plait over one shoulder. A young Indian in a green corduroy suit was seated beside her.

'Mother, are you all right?'

'You're too late,' said Madge.

'Everything is all right,' said the Indian.

Everything looked far from all right. One of the window-panes was cracked, and things had been flung all over the floor – books, clothes, a tea pot.

'I need some paper . . .' said Madge, pointing towards the Kleenex for Men.

'Shall I get one?' said Richeldis.

'Don't touch it! Why *won't* you do what I say?'

'It's all right, Mrs. Cruden.' The Indian's voice was quiet, soothing.

'It's *not* all right. If she touches that box, the whole room will blow up.'

Richeldis, whose hand was stretched out towards the box of paper handkerchiefs, hesitated. She felt that, if she touched the box, there might actually be an explosion. Her mother had always spoken with authority. Now, more so than ever. Nor had she ever been more theatrical. It was as if she were acting the role of a mad woman. Her hair, when not piled on top of her head, looked wild and alarming. The dressing gown was open at the front to reveal all her pathetic nakedness. The eyes were no longer the bright little eyes of a cockney sparrow. They darted stormy untrusting glances, first at the doctor, then at Richeldis, then at nothing in particular.

'This man isn't a doctor at all,' she said.

'What am I?'

'I rather think, sir, that you have been sent by General de Gaulle. That's what they call him, but of course he isn't the *real* general. Oh!' Suddenly her patience snapped. 'Don't ask me! They say one thing and do another, do you see, trying to confuse me. I knew that I was waiting for Mr. Bardell to do my feet, do you see, but he wouldn't come on a Tuesday he came on a different day. Well, I wasn't confused when I heard the Whizz-Kids. Then I knew.'

'And they were speaking to you through the radiators, were they, Mrs. Cruden?'

'Tatty Coram was the one who did it.'

'She keeps talking about this Tatty Coram,' explained the doctor.

'She planted a computer in the hall. On, off, on, off.'

'Tatty Coram did you no harm, mother. She's in Paris.'

'Of course she is. This is another Tatty Coram. The first was guillotined by the general. In the purge. But, do you see, nobody realises that I am on double time, so when she came to me the other evening. And then that other man. The one who's married to Richeldis.'

'I'm Richeldis, mother.'

'I *had* to take my clothes off because they were very severely contaminated.'

'Mrs. Cruden, I think you are tired,' said the doctor. 'And I think you need some rest. It would be better for you if you came to hospital.'

'What sort of hospital?'

'Just for a few days, Mrs. Cruden.'

'Eric could never look after the house. He's out all the time at the dentist, do you see, or snatching bodies out of the river. Did you know that my husband was a body-snatcher?'

'No,' said the doctor.

'I couldn't come without my state papers, and my share certificates.' She lowered her voice to a whisper and winked at Richeldis. She pointed to the doctor and said, in case her daughter had been too stupid to recognise him, 'Jonathan Cape.'

'Jonathan Cape was a publisher, mother.'

'A very good friend of mine. Absolute darling. But he's trying to take me over, and I'm going to hold on to my share certificates. Magna Carta says that you cannot take away the tools of a man's trade. Well, my tools are my share certificates.'

'Of course you can bring your certificates,' said the young man.

'Jonathan Cape,' she whispered again, 'Cape of Good Hope.'

'Jonathan Cape is dead, mother.' Richeldis said it aloud, it was absurd to be whispering.

'I know,' said her mother with a wink which triumphantly suggested that she had clinched the argument. 'What day is it?'

'Tuesday,' said the doctor.

'So I add five?'

'If you want to.'

'How do you know that there are seven days in a week?'

'It's just a convention,' he said.

'What about the eighth day? On the eighth day I rose again from the dead, and then I added five. Well, this annoyed the Whizz-Kids and other undesirable persons of this sort, most considerably. They thought they'd put the computer in the hall, but as this lady says, Tatty Coram is in *Paris*. Now I decided to call up Tatty Coram in Paris on the computer, for this lady . . .'

Richeldis now found herself fighting back tears.

'. . . and it turned out that there were five Tatty Corams all riding on a . . .'

'Horse?'

'Carousel. Five of them!'

'It seems a lot.'

'*Far* too many, do you see. But by then I could hear all the explosions.'

'That was the thunderstorm,' glossed the doctor for Richeldis's benefit.

'Of course it was the thunderstorm,' snapped back Madge. 'I'm not a fool.'

'No one said you were a fool, Mrs. Cruden.'

'It's just that I'm the only publisher in London who will not print porno-filth by these various Whizz-Kids. Did you say you *met* Hore-Belisha?'

'It really would be better if you came with me,' said the doctor.

She would not admit defeat, but she looked at him with puzzlement. 'Do you really think so?'

'I'll come with you, mother.'

'I can see myself to hospital,' Madge said magisterially. 'You might help Rogue Riderhood gather together my documents and my certificates, and my papers.'

'You can come in my car, Mrs. Cruden,' said the doctor.

'Very nice. So long as you allow this lady to collect up my files and documents. She's my daughter, you know.'

With a vivid indication that she thought Richeldis wasn't right in the head, Mrs. Cruden made screwy gestures with a finger at her temple.

'We shall just pack a few things,' said the doctor. 'We shall only take you in for a few days, just so that you can get some rest.'

'Oh, mother!' Richeldis ran to the old woman and held her tiny, palpitating little body in her arms.'

In the event, the doctor spent a further hour and a half persuading Madge to get dressed. Most of the clothes were contaminated, and all the suitcases. They ended up stuffing belongings into plastic carrier bags.

Richeldis, while all this was going on, felt completely overcome by dismay and incredulity. It surely was not possible that her mother believed that a gang had fitted some sort of bugging device into all the radiators. Yet, in spite of her distress, Richeldis found herself seized with nervous giggles. When Madge advised the doctor not to buy shares in Jonathan Cape, Richeldis turned aside and moaned with laughter, hating herself for doing so, and knowing that it was all terribly sad. Leaving her mother for much of the time with the doctor, Richeldis sought out Bartle.

'I don't know whether to go to the hospital or not,' she said.

'Better for her to go with the doctor. You can drive over and see her a bit later on. When she's settled.'

'Mr. Bartle is quite right,' the doctor agreed. 'It would be better if I alone took Mrs. Cruden.'

The doctor took the wheel of the car, and Madge sat beside him, allowing him to attach her seat belt. Her hair was still down. She was dressed in the few items of her wardrobe not suffering from radiation, a splashy summer frock, once worn to a Buckingham Palace garden party; a very chunky blue cardigan; a dressing gown; a yellow sou'wester and some fur-lined bootees. The curtains of houses opposite flickered gingerly at her appearance. Richeldis and Bartle watched from the front door as Madge was driven away.

Then both of them had an ungovernable need to talk about Madge. They wanted to go into every detail of their bad experiences with her over the previous weeks and months.

'She never kept on one topic for long, did you notice?'

'And when she came to Sandilands that day with you it was manic stuff, wasn't it? She just jabbered and jabbered . . .'

They did not speak like people interested in what the other was saying. They spoke from an unstoppable desire to speak. After about an hour and a half, Richeldis suggested that they should get to work tidying the house. Among the chaos of the broom cupboard she managed to find a number of buckets, and mops and brushes. The kitchen was the room they tackled first. Bartle brought an old dustbin up from the area and filled it with rubbish. There were dozens of half-used tins, fluffy with mould, lidless jamjars, flyblown bits of grease-proof paper, empty plastic bottles of washing-up liquid, almost-finished cornflake packets. The Frigidaire was alive with cartons of congealed milk, bulging old yoghurts three months past their date stamp, blue bacon and worm-infested sausages.

'The liver's fresher than it looks, actually,' he said, as she tossed into the bin some black rubbery offal clinging to its paper.

When surfaces had been scrubbed and wiped, swabbed and scrubbed, they completed the washing-up of weeks and put away crockery into cupboards. Attacking the other rooms with dusters and vacuum cleaner was easier. And on hall and landings they collected dustbins full of burnables – old newspapers, packets and magazines. Richeldis found the work therapeutic. There was nothing they could *do* about mother. She found that it was positively enjoyable to work with Bartle. He was so much less *difficult* than Simon. Her husband's behaviour towards her in recent weeks had been the limit. It had hurt her, but only now, in the midst of another set of difficulties, did she see Simon clearly. She had been spoiling him, letting him walk all over her. It wasn't good for him or for her. He jolly well shouldn't be allowed to lose his temper all the time; nor should he behave as though his time was all-important and hers did not matter. The worm, Richeldis discovered, could turn. For the time being, she was happy with Bartle.

'I can put all these old *Church Times* out,' he said, chucking a huge pile of them into the bin. 'They'll make a good bonfire.'

She smiled at him, knowing that he used to order the paper to look for jobs. '*Lively member of team ministry required. Central church- manship. Vestments. Opportunities for outreach. Cardriver essential.*' No wonder he never got any of the jobs he applied for.

'We'll have a good bonfire, won't we?' she said.

He thought how lucky his brother was to be married to this nice sensible woman. He tried not to be bitter. But Richeldis, with her full sensual lips, her lovely smile and gorgeous eyes, was much better looking than Vera. She noticed the 'funny' expression in his eyes, and added briskly, 'We'd better get on with our bonfire. The days are drawing in.'

13

'She can't *know*, can she?'

'Not possibly,' said Simon.

Already, within the space of two days, Monica Cunningham's oldest friend had become an unnameable 'she'. The undemanding comrade of twenty years had now become a rival, capable of destroying all her happiness. One consequence of this was that Monica began to endow Richeldis with almost supernatural powers of intuition. For twenty years, as a friend, she had always made it clear that she thought Richeldis a bit thick. As a rival, she imagined her as brilliantly devious, and even wondered whether Madge's alleged nervous breakdown had not been engineered as a way of taking Simon away.

Monica knew that her response was irrational. It was just so hard to bear anyone taking up any of Simon's time. Their happy love had been interrupted by telephone calls which nagged Simon back into the world of prose. In any other circumstances, the news that Madge had been taken to a lunatic asylum would have filled Monica with grief. But the possibility that it was all some elaborate trick by Richeldis was hard to dismiss. The very fact of her coming to London was terrifying. Monica had spent a frantic hour in the flat changing sheets on the bed, tidying the bathroom, scouring the bedroom carpet for incriminating details, an earring, a hairpin. She honestly considered it a possibility that Richeldis, in the midst of her worries about her mother, might come to the flat in St Petersburgh Place and comb it with the thoroughness of a private detective, for evidence of Simon's infidelity. In fact, Richeldis had not been near the flat. She stayed in Putney, beating carpets, taking loose-covers to the dry-cleaners, and ringing up commercial cleaning agencies. When Simon had visited them there, he had found her and Bartle making a huge bonfire in the garden. They had given him the very firm impression that he was in the way. He had been told that, if he really wanted to make himself useful, he should go home to Sandilands and help Mrs. Turbot to look after Marcus.

Once more, it was hard not to see cunning in this obvious reaction. In London, with discretion, it was possible to meet in hotels. But there was no chance of Monica calling at Sandilands without the visit being noticed. She installed herself at the local motel. Simon did not have the heart to tell her that he had been there before with Miss Jolly. Most of his days were occupied either at the works or at home, playing with Marcus, and watching the little boy's electric racing cars whizzing around the Scalex-tric track. Only when the child was having his bath and could be left with Mrs. Turbot, could Simon repair to the motel for the evening. It was in this hole-in-corner venue that Monica asked, 'She can't know, can she?'

'Not possibly.'

'And yet she has *seen* you since Tuesday. You're so different.'

'Only to you.'

'You sort of *glow*. She must have noticed.'

He was privately worried by Monica's glowing. Hitherto, her smiles had always been satirical, as if she were biting back some observation on human idiocy. Now, she smiled with an almost cretinous happiness. It was flattering to see how much she was in love with him, but he felt troubled by it too, particularly in that nasty little room. He looked about, the strip-light over the bed, the Scandinavian-style bedside lockers, the Gideon Bible, the orange curtains. In just such a room – perhaps this very one – and so recently, he had seen just such a smile on the face of Ruth Jolly. With Ruth, as with other girls, he had known that ghastly chain of emotions to follow one another within half an hour: longing melted into tenderness; tenderness to pity; pity very quickly changed to despising. Oh, how he wished that Monica would not look at him like that! She looked so *silly*.

He closed his eyes and held her hand tightly, full of the feelings of the most dangerous tenderness. He wanted to be deeply in love, and for that feeling to last. He wanted to be a nice guy, and to be loved by this vulnerable, mysterious little being who lay beside him and placed her whole confidence and trust in him.

'I want us to be together always,' she said.

'So do I.'

'And yet I don't want it to be difficult for you, beloved.'

He wished she didn't call him 'beloved'. It sounded so affected and unnatural.

'I don't want to drag you away from your children,' she added, 'your house . . .'

'I don't know what I want,' he said. 'Except to be with you.'

'And I want to be with you, beloved. I just can't *understand* it all!'
She giggled, with a blend of her new-found silly sort of happiness and
her old satirical way of viewing the world. 'It's mad, isn't it, that two
people taking their clothes off and lying together can produce such
intense experiences.'

'Crazy.'

'And to think of all the *millions* of people we pass each day in the
street. They've all been doing it.'

'Some of them.'

'And feeling as we feel now? Why doesn't the world blow *up* with
happiness?'

'Because they don't feel as we feel now. They've writhed about for
five or ten minutes with people who stank, or bored them stiff. They've
had brutalised little fumblings with people they don't really like.
They've done it casually, without feeling, so often that the very act
bores them, nauseates them . . .'

They lay silent for a while. She was disturbed by his words, and did
not dare to look at him. He had his eyes shut, but his hand, still
clasping hers, slowly began once more to caress her body. The gentle
strokes, casual and low at first, became rhythmical. Monica, in a
frenzy of self-abandonment, let out a high scream, as if she were some
temple virgin being slaughtered on an altar of sacrifice.

Long afterwards, when they were able to speak again, she said, 'I
can't let you go. I won't. We must tell her, somehow.'

'Somehow,' agreed Simon.

Richeldis, the while, though not having forgotten the sad reasons
for her being in Putney, felt refreshed by her time there. On the
third day, Bartle suggested that it was time to visit Madge. The
ward, whenever they rang up, said that she was 'fine'; and, which
was not necessarily the same thing, 'settling in'. Richeldis, who had
never visited such a place, had an instinctive fear of mental
hospitals. She was glad that she had Bartle to accompany her. They
parked the car, and approached the girl at the reception desk with
some misgivings.

'We're looking for a Mrs. Cruden,' said Bartle.

'She's in Cruden,' said the girl.

Bartle stared at her. Was she a *bona fide* receptionist, or was she a
nutter?

'No,' he said, '*Mrs.* Cruden. It's the name of a patient.'

'She's in Cruden Ward,' said the girl. 'Unbelievable, isn't it?'

They walked down a corridor. Somehow it didn't augur well that
there was a ward with Madge's name. Richeldis, with sweating palm,

clung tightly to Bartle's hand. They passed a tall, thin man in a suit. Loony? Visitor? Doctor? Who could tell?

Halfway down the corridor they came to a hanging notice: Witts Ward to the right, Harris straight on; Cruden to the left. They turned the corner, approached some glass doors, and Bartle said, 'There's Madge.'

She was standing up, engaged in conversation with a much younger woman who was seated on a chair in the corridor. Both of them were smoking cigarettes. As they approached, Richeldis had an uncanny sense of displacement. This both was and was not Madge. She had achieved the strange feat of ageing by about a decade and reverting to childhood, both at once. She looked older than ever. And yet she seemed like a little girl, an impression increased by the plait of hair hanging down to her waist. The colour had vanished from her face. The expressionless eyes were red with exhaustion and tears. She waved as she saw them approach.

'There's a sign up on the door,' said Richeldis, 'about not speaking to patients without permission from a member of staff.'

'I'm staff,' said the young woman, plump in slacks with a very splashy 'top'.

Mad?

'Thank you very much,' said Bartle.

At the farther end of the corridor, a bleary-eyed old man whose face was covered in cuts jumped up from his chair and said, 'Think I'll just go for a walk.'

He marched almost up to Richeldis, and then did an about-turn and marched back to his chair. Then up and along again. Up and down, like a guardsman on sentry duty.

'A wanderer is man from his birth,' said Madge.

'Try sitting down a bit longer,' said the younger woman.

'I'll have a little sit then,' said the man. After half a minute he was up again. A novel idea had dawned. 'Think I'll go for a walk,' he said. Up and along. About-turn. Back again.

'You could sit in your room, Madge,' said the cigarette-smoker. 'Why don't you take your friends in your room?'

'I'm her daughter,' said Richeldis.

'Would you like to go in your room, Madge?' asked Bartle.

'Can't.'

'You can,' cooed the other woman, who they began to think might really be a nurse. 'You can show your daughter and her husband all your things.'

'This very nice young lady thinks we are in an art gallery,' said

Madge. 'She thinks all these pictures are genuine. As a matter of fact they are fakes.'

To cheer things up, block-mounted reproductions of great paintings had been hung at intervals in the corridors. Van Gogh's *Café at Arles*, Renoir's *Les Parapluies*, and a rather harmless Dutch flower painting by which Madge paused. Her manner recalled to Richeldis many a continental holiday spent with her mother expounding with almost Germanic thoroughness the artefacts worthy of their attention.

'This young lady considers this picture to be the work of Cézanne,' said Madge. 'I cannot agree with her.'

'It's Dutch,' said Bartle.

'You see the cauliflowers?' Madge laughed, pointing out some blowsy white roses. 'Now I can see mice running up the stems and into those cauliflowers, and then they are coming down the stalks as rats, do you see, and they're just about to leap out of the picture. No, they aren't rats any more, they're bison. Getting bigger all the time.'

'Sounds frightening.'

'It would be if it were a genuine picture. But it's what They've foisted on us. Only I have seen through the trick – *that's* the dangerous thing.'

'Go in your room Madge, do,' pleaded the younger cigarette-smoker.

'Can't,' Madge said.

'You can.'

'Can't go in there. It's all wired up and it's much too hot, just as out here, do you see, it's much, much too cold.'

'It *is* chilly,' Bartle agreed.

'Frightfully chilly. This is Mr. Rogue Riderhood,' she explained to the younger woman. 'Sometimes known as Eric.'

'We can always stay in the corridor,' said Richeldis.

'Or there's the day room, Madge. You could take Eric in the day room.'

'Well, I could,' Madge admitted cautiously. Fixing a beady eye on Bartle, she asked, 'You don't have a nice little drop of whisky, I suppose?'

'I'm afraid not.'

She was evidently disappointed.

'Well, I've a cigarette in my room. You can come in there, both of you, but I must warn you of the very intense heat.'

They followed her along the corridor, which was lined with doors, and as she walked she sang. Bartle took up the hymn, and they stood together to render their duet, while Richeldis, blinking back tears, looked out of a window across a bit of lawn and some flower beds.

My song is Love Unknown,
My Saviour's Love for Me:
Love to the loveless shown
That they might lo-o-vely be.
O who am I,
That for my sake
My Lord should take frail flesh and die?

Bartle sang in a flutey sort of tenor, Madge in a deep croak, a cigaretty baritone.

'You'd better come in,' she said, when the song was over.

Just for a moment, Richeldis thought, 'Perhaps, after all, she's much better. Perhaps she was just having a little joke about the cauliflowers and the bison.'

Madge's room was small and high-ceilinged. It had been made sordid by her throwing dozens of folded paper handkerchiefs about the place.

'They are at it day and night, they *won't* leave me alone,' she said, stubbing a cigarette onto a saucer, and opening a drawer in search of another packet. 'That man outside, for instance, on guard duty. I made a little joke to put him off the scent, but he's guarding me all the time. They'd kill me if they could. That light switch over there . . .'

'This one?' Richeldis asked.

'Don't touch it,' her mother roared. 'I got up in the middle of the night and moved it down as low as I could. If I hadn't moved it, the whole world would have blown up. Of course, I had to stand on my bed and then they came in and tried to beat me. I struggled with them because I had to move it, do you see. In the morning the doctor came in and congratulated me warmly, and just didn't know how I'd done it. "We would all have gone up in smoke if it hadn't been for you, Mrs. Cruden," he said. But even he would not realise about *time*. Questions, questions, questions, they ask endless questions trying to catch me out. And it's all this business, do you see, of saying one thing and doing another.'

'Of course it is,' said Bartle.

The humiliation of her mother was the most dreadful thing she had ever witnessed, but Richeldis could not stop giggling. She found herself chewing the back of her hand to prevent an actual outburst of laughter.

'I have to add five. And this is what these people will not recognise. Of course I saw through it all long ago. I know what they are up to. I know who you are.'

'I'm Bartle.'

'Certainly not. But aren't you boiling hot in here?'

'It seems just about right to me,' Bartle said.

'You must be mad.'

'Perhaps.'

'What do you expect?' Madge asked. 'This is a National Health Lunatic Asylum. Otherwise known as the loony bin.'

'Do you want a hand, Madge?'

Bartle tried to steady her as she heaved herself on to the bed.

'I can hardly move after last night. Getting off the bed. Getting back on the bed.'

'You can rest now.'

'I've got half the room more or less straight. From the ceiling down to about there!' she waved a hand airily to indicate a distance somewhere above their heads. 'The next thing I want to control is the sun.'

'Could be difficult.'

'Extremely. If you will watch me, I fold one of these proof copies . . .'

She swung herself off the bed and took a Kleenex from the box. She laboriously tottered to the wash basin.

'Now I think if I just dip this in the water. Are you watching?'

'Yes, Madge.'

'And then I press the paper to my eyes.'

She turned round. Her face was covered with the damp tissue. When she lowered it, she looked more gleamingly mad than ever.

'Now you,' she said commandingly.

With a bit of a sigh Bartle reached for the Kleenex. Madge shouted instructions all the time. 'Not that way round, you idiot! Remember which tap to turn on. Oh, you fool, don't you know the difference between contaminated and uncontaminated water?' Bartle turned round with the soggy paper handkerchief stuck to his glasses.

'Take it off,' said Richeldis.

'You'll be a fool if you do,' said Madge. Such was her tone of authority that Bartle, in that moment, really believed that it would be advisable to keep a damp tissue over his face.

'Mother, we ought to go. We'll come again and bring you some cigarettes.'

'It was Tatty Coram who got me here,' Madge hissed. 'It was *she* who betrayed me. She found out about my adding five and then she altered the computer in Rockingham Crescent. First hot, then cold. General de Gaulle, he tried to kill her. He *saw* what she was doing to

France. Watch out for her, she'll steal your husband. I know her ways.'
A parody of lasciviousness came over Madge's face. 'Hallo, dearie.
Like to come upstairs?' she said, acting the cockney tart. To
Richeldis's horror, Madge lifted up her skirts to reveal a pair of
incontinence knickers.

14

The whole texture of existence was altered by what had happened to Madge: for Bartle, for Simon and Richeldis, for all of them. The first week, Richeldis stayed in Putney, tidying the house, visiting the hospital. Then she came home, but all her concentration was devoted to Madge. She forgot that there had ever been a time when she thought of anything else. She no longer noticed what mood Simon was in. She did the shopping and the housekeeping, and the looking after Marcus, but she did these things automatically, while thinking about Madge. She was on the telephone for hours about it to Bartle, and to the old woman's doctors. Her condition completely baffled the hospital. They assumed at first that it was all 'alcohol related'. Then they fell back on saying that Madge was 'manic' – but half London had known that for seventy years. Richeldis and Bartle, in their talk, veered between thinking the doctors were rather useless and Madge rather marvellous for defying any attempts to define her. Though Bartle had nothing but praise for the ward, and the nurses, his bulletins were always disturbing, because nothing stayed the same. Sometimes, apparently, Madge was very energetic, running up and down the corridors of Cruden Ward and being led back to the day room by the nurses. On other days, she was hardly able to move, and lay on her bed moaning and crying. On some days, the madness seemed to leave her, and she held coherent conversations about books or the past. Then it would descend, worse than before.

Each development of her mother's condition obsessed Richeldis, and in so far as she noticed Simon's silent, withdrawn reaction to the crisis she was annoyed by it. Oh, he occasionally gave Marcus an hour or two of his time, and he had offered to man the fort whenever Richeldis wanted to go to Putney, but he was not really pulling his *weight*. He was sulking. As though Madge's illness had been designed to upset *him*.

Richeldis did not want to risk a major row by repeating her suggestion that Monica be asked for Christmas. (He was horrid about her friends, she had now decided.) It worried her, nonetheless, that

Monica had not replied to her invitation, scribbled on a post-card. Normally, she was such a punctilious correspondent; Richeldis began to wonder if her friend was ill. It was not a worry which dominated. There were plenty of other things to occupy Richeldis's mind. When there wasn't mother, there was Marcus, there was the house itself; and when there was not Sandilands there was Christmas which, hellishly soon, would be upon them. Luckily, Richeldis was a planner. A local butcher got her a goose and Mrs. Turbot's puddings were a thousand times better than Harrods'. Some of the children's presents – computer software, and a walkman with headphones – had been bought as long ago as September. The cards were printed locally. On one of their rare evenings together, she and Simon had signed them.

'We'll send one to Monica, funny old thing, even though she hasn't seen fit to reply to my invitation,' said Richeldis. Simon had merely grunted. Really, much of the time, he wasn't all *there*.

The day following, they drove together up to London. He had to have a morning of business in the City. She decided to do some last-minute shopping, and luncheon with Lady Mason.

Belinda's flat, the legacy of her last marriage, was in Elgin Crescent. Richeldis, fur-hatted and parcel-laden, began to talk almost before she got out of the taxi and she talked and talked and talked throughout the meal, barely noticing the expressions which passed, or failed to pass, over Lady Mason's face. She talked chiefly of her mother's madness. She wanted to cover every detail of it, from the first incipient signs in her behaviour years before, to the most recent bulletins from Bartle. With almost equal fervour, she talked of her domestic arrangements at Sandilands: having Emma's room redecorated, having to 'stay in' for plasterers. She knew that she should stop and ask about Belinda's life. She suspected that she had stopped, at some juncture of her monologue, being interesting. But she could not stop the flow of words, words which came spouting out of her mouth.

It was a nice little lunch – some cheese quiche (Belinda considered her local 'delly' *marvellous*), a tiny salad, mainly iceberg lettuce and chicory, tons of vodka before the meal and a bottle of Oddbins Riesling with the food. Cheese, nectarines, coffee. Jabber, jabber, jabber. It was only when the forthcoming Christmas holidays were mentioned that there was a little pause, and Richeldis said, 'Do you know *the* strangest thing about Monica?'

Belinda, fussing with a coffee-filter near the sink, dropped everything with a clatter.

'What about Monica?' she enquired gingerly.

'I asked her to stay at Sandilands for Christmas. I don't know why –
I suppose it was because she used to be so close to mother. Somehow or
another . . .'

'The impulse took you, anyway,' said Belinda, trying to cut
Richeldis's long story short.

'I know Simon would be a bit fed up because he likes Christmas to
be just a family affair. And you know the way he always grumbles
about her. Actually, I think they get on quite well without either of
them wanting to admit it.'

'I didn't know that Simon *did* grumble about Monica.'

'Lord, yes, thinks she's *weird*, regards her association with Madge
as sinister. Actually I've always thought Simon was just a bit
threatened by dear Mona. But you know what he's *like*.'

'Do I?' asked Belinda.

'I wrote to Monica, anyway, just a card. Normally, she's almost *too*
conscientious about replying and you know the way one feels she can't
have enough to fill her day if she answers a letter so promptly and quite
so fully. I just wondered if she was ill, that's all. It's occurred to me, if
Monica were really ill, none of us would necessarily be told, would
we? She doesn't have any next of kin any more. We are probably the
closest connexions she has in the world.'

'I suppose we are.'

'Rather sad, really. I just wondered if you'd heard, because if you
hadn't, we might . . .'

Belinda never knew what made her blurt out, 'She was all right
when I saw her last week.'

'You mean when you went to Paris.'

'Oh, yes.'

'That was two weeks ago. Belinda, she hasn't been over without
seeing me?'

'Christmas shopping probably,' said Belinda.

'She doesn't know anyone to give presents to,' said Richeldis. 'She
always sends money to the children. Who'd come Christmas shopping
in London if they could do it in Paris? Belinda, what *is* this? You're
keeping something from me!'

'Of course not.'

'Does she know about mother?'

'Yes. No. I don't know.'

'You see, mother *said* that she called, one evening when Bartle was
out. Tatty Coram, she calls her. Well, of course, I just assumed this was
fantasy. Everything else that mother has said has been so wild . . . Poor

mother has an absolute fixation about Monica at the moment. She thinks she's responsible for everything that's gone wrong. She thinks we've all betrayed her, but that Monica has been a secret Whizz-Kid all these years.'

'Perhaps there's something in that.'

'Oh, Belinda, you shouldn't have kept all this from me, truly you shouldn't. This is awful. I now see it all.'

'You do?'

'Well, Monica came over to London and she saw mother. Mother probably said something which was so absolutely frightful that she feels she can't come and see us. Or perhaps she holds me responsible for not looking after mother. You see, Monica was very close to mother when she worked at Rosen and Starmer. Oh, God, she's probably feeling wretched. Poor old Mona, and no one to *talk* to about it.'

'It isn't necessarily as you say, darling.'

'Did she say anything, when she met you? Anything at all about me?'

Lady Mason fumbled for a Falstaff, and after the requisite silence stared at her friend through a haze of smoke.

'I know that Monica is a very bottled-up person,' she said, 'but she didn't say anything to me about any of this.'

'But it is pretty extraordinary, isn't it? Her not coming to see me? I mean, if she'd seen mother, you'd think she'd be *bound* to get in touch with me. When was this? When *was* she in London?'

'You're probably making a mountain out of a molehill, darling.'

'I'm going to ring her up here – and – now.'

'She might be out.'

'But, if she isn't out, I can speak to her and reassure her that mother really isn't accountable for the things she's saying. I mean she could have told Mona that I don't like her, or something like that. Mother's very persuasive you know, even now.'

'I don't think we should ring Monica,' said Belinda.

'I'll pay for the call.'

'That's not the point.'

'Please let me, Linda.'

'Well, don't make a *thing* of it,' said Lady Mason, handing Richeldis the receiver with quivering hand.

Richeldis peered for the long international dialling code, transcribed in her little engagement book. With miraculous speed, the gulf was bridged between London W.11 and the Seventh Arondissement of Paris.

'Quatre vingt dix-sept,' said Monica's high-pitched, well-modulated voice.

'Monica, it's me.'

'Oh, I thought you might ring.'

'You did?'

'So you know?'

'You mean about your visit to London?'

'Yes.'

'Monica, darling, about mother.'

'Is she dead?'

'No. Look, darling, I gather that you called on mother in Putney. I don't know what happened during that visit, but that's why I'm ringing you up. You aren't to take seriously what she said then . . .'

'I don't . . .'

'I knew something was wrong when you didn't answer my postcard. You should have *said* you'd had a visit to mother. She's been going quietly downhill for some months now, and I'm sorry to tell you . . .'

With relentless thoroughness, Richeldis rehearsed Mrs. Cruden's psychological history for the previous fortnight. 'You see,' she concluded, 'when I heard you'd been to see her I was afraid she'd said something hurtful, and that might have been the reason for your silence.'

'Sorry, I've neglected letters lately.'

'That's not like you.'

'Richeldis, are you all right?'

'Well, it's all been very exhausting. Marcus woke us up screaming at five o'clock this morning. Simon said, "Why don't they fit children with silencers?" – priceless, wasn't it?'

'And you're all right apart from that? Both of you?'

'Oh, we're in fine fettle. Actually, Mona, now I've got you on the line how *about* Christmas? Simon really brightened when I suggested you coming to stay . . . Hallo? Hallo?'

'Hallo.'

'I thought we'd got cut off.'

'I'm sorry, Richeldis. I can't come for Christmas. I'm busy.'

'Oh, come off it, Monica Cunningham.'

'Look, Richeldis, this call must be costing you a fortune.'

'Belinda a fortune actually. She can afford it.' An hilarious shriek accompanied the quip.

'Is she with you?'

'*Rather*. Why?'

'Oh, give her my love. 'Bye, Richeldis.'

'Monica! Mona!'

The line went dead.

'I think that reassured her,' said Richeldis. 'But I still couldn't help thinking that she was keeping something from me. Perhaps one always felt that about old Mona. You don't know of any other reason why she might be being funny? Do you, old bean?'

Lady Mason drew back the corners of her mouth in an attempted grin and offered her guest another cup of coffee.

*   *   *

Simon, meanwhile, had eaten a quite excellent steak and kidney pie, and finished off a bottle of Châteauneuf du Pape, in a restaurant off Lombard Street. He was lunching alone. He had spent the morning with the chairman of the conglomerate of which Longworth was a subsidiary. At several points during their hour together, Simon had wondered whether to resign as joint managing director of the old works. It was not that he objected to drawing a salary of £79,000 per annum for what was in effect a part-time job. It was that he was now forty-eight years old, and even if he had not been in love with Monica he would have been beginning to wonder whether he wanted to spend the rest of his life presiding over a sand pit.

Now, as he digested his pie, and idly scanned the pink pages of his newspaper, Simon began to tot up, inside his head, whether he could *afford* to abandon his salary. How much was he worth? This was a little sum he often did, with the automatic semi-concentration which another man might devote to prayer. There was Sandilands, but he left that out of account. He had made it over to Richeldis many years before. This was so that he could claim the St Petersburgh Place flat as his principal residence thereby avoiding capital gains tax if it ever had to be sold. So, what was the flat worth? They had paid £13,000 for it in 1970. Similar properties were now on the market for around £95,000. He had a mortgage on the flat of £40,000 to claim against tax. He belonged to a syndicate of underwriters at Lloyd's and had sunk some £200,000-worth of capital into this. It brought in a decent income which he generally ploughed back into investments. You are not allowed to invest money in Lloyd's unless you can guarantee the entire sum against loss. Most of his *other* £200,000 was invested in a boringly sensible portfolio, spread mainly between gilts and British equities. He left the management of this portfolio to a broker. For purely personal amusement, he kept another £50,000 to play with. He used it for speculative investments. Last year, as we observed, he had made a killing in cocoa futures: money which was spirited away into an account in Jersey, administered as a trust fund for his children, who had each been left a certain amount by his old father. So, this money he did not really count as *his*. Not counting the £17,000 or so which he kept in the bank for day-to-day expenses such as the cars, repairs to the house and school fees, he perhaps had £450,000.

Since many of the men with whom he lunched in the City were worth considerably more than this sum, Simon did not consider himself particularly wealthy. But his money was the most crucially important thing in his life. He knew that he was richer than the huge majority of his fellow-countrymen. But he was always bitterly conscious that, had he hung on to the company for five or six years longer, he would have been five or even ten times richer than he was today. He had sold at a bad time, before the really huge inflation caused by Edward Heath – a figure whom he detested, passionately.

Falling in love with Monica had revealed to Simon new truths about his little fortune. Monica too had 'a bit of her own money'. She led an independent life. No one had the slightest idea how much old Allison had left her, but clearly there was no question of Monica ever needing to work. Money has a tremendous power over its possessors, much stronger than we, the moneyless, could guess. Simon reckoned that Bartle talked a great deal of irritating claptrap about the way of 'dispossession'. Both brothers considered the other's attitude to money disgraceful. Simon believed that Bartle's cut of the family fortune had been ludicrously over-generous, since he had never taken the slightest interest in the works. He had, moreover, allowed his dreary wife to waste most of it. Bartle now possessed nothing except the rather malodorous clothes he occasionally stood up in – if you could describe that limp figure with hunched shoulders as standing up. He drew money from the dole. He said he felt free, being apparently unaware that he was sponging off the taxpayer. And where would he have to live if he did not sponge off Madge? Simon distrusted Bartle's so-called other-worldly attitude. For his own part, Simon was glad to be held in the comforting but inescapable tentacles of money, glad that his house, his flat, his children's education, his wife's clothes and the family holidays could all be provided with ease. At the same time, this had always rankled. When he first met Richeldis, he assumed that Madge 'ran' Rosen and Starmer in the sense of owning it, and that there was plenty of money in the picture. It was a bit of a shock to discover that Madge had no money at all – again, the mysterious phrase 'of her own'. He disliked in himself the vulgarity of minding, but he *did* mind. It annoyed him that he had no choice about signing the cheques. When Richeldis bumped the car or 'did the ton' at Waitrose (i.e. spent more than £100 in one shopping spree) or booked them all in to some expensive holiday, it was always he who provided the money. Richeldis had no money 'of her own'. Indeed, she seemed almost proud of her mother's disastrous inability to handle money. Simon shuddered at such blasphemy.

Falling in love with Monica, far from diminishing the importance of money, heightened its significance for him. For the first time in his life he was being offered relations with a woman which involved no commercial transaction. With some of the more disastrous adventures – 'fishing', as he thought of it, in the typing pool – he had actually calculated how much it was all costing. Sometimes he realised that he could do it all much more cheaply with a high-grade 'call girl', but his self-esteem would not allow him to sink to that. Even with his wife, there was this nasty sense that he provided all the money. But, with Monica, it was different. During their 'first' and momentous lunch, neither had cared who paid for it. Monica's money provided Simon with all the spiritual joy of dispossession without the absurdly obvious material disadvantages of living like Bartle.

In Monica, he had found a companion who had the same attitude to money as his own. This was just as important as the fact that they both *had* money. They both believed that money was the only thing in this world which could guarantee personal freedom; and it was this freedom which they both intelligently claimed and wanted. For poor Richeldis, money was simply a method of exchange. She was like a child with the stuff. The discovery that she had £200 in her current account would make her rush to Peter Jones to spend £250 on unnecessary new duvet-covers, or saucepans, or towels or garden chairs. She was an incorrigibly silly *spender*. Over the years, he had noted with distaste that she was rather greedy and self-indulgent. She changed wallpapers and lampshades the way some women changed their underwear. It was *his* money that she splashed about in this way, and she seemed so stupidly unaware of what made their money so special.

Simon's money did not give him power, it merely offered him the chance of privacy. He could not become the proprietor of *The Daily Mail* or make 'significant contributions' to Conservative Party Funds. He could not threaten companies with take-over. To that extent he was a very small fish. He was happy to be one. His money merely enabled him to be cocooned from some of the worst horrors of modern life; if necessary to escape them altogether.

'I hate the world,' he had said to Monica, one day in bed.

'Not forests and mountains, but politicians and multi-storey car-parks,' she had agreed, not needing to have his words explained.

'Of course, not mountains. Let's see some mountains together. In the Auvergne? Haute-Savoie? You say.'

'I'd love to, beloved. But you don't have to explain to me, of all people, about keeping the world at bay. I've lived for fifteen years in Paris, doing little else.

'Wimpies,' he said, giving great loathing to both syllables.

'Wimpies avec les french fries – expanded polystyrene, motorways, three-piece suites,' she said. 'Keeping all that at bay.'

'Everything *looks* and *smells* and *is* so horrible,' he said.

Their destiny was to escape this everything, or so it had seemed at that moment. When he was assailed by feelings of dreadful doubt about whether he *could* love any more, this kinship inspired him. He and she saw the same truth. Not only did he find her beautiful, he found himself absolutely at one with her, in a way that he had never been with Richeldis.

And now, for three days, they had been apart. Monica had insisted upon leaving him; she found, now that Richeldis had returned to Sandilands, that there was deep ignominy in deceiving her oldest friend. It was demeaning. Sooner or later Richeldis would find out, and in Miss Cunningham's sharp rather hard way of seeing things this sooner or later was not good enough. They owed it to Richeldis to tell her. Properly. Until Simon did so, Monica would skulk off to Paris for a while. Besides, much as she loved him, she began to tire of her purdah in the motel. Nothing could stop the true Parisian being hungry for the very light of the city she loved, homesick for even the smell of it; for grey straight streets; crumbling stucco; paint peeling off old shutters; neo-classical magnificence to the front; to the rear, on high ledges at great heights, washing lines, cats, potted plants: all the soulless, heartless dignity and squalor of the French capital was what she missed. So she went, not knowing how she dared to explain her absence to Agafya Mikhailovna, and leaving Simon with the task of telling Richeldis.

The pie consumed, and the Burgundy, he paid his bill and walked out into the frosty air. A busker, claiming to be a war veteran, was playing 'O Little Town of Bethlehem' on a mouth organ. The ill-executed but haunting melody reminded Simon with miserable clarity of the approaching festivities: the absurd present-buying; the wrapping and unwrapping; the over-eating; the agonising sense of being imprisoned in a houseful of people one did not really like; the bonhomie; Richeldis, glowing and smiling and loving every second of it.

When he contemplated that stupid, smiling face of hers, he now remembered how easily he had been able to make it crumple with tears. She quivered with grief just because he had lost his temper around the house. How was she going to respond when he told her that his whole life with her was unendurable? He would *have* to tell her that he did not love her, never really *had* loved her, that he did love Monica . . . Then he thought of the pain this would cause. Presumably he would have to tell her soon, sometime over Christmas, with the children to witness her suffering. And they, too, would have to be told.

Since he did not hate Richeldis, in fact felt some pity and tenderness for her, he could not look forward to these tasks. He began to ask himself what would be wrong with killing Richeldis. If one discounted any preconceived claptrap about the absolute sanctity of each individual existence, was not murder the obvious answer in this case? Why should he torture this harmless creature with excruciating, humiliating, disclosure? On the other hand, why should she be allowed to spoil his happiness?

He hailed a taxi and asked it to take him to Elgin Crescent. He had promised to meet Richeldis and accompany her on an afternoon visit to the lunatic asylum. But now he tingled with excitement at his new idea. He would have to make it *look* like an accident . . . Or a suicide. Pushing her car into a river? Something would be worked out. It would spare her so much unhappiness.

15

Before making his Christmas confession, Bartle sat at the back of the church, straining to read his office by the illumination of a distant, solitary electric bulb. The last psalm appointed for that evening was *Misericordium et judicium*, the one hundred and first . . . *I will walk in my house with a perfect heart. I will take no wicked thing in hand; I hate the sins of unfaithfulness: there shall no such cleave unto me.* The words returned and returned to him as he sat, prayer-book shut, and meditated, and the sins of unfaithfulness clung to him like burrs: unfaithfulness to God; unfaithfulness to his own heart's darling; unfaithfulness to his vocation . . . These things in themsleves were not necessarily compatible.

He hated going to confession, but he knew his life would fall to pieces if he stopped. In the old days, as a young parish priest, he had gone each month – sometimes every week. Now, he dragged himself off before Easter, Whit and Christmas. For some reason he always returned to the same confessional, in a blackened brick church half a mile north of King's Cross Station. The familiarity of the surroundings made it more possible to go through with this hated proceeding. He hated drawing attention to himself in this way. He hated having to confront his own imperfections, which were for the most part unchangeable. Nothing, for example, would reconcile him with Vera. Nothing, more generally, would make him any less 'hopeless' an individual. He was more conscious than any detractor of his famed ability to make a mess of just about anything. His own judgement of himself was harsher than anyone else's, excepting perhaps the judgement of God. Before that judgement he trembled, as he now recalled the mightiness of the thunderstorm. The feelings of awe which this inspired had lasted two days. Quite a lot had happened since then. In so far as he hated to see the humiliation of a fellow-human, Madge's madness distressed him. But he did not really mind the madness itself, or the crazy things she said. She had quietened down. Though still suffering from delusions, they had been pushed to the background of consciousness. She still believed that the central heating system in

Rockingham Crescent had been infiltrated by Whizz-Kids, but this was a fact on the same level of interest as the name of the Prime Minister: not something one talked about all the time. She talked to him chiefly about God. Where was He? How was He to be known? She had started to attend the chapel services at the hospital. But still she could not find Him, and it pained Bartle that he could do nothing to help her in her quest.

In spite of feeling so certain, during the thunderstorm, of God's presence, Bartle remained in a muddle, a muddle which coming to confession merely focussed more sharply. The psalmist longed to walk in his house with a perfect heart. But, by the searching judgements of Christ, none of us have perfect hearts. It was said by them of old time that he who divorced his wife could marry another. Technically, it was Vera who divorced him. But the man who is divorced and marries again, in the New Testament, commits adultery. And the man who lusts after another woman has already committed adultery in his heart. Oh, sizzling beef and noodles Cantonese style! Oh, touching of fingers while eating toffee bananas!

Since Madge went mad, Bartle had made no effort to get in touch with Stephanie. Perhaps he would now be given the strength to renounce her. When he went into the confessional, he would be absolved of all his offences, even of the adultery in his heart. But this was the difficulty, for him, about God, and God's laws, and God's forgiveness. For when he emerged again from the confessional, technically speaking absolved, he would still have an imperfect heart, and no act of will could alter it. What was the point in trying to fulfil God's law, which was an impossible counsel of perfection? And, when he failed, why did *he* deserve to be singled out for forgiveness? What of the thousands and thousands of sinners who do not ask for forgiveness?

He was tempted by such thoughts into the sin of absolute unfaithfulness. That is, he was tempted to doubt the very gift of grace itself. And it was here that the will played its part. His mind could not explain it. Feelings of guilt, or the stirrings of conscience, only played the smallest part in recalling him, time and again, to this sacrament. He knew only that he owed this to God. He had a vision of perfection; of absolute good, complete truth, pure love. 'My strength is made perfect in weakness.' These words, for Bartle, were the first stage of a journey leading up to the only Love who was fully good and true.

'Lord God,' said Bartle in his inmost soul, 'My priesthood is a gift which, like all your other gifts, I have wasted and squandered and spoilt. But, even now, let my very imperfection be itself priestly. I know nothing of you. My attempts to follow you have all failed, again and again and again. But, somehow, use me. Let my weaknesses fill up what is missing in the perpetual atoning work of Christ. Let my tiny and inadequate act of penitence be not only my act of penitence, but also the penitence of all those who are better than I but who doubt your grace or do not understand it as you have given me to understand it. When I am absolved, let the absolution be as a healing to Madge, a comfort to Richeldis, an illumination to Simon; let poor Vera's sins be forgiven with my sins; and, if she has committed any sins, let Stephanie's sins be forgiven here with mine. O God, who loves us all with an equal and unsearchable love, who casts none of us away, do not let them judge your truth and your Gospel by my foolish words, my feeble misdemeanours. But let my prayer come before you as the incense, the lifting up of my hands as an evening sacrifice. My life is no example. My words do not persuade. Even now, as I promise to do better, I know that I have nothing to look forward to but failure and more failure. But it is to you that I come, dear Physician of life. I no longer dare to ask to be perfect, even as you are perfect. I dare only to kneel in your presence in all my muddle and impurity and doubt and offer these things to you. Muddle, impurity and doubt is all that I have to offer you, O holy child of Bethlehem. O friend of sinners, O helpless child, this is my offering to you.'

While he was still at prayer, someone switched on the lights of the aisle where he was kneeling. He saw that by now there were about half a dozen penitents waiting by the confessional. At two minutes to six, the priest emerged from the sacristy wearing a 'shorty' black car-coat over his cassock and shivering with cold. He was an old priest who had heard Bartle's confessions many times. During this man's Italian holidays, Bartle had sometimes 'helped out' in the church by saying mass there. The priest knelt for a while in prayer before the Blessed Sacrament, and then put on his stole over his car-coat. One by one the penitents approached the grille. Bartle was always touched by the sight of people queueing at a confessional. Almost certainly they had thought of their sins as deeply secret, though one could tell from looking at them what kind of sins they had come to confess. The young man with lacquered hair and tight jeans was worried about gay sex; and the old woman with a hairnet was mean as hell and kept losing her temper with her sister; and the rather impeccable man in a camelhair coat worshipped Mammon. Probably he drew a shady line between tax evasion and tax avoidance and found himself being tempted by 'massage parlours'. And the harmless old fatty who was in the confessional at the moment had probably never committed any sins except ones of gluttony and came to confession chiefly because she was lonely and wanted someone to talk to. She was in there ages.

Bartle never entered the confessional without acute feelings of embarrassment, and a childish wish that he had any other sins but his own to confess. His own were so humiliating. Probably they weren't more serious than anyone else's, but that was one of the most humiliating things about them. Yet, once he was kneeling at the grille and repeating them, all doubts about it fell away. He knew that he was in the presence of the ultimate reality, the all-seeing and the all-forgiving Judge. Only a few minutes before, he had been seriously wondering whether he might not hold some of the sins back. It was really too ridiculous to have been caught out by these old sins yet *again*. But, once he was kneeling in the box, the very notion of concealment was what became ridiculous, since he was in the presence of one from whom no secrets are hid.

When he had finished, there came a few words of advice from the old priest.

'We keep *saying* that God loves us,' said the priest, 'but it is really the hardest thing of all to believe. What makes it so hard to imagine is that he goes on loving us whatever we do, and even if we cease to think about him; we can spurn God's love, we can run away from it, as you are trying to do. Well,' a little laugh came from behind the grille, 'we *all* are. We are all Jonahs running away from Nineveh, especially us priests. We don't do anything to *merit* God's love, and we are not trying to *win* God's love by coming to confession. It is his love which draws us here, and his love which sends us out again, absolved and healed, to build up His Kingdom. And that's what we must hold on to.'

'But, father . . .'

'Yes?'

'What if we want something which is contrary to the Gospel of the Kingdom, contrary to the law of Christ, and yet we *know* that our whole lives will be incomplete until we have it?'

'What is this "something"?'

Bartle told him, and added, 'For me it would be a *good*. And yet the whole law of the church is against it.'

'Remember that we are called to follow the way of the Cross,' said the priest. 'That is our privilege as Christian men. God knows all your desires. He knows all your good. He puts into our minds the knowledge of what is right for each one of us, and sometimes that clashes with what we might have supposed to be right.'

'That's what this feels like,' said Bartle.

'Well, be patient. It may be that you must follow the way of the Cross. In which case your act of self-sacrifice will work for good in God's hidden purposes. But Our Lord Himself fell three times on the way of the Cross. And He alone, in his crucifixion, bears all *our* failures, all our fallings. We must not attempt ourselves to be crucified. We must not attempt to bear our sins. They cannot be borne, except by Him. If you do what is wrong, God still goes on loving you.'

'So you cannot advise me what to do?'

'You don't really want me to, do you, father?'

To be addressed as 'father' by his own confessor made Bartle feel choked with emotion.

'It sounds rather an awful thing to say,' the priest said, 'but sometimes I think God *lets* us get into a jam, just to cut us down to size. It is when we are conscious of our own failure that we are most conscious of His love. And all of us are failures, aren't we?'

'Yes, father.'

'Now, is there anything else?'

'No, father.'

'For your penance, say the collect for the fourth Sunday in Advent.'

There followed the words of absolution, and then the prayer which moved Bartle above all others:

The Passion of our Lord Jesus Christ and his Infinite Love, the merits of the blessed Virgin Mary and all the saints, whatsoever good thou hast done or evil thou has endured, be to thee for the remission of sins, the increase of grace, and the reward of eternal life. And the blessing . . .

When he came out of the church into the dark, dewy evening, the garish shop-fronts, the jostling 'bus queue, Bartle felt the world transfigured.

16

Simon picked up Richeldis at Belinda's flat. He didn't stay: they were both going to see Madge in the bin. Their visit lasted about twenty minutes, and they found the old woman much calmer. The delusions had died down. She was never going to be restored to her former terrifying vigour, but she no longer seemed, exactly, mad. It should have been obvious that Cruden Ward was no longer the place for Madge. She had started to become understandably frightened of her fellow patients. The young woman in the next-door bed ran up and down the corridor with no clothes on screaming, 'Glory, Mercy, Glory,' at unpredictable hours. She struggled and kicked and screamed and had to be held down on her bed by nurses. On the other side, an enormous Jamaican man, aged about thirty, brooded in total silence. Bartle, on what authority no one knew, had described this man, in his last telephone call, as an arsonist. The mixture of races and sexes and classes was not, nowadays, something about which one could complain. Where *else* could Madge go? Both Simon and Richeldis had been supposing that the old woman would remain there until someone – the doctors perhaps – moved her somewhere else. They were amazed when, after today's visit, the nurse took them into the office and began to discuss Madge's condition. He was quite a nice intelligent nurse; short curly hair, a Canadian accent, gay probably, they both decided. He told them that Madge had responded well to treatment but that they no longer thought it was appropriate for her to remain in Cruden Ward. She had been assessed by a geriatric psychiatrist. The verdict was that she would never be other than demented. The brain cells were no longer there. The fact that she had good 'linguistic skills' disguised the fact that she was actually very far 'gone' and could only get worse. But she was less deluded, less unhappy. They had decided that it would be disastrous if she ever drank alcohol again, but they were unable to say whether her condition had been caused, or merely aggravated, by alcohol. Probably Madge would be better off in a nursing home, 'if you can't manage her yourselves – you've got kids, I suppose? She talks about her grandchildren.'

Even as he was speaking, neither Simon nor Richeldis could realise what the young man was saying to them. He had to spell it out. They were discharging Madge in about a week. They did not want her to spend Christmas in the hospital.

Richeldis and Simon walked back to the car park in a condition of panic. They just *couldn't* have Madge at Sandilands in her present condition, they really couldn't. They both agreed that it wouldn't be fair on the children. Nor would it be fair on their neighbours for whom they normally held a little cocktail party on Boxing Day. Her conversation was no longer wildly, wildly *deluded*, but it was still muddled, and she had started to take a childish pride in an ability to fart at will. 'Is there anything I can do for you, dear?' she had asked that afternoon. 'I can make a rude noise.' And then she had. Simon remembered that there had been boys at school with a similar capacity. While it might be a fascinating accomplishment in a coeval aged ten, it was not something of which one could be proud when introducing one's mother-in-law to other people in the Lane. Also, poor old thing, she had started to dribble.

They sat for fifty minutes in heavy traffic discussing it, all differences between them forgotten. They decided that they must go at once to Rockingham Crescent and tell Bartle that he must look after her there.

'She'd be fussed in our house,' Richeldis said. 'Much better that she should be among her own things.'

'Then after Christmas we'll find her a nice nursing home,' said Simon. 'Bartle will simply have to cope until then.'

His tone implied that this was the least, in the circumstances, that Bartle could do.

'Don't be cross with him,' said Richeldis. But when they got to the house, and found it empty, it was she who exclaimed truculently, 'Well, really, he *is* the limit.'

'We'd better hang around until he deigns to turn up,' said Simon.

'It's really better that she should come here,' said Richeldis. 'She wouldn't *want* to come to Sandilands.'

And then, almost word for word, they repeated the conversation they had been having in the car. Richeldis seemed oddly jumpy, Simon thought. She revealed, earlier in the afternoon, that she'd been on the telephone to Monica, and he began to suspect that she *knew*. Was it really possible for a woman to live with a man for twenty years and be so *stupid* that she didn't guess such a thing? He began to see that the conversation about Madge was a way of avoiding a conversation about Monica. That, surely, was why they both clung to it so desperately. When it came to it, obviously, they were both too terrified to discuss the Big Thing.

'We've had such a hell of a time these last few weeks,' Richeldis said, 'we really *owe* it to the children to give them a decent Christmas at Sandilands.'

There was a ring at the door-bell, and Richeldis jumped up with, 'That will be him.'

'Even he can't be such a fool as to ring the bell of a house which he believes to be empty.'

'He probably saw the lights on. I bet he's forgotten his key, bless him.'

Simon emitted a mirthless laugh as he went out into the hall. Through the frosted glass of the front door he could see a shape which was not his brother. It was about six inches shorter than Bartle and very much stouter. Before Simon got to the door the bell rang again.

'Mr. Longworth?' said his visitor.

'Yes.'

'Mind if I come in?'

'Who are you?'

'First things first, Mr. Longworth,' said the man, stepping into the hall and not removing his white golfing cap. 'First things first, if I may say so.'

He was perhaps five foot six inches in height. In addition to a golfing cap, he wore a brown anorak with a nylon fur collar, and some pale blue moccassins on his feet. He was a man of about fifty with enormous ears whose lobes and crevices were covered with thick tufts of fur. The top of his chest, just visible above his vest and an open-necked shirt, was similarly furry. The face itself was honest, fleshy, well-shaven, but his bristles were so profuse that the lower part of his face was darkened with bluish shadows. Brown eyes, quivering with emotion, stared at Simon from either side of a noble nose. He was very angry.

'I mean, you can't just play around, can you, not with women.'

Simon felt a jolt of sickening fear. This was worse than any nightmare. This was some sort of blackmailer who had spotted him with Monica in the motel: or some sort of moral fanatic – worse – who wished to preach the error of their ways. Richeldis was, presumably, within earshot. Simon wondered whether the mere sight of cash would shut the man up, and began to fumble for his pocket book.

'I mean this sort of behaviour. I'm a decent man, Mr. Longworth.'

'I don't know if a cheque would make any difference to you,' said Simon. 'I might add that I have absolutely no idea what you are talking about and, that if you come here again or attempt to bother me in any way, I shall call the police.'

'Now look, moosh, who d'you think you're talking to?'

'Since you haven't introduced yourself I have no way of ascertaining.'

'Don't try and get clever with me, Mr. Longworth. Just don't try and get clever with me. If you think this is a cheque-book matter, then you don't know Leonard Bernstein.'

'I don't know Leonard Bernstein.'

'Very clever, *very* clever.'

'Look, I'm completely in the dark.'

'So are we, Mr. Longworth, so are we. But let me tell you *this*. If you think you can dabble with a young girl's affections and then just chuck her on one side like an old sock . . .'

'That isn't my belief,' said Simon. He suddenly guessed who this man must be. Ruth Jolly's father. Oh, *God*!

'I mean we're talking about a young girl who's pregnant. Mr. Longworth.'

Oh, *Christ*! In his head he hastily counted the weeks since his holiday in Paris with Ruth Jolly. Seven weeks. Too late for an abortion? Oh, the stupid, vindictive little bitch.

'Look,' he said. He was almost whispering now, half pleading with the man to keep his voice down. 'I'm sure that if we talk this thing through rationally, Mr. . . .'

'Bernstein. I've told you my name, haven't I?'

'I didn't realise.'

'Quite a lot you don't realise, Mr. Longworth, if I've got your number right. Like people having feelings. Ever thought what it must feel like to be a young girl in love with an older man, know what I mean, you give her expectations . . .'

'Yes, yes, I know what you are talking about . . .'

'And then you turn round and say you don't want to know, or rather, you don't say *anything*. That's what hurts, Mr. Longworth, you're just walking away from this situation.'

Mr. Bernstein's large frank countenance did not lose its expression of wrath; but into the anger there flowed an intermingling of sorrow.

'Break a lot of hearts, do you?' he asked.

'No.'

'If you could see that girl now, Mr. Longworth, if you could see her, I mean, it really is pitiful. No other word for it. It's mope, mope, mope. "Go out," I say. "Go and see your friends. Maybe see a film. Go and buy yourself some nice food." And if I've said it before, Mr. Longworth, I make no apology, that behaviour is *shabby*.'

'What is it, darling?' said Richeldis, coming out into the hall.

'Nothing,' said Simon. He felt himself turning to gooseflesh. How often, in the last weeks, had he imagined what it was going to be like when he told Richeldis that their marriage was at an end. It would have been hard to explain about Monica, but the moment would come, in its way rather a grand, tragic moment in all their lives. The present moment was one of sordid farce. Ruth *Jolly*, for Christ's sake. He had more or less forgotten that she existed.

'She's got a good job, she's a clean-living girl, and she's a *good* girl, Mr. Longworth. There's never been anything like this, if you know what I mean.'

Simon thought that he *did* know what Mr. Bernstein meant, in which case it was absurd to pretend that Ruth had been clean-living and good by that gentleman's rather high moralistic definitions. He wanted to say that the girl had been lying, but he couldn't, not with Richeldis there.

'Good evening,' said Richeldis, smiling pleasantly as she always did at everyone.

Mr. Bernstein raised his golfing cap to reveal a shiny bald head, with two scrubs of curly black hair on each side of it. In a courtly manner, quite at variance with his way of speaking to Simon, he said, 'And who do I have the pleasure of addressing?'

'This is my wife,' said Simon quietly.

There was a shocked silence, during which it would not have been surprising if Mr. Bernstein's eyes had stood out on stalks.

'Excuse me, Mr. Longworth, but did I hear you correctly?'

'Yes, I'm afraid you did.'

'Afraid,' said Richeldis, 'Why ever . . . ?'

'I am sorry, Mrs. Longworth, but I must say this to your husband, and not having been previously informed of your existence, I had not reckoned on having to say this in your presence. But if I had known you was married. If she'd known you was married . . .'

'Who?' asked Richeldis.

'Spun her a yarn he was a divorced man. Quite a sob story by all accounts. Quite a little work of art, wasn't it, eh, Mr. Longworth? Eh? Eh?'

'Simon!' Richeldis exclaimed.

'It's all some dreadful mistake.'

'Too right it's a mistake,' said the persistent Mr. Bernstein. 'It's the biggest mistake a certain person ever made in his life.'

He advanced on Simon and took him by the lapels. Richeldis let out a little squeak, in deference to which Mr. Bernstein released her husband and muttered, 'If I was a younger man . . .'

'Well, neither of us is young.'

'Do you know this, Mrs. Longworth? This certain individual is old enough to be that girl's father?'

'Simon, you really had better explain,' said Richeldis.

'And you call yourself a Reverend!' added Leonard Bernstein with withering scorn.

'But I don't —' said Simon. His face, which displayed immediate tokens of relief and amusement, quickly became taut, as he returned into the familiar groove of being furious with bloody Bartle. 'It's my brother who is the Reverend.'

'So you aren't Mr. Bartle Longworth.'

'No, no, I'm Simon.'

The news discountenanced Mr. Bernstein considerably. He began to murmur that he did not know what to say, and that his mistake had been 'highly unfortunate'.

'I perfectly understand your anxiety,' said Simon self-righteously. 'And I can assure you that, if my brother has been responsible for this . . . *unfortunate* state of things, my family will do all in its power to help you and your family . . .'

'If . . . you say *if*, Mr. Longworth, but there's no if about Stephanie's being in the family way, is there?'

'And no *if* about the father?'

'I told you, Mr. Longworth, she's a good girl. I don't know what to say to you, I don't really. I mean, coming here and making accusations. My wife, she says, Lenny, she says, you will make a fool of yourself calling on people you've never met . . . Well . . .'

'Surely it's all some *mistake*!' said Richeldis earnestly. '*Bartle*! I mean, you're not seriously saying that Bartle and your daughter . . .'

'My niece, madam. My niece Stephanie. My wife and I never had any children, and then the wife's sister and her husband passed away when Stephanie was six and a half. Well, she's been more like a daughter to us than one of our own.'

'But you can't think Bartle . . .'

'Let's ask him,' said Simon, as they heard the key turning in the latch.

Bartle was still glowing, his absolution of an hour earlier not having had time to wear off. He smiled, not the natural open smile he had for Stephanie and Madge, but the tight-lipped unhappy smile — screwed-up eyes and set jaw — which he used to produce for greeting parishioners at his church door.

'Hullo, there,' he said. And seeing a stranger (a workman? a plumber? Oh, Lord, had he left a tap running?) he saluted Leonard Bernstein with a nod.

'This is Mr. Bernstein, Bartle,' said Richeldis with a trembling voice.

'Mr. Lenny Bernstein?' The taut smile flowered into something more natural. 'Stephanie's uncle?'

'I'm afraid it's bad news, Bartle,' said Richeldis.

'Is she ill? She's not . . .'

The desolation in Bartle's face at the prospect of Stephanie's suffering should have told it's own story. But Simon bossily said, 'You'd better go in the sitting room. Mr. Bernstein has something to say to you. We'll be in the kitchen, Mr. Bernstein, when you've finished. As I said to you, we support you completely and fully take our share of responsibility as a family . . .'

Simon was boiling with rage. This business of Bartle's baby could conceivably be used as an excuse for not looking after Madge over Christmas.

Bartle led Mr. Bernstein into the sitting room and apologised about the mess. He offered Mr. Bernstein a chair but that gentleman said that he would rather stand. Bartle pressed him for news of Stephanie and, when he heard it, he himself sat down.

'I take it you wouldn't think of denying your responsibility,' said Mr. Bernstein.

'Of course I feel responsible for helping Stephanie in every way I can . . .'

'That's not what I said, Mr. Longworth. Are you a Jesuit as well as everything else?'

'No, I'm afraid we don't have Jesuits in our church.'

'Cards on the table, Mr. Longworth, do you deny you are the father of Stephanie's baby?'

'Does Stephanie say that I am?'

'Never mind what Stephanie says.'

'I mind what Stephanie says,' said Bartle, his eyes aflame. 'Has she told you that I am the father?'

'That's a private matter between the family.'

'No, it's not! It might be a private matter between me and Stephanie, but it certainly is not the exclusive concern of her uncle.'

'Now look, Mr. Longworth.'

'I love Stephanie!' His face was wild, terrible, and full of grief as he said it. 'Now can you please tell me. Did she say I was the father of this child? . . .'

'No, not in so many words. She won't say who the father is, will she? She's clammed up on us, hasn't she? But as far as her aunt and I can see she's not had a serious boyfriend for years, not for three years at least. There was a man called Kevin but Ray put a stop to that; my wife can be very firm, Mr. Longworth.'

'Do you mean to say Stephanie hasn't got any boyfriends at *all*?'

This was so cheering that, in spite of the awful news about the baby, Bartle could not help himself grinning.

'Oh,' he said, 'but that's wonderful.'

'Well, of course we knew you took her out on a regular basis – she'd come back talking about her Chinese meals and what was it – the Church Union? I'm a broad-minded man, Mr. Longworth, Ray and I were worried she didn't seem to like any Jewish boys, but as Rachel said to me, we'd rather have her go out with a Reverend than some man we couldn't trust. You see that's what you *had*, Mr. Longworth, a position of trust.'

'I see that.'

Bartle was still grinning at the fact that, in the Bernstein household, he was Stephanie's official boyfriend.

'I haven't seen Stephanie for nearly a month,' said Bartle.

'That she *would* admit. "Going out for a Chinese?" I would ask her. You know, Mr. Longworth, we don't like to pry. I would never ask her who she was going out with. But Rachel or I would usually say, "Going out for a Chinese?" and she'd say, "Yes." But, just lately, a week went by without her going for a Chinese.'

'A week quite often goes by without our seeing each other,' said Bartle artlessly.

'Every week, sometimes twice a week, regular as clockwork that girl's been out with you and don't you tell me otherwise,' said Leonard Bernstein fiercely. The fact that Bartle knew this to be untrue filled him anew with the jealous certainty that she had been out with another man (other men?) and used her friendship with him as a cover . . . 'Then a whole month goes by, and she never seems to have gone for a Chinese, and I say to her, what's the matter, and she bursts into tears and she tells us she's pregnant and she doesn't know what to do and she doesn't want to talk about it. And what does Mr. Longworth say to *that*? asks Rachel, because my wife, Mr. Longworth, is a very direct person, very warm, very honest, and little Stephanie cries even more. And, *Right*! I says to Rachel, I drive straight off to see Mr. Longworth. You'd have a job, she says, since you don't know where he lives, but Stephanie has left her handbag in the lounge, and fair's fair, Mr. Longworth, in an emergency. We found your address in her little pocket diary.'

'You did?' Then there was some ray of comfort. She must care for him a *little*.

'What do you propose to do, Mr. Longworth? You understand an uncle's anxiety?'

'Of course I do. Will you tell Stephanie – ask Stephanie – to get in touch with me? Please?'

'Is that all you're going to say to me?'

'Mr. Bernstein, you have made some very serious allegations which have no foundation in fact or in law.'

'If you are going to start waving the law book, Mr. Longworth, I know some very good solicitors. Ever heard of Oscar Bueslinck?'

'No,' said Bartle. 'Stephanie is twenty-six years old. If she doesn't want to talk about her life to you, then neither do I. Tell her that I shall be writing to her. Tell her to come and see me if she needs me. Tell her I will do anything – *anything* – she wants me to do, *anything* to help her. And now I would like to be alone.'

Mr. Bernstein was so surprised by this speech that he arose, and saying that Mr. Longworth would be hearing more of all this, and that other people in the world beside Mr. Longworth had solicitors, he let himself out of the front door. Bartle was in tears. He did not know *what* had happened. Beyond a complete certainty that he was not, and could not be, the father of Stephanie's baby, he felt woundedly ignorant. If only she had told *him*!

'*How can this be, seeing I know not a man?*'

The sentence had re-echoed bitterly inside his head while Mr. Bernstein had spoken.

Richeldis, when she opened the sitting-room door, found Bartle with moist red eyes, sitting on the sofa and smoking a cigarette.

'Bartle' she said cooingly, 'love, hope everything's all right. Bartle, it's about Madge, and Christmas.'

17

The family rituals had been gone through. The tree had been bought, the frozen goose defrosted and roasted in the Neff oven, the presents exchanged, the Wine Society champagne popped and quaffed, the boring neighbours entertained. Sandilands sank into torpor, the children languidly staying in bed until lunch-time. Someone had unwisely given Marcus a whistle, but otherwise things were tranquil. The eruptions of ill-humour between Emma and Thomas were resolved by Emma going away for a few days to stay with a school friend.

Throughout all these days, Simon felt the moment of truth approaching. He was going to have to tell Richeldis, tell her everything. Dread of this disclosure made him unable to concentrate on any of the Christmas absurdity. He had pulled crackers and corks, played board-games, allowed himself to be kissed under the mistletoe by their pretentious neighbour, Mrs. Vaughan: but all in a sort of daze. During Monopoly there had been cries of, 'Oh, *Dad*!'

'Sorry, was it my go?'

Abstractedly, he had thrown the dice. It felt terrible to be leaving them all, to be breaking the whole thing up. So, this was the last Sandilands Christmas. He alone knew it. This was the last occasion when they would be together as a family, and even this was marred by Daniel's absence in Canada. Of course, the older children would cope. And Marcus, poor little sod, did not know *what* was going on. Simon wondered about the effect of the break-up on Thomas, the third child, a curly-headed little urchin who had been rather slow in growing and whose only interest at present appeared to be peering at some bleeping computer-game. Last term's school report suggested that he *was* settling down at Allhallows. But, if only he'd got decent results in Common Entrance and been able to go to Pangham like Daniel. The trouble was, Thomas was such a funny, silent chap that you just couldn't tell what was going on inside his head. For instance, in the middle of Christmas dinner when they had all been sitting there with paper hats on their heads, he had blurted out, 'I'm missing granny.'

In the event, one felt rather a shit leaving granny with Bartle, but what else could they *do*? Richeldis had rung up a temporary nursing home to see if they would have Madge for a short spell, but it was eight *hundred* pounds for a week. Anyway, Bartle had rung up on Christmas Day and obviously they were coping. Their nearby Italian restaurant was closed on Christmas day itself, but he'd found an Indian place which did 'take-away', in many ways preferable with Madge in her present condition.

They had all seen Madge merely as a problem. Only little Thomas had said the human thing. There had been a nasty moment at the dinner table when Simon had thought the child might weep. He had gone very red and rubbed the top of his sadly-beginning-to-be-spotty forehead with the back of a hand which was still clutching a forkful of sausage.

Later, in bed that night, the husband and wife had talked of the moment. They both realised how sad they were that Thomas was at boarding school. Neither of them *understood* him, and now the chances were that he would remain a stranger to both his parents forever. They had no idea whether or not he was happy. Simon had ended this conversation rather abruptly, and then turned over and closed his eyes. He felt instinctively that holding any unnecessary conversation with his wife, particularly if it was amicable conversation, represented a betrayal of Monica. Since her return to Paris, he felt a wild ghastly love for her which was as strong as ever. In spite of it, however, he wanted to talk to Richeldis about the children. He missed her customary burbling commentary on the family's doings. Somehow – it only dawned on him with hurtful slowness – she didn't *want* to talk to him as much as she used to.

On Boxing Day, while the others were out at Mrs. Vaughan's ('I'll follow you over'), Simon had decided to take a risk. Closeting himself in the study, he had rung Monica.

'What did you do yesterday?'

'I had a Russian lesson.'

'On Christmas Day?'

'It isn't Christmas Day for them.'

'How very Soviet of you.'

'You miss my point. It's the last Wednesday in Advent. It's not Christmas for *them* for over a week. I miss you.'

'I miss you, too.'

'Have you spoken yet to Richeldis?'

'I can't just yet.'

'Try to, beloved. Please. It will be better, truly it will, when you have told her. The worst thing is the deception, the lying. She's my oldest friend, don't forget, as well as your wife. I can bear the idea of taking you from her, because that has been inevitable. We couldn't escape it. I think she might *see* that, I really do. She's a great romantic, Richeldis. But I can't *bear* the idea of lying to her.'

'No.'

'As soon as you've told her, come over here.'

'Someone's coming. 'Bye.'

But it had only been Mrs. Turbot coming in to tidy the bedrooms and wash some pots and pans.

A day or two had passed, and still the moment was not right for telling Richeldis. It wasn't just Simon's cowardice. Family or neighbours were *about* all the time. Richeldis was never alone, except late at night. They were so *sleepy* after eleven o'clock. It was no moment for important discussions.

And then, unambiguously, the Moment came. It was provoked by Richeldis herself. He felt very much surprised when one day, after luncheon, she put on her silly woollen hat and her Windsmoor and said, 'Darling, come and have a walk with me. We've got to have a talk.'

They walked in single file, as was necessary, down the little lane, and out into the edge of Bunyan's Field. He wore clumping brown walking shoes, corduroy trousers, a Barbour and a tweed cap: every inch the suburban squire. She, the dewy air settling on her fluffy hat like gossamer, looked a meet spouse for the figure he was trying to cut.

In the field, she stood and looked at him, and took one of his gloved hands in her mitten. She realised then that she had been avoiding his gaze for about a week. They had hardly looked at each other all Christmas. And now she was staring at him with serious intentness, and he could see her kind, worried eyes peering deeply into his.

'We can't go on like this,' she said, 'being cross with each other.'

'Richeldis.'

'No, I know what you are going to say.'

'You do?'

'Of course. But let me have my say first. You see, I don't think you have quite realised how utterly disturbed I have felt for weeks: worried about mother, worried about Marcus in the way one is, worried about Monica.'

'Oh.'

'Not very worried, but worried, yes. Perhaps that didn't occur to you.'

She laughed, and he wondered at her *coolness*. It rather annoyed him that she was taking charge and Behaving Well. It was typical of Richeldis and, while being angered by her bravery, he could not but admire it. Other men's wives, when they discovered that their husbands were in love with other women, behaved like frantic loonies. Not Richeldis. Not very worried, but worried about Monica! This was rich.

'I'm not trying to excuse my behaviour, Simon. I don't want to excuse it.'

'It's not *your* fault,' he said, faintly puzzled by her attitude, but allowing her to talk because he did not himself know what to say.

'When that little man came to the house and started talking about Bartle, I just felt so guilty! It seemed like a judgement on *me*. It's funny. Mother always said that Bartle had a floozy girl, but I thought it was just one of her little ideas.'

Simon was silent. He wondered why they were talking about Bartle, rather than about him and Monica.

'Isn't it funny, being married,' continued Richeldis, who would not let go of his hand. Their feet crunched on the hard frosty mud of the field. All around, the strange landscape spread itself out in a starkly featureless composition of greys and duns. 'I mean, one just doesn't *need* to spell everything out – we both know what is happening by *feeling*.'

'Yes.'

'The trouble with not talking, though, is that things get out of perspective.'

'I don't think this is out of perspective, Richeldis.'

'At first, I wasn't going to tell you,' she said. 'After all I've been under strain, and it just wasn't important. I have never done such a thing before and it won't happen again. I can't exactly feel guilty about it, either, because it was so, in a way, innocent. But of course your whole attitude to me has been different since that day, completely different. Darling, don't be hurt. I know I ought to be kneeling at your feet and imploring forgiveness. But I don't think it's necessary. For one thing I am rather moved by your attitude. It demonstrates, in spite of everything, what an extraordinarily solid marriage we have: your *knowing* instinctively, your minding so frightfully. Perhaps something *has* disappeared from our marriage, but we are still jolly good friends. It's silly for us not to be happy.'

Simon was turning to gooseflesh. She was playing a totally surprising card. He had begun to suspect that she had some trump up her sleeve, but this was a card from a different pack: not the ace of spades, but something from Happy Families. Moreover, his intelligence was on trial. She was condescendingly congratulating him for having intuited something which *she* had done. Surely she was not trying to call his bluff by claiming that she had found another man? What he would have called 'the logistics' were impossible. She had been so fully occupied, looking after him, seeing to the children, going to see her mother, helping Bartle tidy up the mess which he had created in Rockingham Crescent . . .

Bartle! ! ! ?

'I take it you're not being serious,' he said cautiously.

Not Bartle!

'Darling, don't let's go on being cross with each other. You've been horrid to me for months, and I minded rather a lot at first. But I dare say you couldn't help it. I've been pretty annoying, I dare say. And perhaps all this has something to do with it. But the fact that you were *so* intuitive made me feel our marriage was really strong . . .'

Not that again! Now was the moment to stop all this dreadful prattle, this self-righteous tosh about how happy they were and how marvellous she was. He could shatter her illusions with a few words. He could tell her about Monica, and announce that he was about to leave for Paris. But he felt cowardly about doing so, and genuinely curious about the matter he was supposed to have deduced with such marital intuition.

'Can you please explain what you are saying?'

'I know you are leaping to all kinds of ridiculous conclusions.'

'Not until now.'

'So I've decided to be totally honest. I have written a little note to Bartle to tell him that I have told you, and we are all going to behave sensibly and just carry on as if nothing had happened.'

'To Bartle? You've written to Bartle . . .'

'Don't look so *worried*, darling. It meant *nothing*. No, that isn't true, it didn't mean nothing, but it didn't mean what these things usually mean.'

'What are you talking about?'

'I'm not in love with Bartle,' she said, gulping seriously and turning to look at him with large serious eyes. 'You'll just have to believe that.'

In normal circumstances, the idea of anyone being in love with Bartle would have produced, from the brother, a belly-laugh. Now, the sensations in Simon's belly were far from merry; he felt as if he had just started a rough ride on the big dipper.

'Do you remember the day mother went funny? I think we all went funny that day. And I went to Putney and you were so busy, and then rather sweetly came back here?'

'Yes.'

'And Bartle and I stayed and cleared up the house, and you can imagine the rest.'

'I can't. I can imagine almost anything more easily than Bartle . . . language fails.'

'You are *awful*.' She squeezed his arm. 'I'm rather flattered that you are so cross.'

'Don't be.'

'It was one evening when we'd been to see mother at the hospital; it was the day she was being the captain of a submarine; no, it wasn't, it was earlier, the Whizz-Kids were still in those radiators . . .'

'It doesn't really matter what *day* it was.'

'Well, it does in a way, because you know, darling, everything became unreal in those few days. Mother was jabbering about being on double time and adding five, and the world was about to blow up. Everything was just – unreal.'

'Nothing more so than this.'

'We went to that crumby little trattoria mother loves so much, just Bartle and I. We drank a bottle of Soave. I had Veal Milanese and he had Chicken Cacciatore.'

'I would rather not know what you both ate.'

'And then we went home and had a cup of coffee. Oh, I know there isn't really an excuse, but I was tired, and a bit drunk, and I just wanted someone to cuddle.'

'You are telling me that you and Bartle . . . did this thing . . . there and then?'

'But you knew – didn't you?'

It should have been easy to say that he did not know, that this was in fact the most astonishing piece of information he had ever received in his life. It should have been easy, but somehow the words did not come. Absurdly enough, it felt at that moment as though the only way he could rescue any dignity for himself was to behave as if he had known about this all along. But he felt shocked, and deeply hurt.

'Has this happened often?' he asked.

'Well, that's what worried me so much because I *guessed* you were thinking that. Darling, you're not to think that Bartle and I are having an affair or anything like that . . .'

'I shall never have him in this house again,' Simon heard himself saying. 'This is outrageous. He is meant to be a *priest*.'

'It was one, tiny, extraordinary incident. As a matter of fact, Bartle thought that much the best thing . . .'

'I do not wish to know what Bartle thought.'

'He thought I shouldn't tell you, that you would be hurt. Poor thing. His own experience of marriage has been so wretched that he didn't understand. He just couldn't see that you would be able to understand,

Simon. I wouldn't have told you if I didn't see it eating into you. I expect you were imagining that it was something much worse!'

'Yes, and no.'

'Will you forgive me, my darling Simon.'

'I don't think you realise . . .'

She turned to him. Her upturned face was both beguiling and infuriating. She was so maddeningly in control. And now, if he told her about Monica, it would look like tit for tat. It would seem as though he was running off to Paris because he was so angry about Bartle. He *had* to explain that *his* affair had started before hers; he owed it to himself. But there was something deeper than that. He could not bear the thought of that bloody creep with her. With *his* Richeldis. Roughly, with a boyish roughness, he took her in his arms, not sure whether he was the lover claiming his own, or a little child running back to his mother. From afar, on her way back to make her husband's tea, Mrs. Turbot saw them, clasped in their embrace, and thought how lovely it would be for two people to be so much in love.

*   *   *

It is so cold here that the Seine is almost frozen. Everything looks very beautiful. I think that Paris is meant to be icy, like Parisians. No telephone calls and no letters for a couple of days. Bother Christmas.

Monica laid down her pen, a fat black Montblanc. Why did she feel such misgivings? The jealousy which she felt at that moment of Richeldis was so strong that she thought it would kill her. She had had so *much* of him. Richeldis had just *hogged* him for twenty-two years; and he had not truly loved her. It was hard, for this, not to hate one's oldest friend. But if she found it hard to forgive the long wasted years, the best years of Simon's life, she could less easily pardon these few days and weeks since everything had begun to happen. When they were together in London, and in the motel, Monica had counselled gentleness. She had wanted to have what she so desperately yearned for without hurting Richeldis or the children. It had been clear, then, that they must wait for the Right Moment for telling them of the decision. But, once she was alone again in Paris, she had been completely overwhelmed by the unjustness of this. It was she who longed for him, ached for him, sobbed for him, needed him, adored him. And why the hell *should* those boring, limited people claim his company for a further ten days, simply because they wished to wear paper hats and eat a lot of disgusting food together? It was hard to be her old brittle, restrained, funny self, when feeling like this. Moreover, she felt, after nearly a fortnight's absence, almost a shyness in writing to him, as though she hardly dared to say directly and simply what she felt.

This afternoon, I shall go to the Luxembourg and sit on 'our' bench and think of 'our' conversation there and this evening I have reserved 'our' table at Chez Paul. But it's not much fun being at our table all alon-io and for the first time in my life I am hating being alone. What have you done to me? I find myself thinking I'd rather be in a motel in Dunstable than strolling down the Boulevard Saint-Michel in the snow. I almost found myself writing to be forgiven for loving you so much, it makes me feel greedy for you. I just want to be with you forever and ever, and every second I am not with you seems empty and pointless. M.

The letter, disguised as best it could be in a typed brown envelope, found a very different Simon who no longer knew what was happening to him. The reminder of how much Monica loved him, though gratifying his vanity, filled him with deep embarrassment and awkwardness. Things had changed so. Marriages, he was now saying to himself, go through these *phases*.

When he heard about Richeldis and Bartle, it should have provided the perfect opportunity of bringing the marriage to a formal end. But he felt so scaldingly humiliated by the thought of his wife in bed with his elder brother that he wanted to establish his *rights*. Richeldis and Simon became lovers again. He was still very angry with her; angry that she had thus reclaimed him, angry that she had betrayed him, angry that she had forced him to 'betray' Monica. But this made it no less exciting to take her. In fact, the marital act now had all the angry passion of adultery with an enemy.

The next morning, still thinking of how she had betrayed him, he had worried at the wound, torn at the scar, and steeled himself to ask the ignominious question: had she *enjoyed* going to bed with Bartle? She amazed him by laughing. Laughing and laughing and laughing.

'Going to *bed* with Bartle! My darling, you must think I'm a nymphomaniac or something.'

'But you *said* . . .'

'I said that I had wanted someone to cuddle. That was all that happened.'

'You mean, you didn't even undress?'

'We lay and cuddled each other in front of the gas fire. That's all. And he, very sweetly and flatteringly, said he wanted us to spend the night together.'

'I'll kill him.'

'Don't be so *silly*. He knew as well as I did that it was out of the question. He was drunk, that's all.'

'He tried it on, though. To think that man once had responsibilities . . .'

'Oh, come on! Darling! One little moment. It was an important little moment for both him and me; and I didn't want it to be a guilty secret. That's why I told you.'

'You mean that you haven't betrayed me at all?'

'Funny language to use.'

Then he felt cheated. Samson shorn of his strength by Delila. But he did not resist when she embraced him, and he felt all the softness of her skin, and the plumpness of her belly and breasts. A repetition of the previous evening's delights was not only unavoidable. It was what, in that early morning darkness, he most profoundly desired.

18

Far away in the suburbs of Leeds, Vera McManus was beginning her day. The new marital routine was a much brisker business than the horrible old days in the vicarage. Keith, her new husband, always brought her some tea at seven o'clock which they drank together while they listened to the *Today* programme on Radio Four. Then, arrayed in track suits and woolly hats, they went out jogging for thirty minutes; down their road, up a footpath, out into the park, past the children's recreation ground, and then home again for a shower, followed by a breakfast of muesli and whole-meal brown bread. They had both become fanatically keen on health food since Vera had been told that she had slight 'blood pressure'.

Keith was a wiry little man with glasses. Malicious observers said that he looked a bit like Bartle but anyone could see, in Vera's opinion, that they were quite different. Keith was altogether less lopsided than Bartle, who was woefully out of training, and would not have been able to run ten yards to save his life.

Keith's track suit was the same colour and design as Vera's, fluorescent green, with sporty white stripes down the legs. On the feet they wore identical white towelling socks, and sneakers; Keith's were size nine, Vera's size five. If you had seen them that morning, you might have taken them for brother and sister, both so bespectacled, both slightly pinched in their neatness. Both, at the bottom of the stairs, looked round admiringly at the open-plan living area of their house: at its immaculate oatmeal carpet, its white walls uncluttered with pictures or ornaments. The furniture was rigidly geometrical in structure. The oblong predominated. There was a hi-fi system in the corner, and a glass coffee-table, neatly piled with *Which?* and *New Society*, both of which they read avidly. The only anarchic shape in the room was Vera's 'cello, neatly hidden behind the sofa.

They liked, too, the trim, gravelly patch at the front, designated a rockery. On the whole, they were pleased with the Avenue, as they called the cul-de-sac of their residence.

'Have you got the key?' she asked sharply, as she asked him every morning. Vera always spoke sharply, probably it was a legacy of long years with Bartle. When she interrogated Keith it still gave her pleasure that she got a proper answer.

'In my pocket, dear.'

If you asked Bartle whether he had remembered the key, he would say either 'yes', and then admit half an hour later that in fact the key was still in his old pair of trousers hanging on the back of a chair in the bedroom. Or he would lose his temper and ask why he should bother with things like keys. You couldn't get a man like Bartle out of your system, not ever. Closing doors was one of the moments when she always thought about him, always with irritation. He was neurotic, she supposed.

Keith and Vera gave off a slightly sweaty smell as they jogged down the Avenue, but this stench would vanish when they returned and took it in turn to stand in the self-assembled shower-unit, and soaped themselves with Lifeguard.

On their runs, they began by having little chats, either about the previous day, or about the coming day. Later on, they would grow breathless and conversation would cease. Today they spoke of the possible arrival of a gas man to service their central heating boiler. They had had this conversation twice before; once on the day that the postcard arrived, announcing the date of the technician's arrival; and once the previous evening.

'They just sent a card,' said Vera, 'saying they would be coming today.'

'Not even,' chimed in Keith, 'whether they would be coming a.m. or p.m.'

'They just assume that women do not have jobs,' said Vera.

'Or that someone will be in all day. Just for them,' said Keith. 'Still,' he added, 'I yield to no one in my belief that gas is the most efficient and economical way of heating a house of our size.'

'Definitely,' said Vera.

'Now, I can remember before the price of oil went up . . . Are you all right, dear?'

'I think I've got a stitch,' said Vera. She was clutching her side and her face was contorted with pain. She looked up at Keith with bulbous, terrible eyes. Having been deathly pale, her face had become dark and purple.

'Are you going to be sick?' asked Keith. 'Very often, running on an empty stomach . . .'

But before he had completed this generalisation Vera had fallen dead by the lamp-post. A detail which Keith was never able to forget was that her hand splatted into a lump of dog-shit as she fell.

Bartle never heard about the dog-shit. It was Keith's secret. Bartle did not even learn that Vera was dead until some four months later when he had a solicitor's letter about it. By then the whole complexion and pattern of his life had altered.

*   *   *

On the morning that Vera died, her husband in the eyes of God was looking after Madge and feeling wretched about Stephanie. Bartle did not blame the hospital for trying to see if Madge could be reinstated into the community, to use the cant phrase. But he was pessimistic about the success of the venture. Her completely manic phase had passed, anyway for the time being, and it had given place to agitated dolefulness. She was under the impression that there were all kinds of rules, relating to the most minute particulars: for example, where she should put her feet. And her brain was too fuddled to keep up with the flood of exacting regulations with which They, the mysterious They, were torturing her. Then, for spells of about an hour, she would become calm, and quiet, and sad. It was as though all the madness left her, then, and she saw herself with purgatorially cruel clarity.

'I suppose Richeldis will have to sell this house,' she said, when one of these moods was upon her.

'Not unless you want to sell it.'

They were slurping their milky coffee at about half past ten in the morning.

'She'll have to. Can't go on like this.'

'I'm here.'

'You're very kind, but why *should* you be?'

'Because I want to be.'

'You don't really want to be. Someone has to be kind, usually the weakest person or the one with the softest heart. That just happens to be you. But I ought to be in a . . . a ward.'

It was horrible that she was able to see this so clearly. By way of expanding the remark, she added, 'Somewhere that I could make extremely rude noises.'

'You can do that at home.'

'Very smelly.'

'No one minds.'

'I mind,' she snapped. Then, coffee cup in mid-air, her mood changed and she was seized once more with a fit of agitation. 'Now, where am I to put *this*?'

'On the saucer.'

'But am I?' she dithered tragically, as though They were going to punish her when she put the cup on the wrong place.

'Oh, put it *anywhere*, Madge.'

'But where's it *meant* to be?' Her eyes started to fill with tears. First, she lowered the cup towards the saucer but, just before putting it down, she jolted it up again. 'Or should I put it on the floor?'

'If you like.'

'If you like's no good. Where am I *meant* to put it?'

'On the saucer.'

'You're sure?'

'Yes.'

She clunked the cup on to the saucer and spilled a little of the coffee. The minor calamity provoked a flood of tears. 'I've done it all wrong,' she moaned. 'I do everything wrong.'

He came over and tried to cuddle her, but she would not be comforted. Once more, They had won. They had caught her out. He could smell that she needed to visit the lavatory. Getting her upright, waddling her along to the loo, removing the underclothes, cleaning her up and putting her into a clean pair of incontinence knickers was a sorry task. At several points he was very close to retching.

'Very disgusting for you,' she murmured.

'Not at all. Now, where would you like to be?'

'Oh, don't ask me!' she said crossly. 'Where am I *meant* to be?'

'You could come back into the sitting room. Or would you like a little lie down?'

'Am I supposed to lie down?'

'You can if you like.'

'I think perhaps I am meant to lie down.'

'Then, let's go to the bedroom.'

'Or am I meant to practise walking? I could try walking in the hall.'

The door bell rang.

'That will be Richeldis,' said Madge.

Bartle hoped that it wasn't. He felt very awkward about Richeldis. Alcohol had prompted him to behave like a fool towards her. His confessor had said that what transpired was hardly sinful: two lonely people hugging each other for an hour or so. But it was not her betrayal of her husband that he had minded about. What made him ache with self-loathing was that he had betrayed Stephanie, betrayed his romantic vision.

'I'll let her in,' said Madge.

'Should you?' The habit was catching.

'Perhaps not.'

'Do if you want to.'

The bell rang insistently once more.

'Oh, why can't she let *herself* in?' asked Madge.

Bartle opened the door. It was Stephanie.

At first, he could not believe his eyes. She had not answered his letter, written after the distressing visit of her uncle. She was carrying another man's baby. Stephanie had made a fool of Bartle, and now she had passed out of his life. He had convinced himself of that. And now, here she was again, her beautiful flames of hair framing her pale face. She wore an anorak, brown corduroy trousers and high-heeled black boots.

'I wasn't sure if you'd be here,' she said, nervously smiling.

'Come in.'

'Richeldis, you're late.' Madge called out.

'This is Mrs. Cruden,' said Bartle.

Stephanie looked at the figure who stood beside Bartle. His attempts to put her hair up had not been successful and the chaos of unwashed locks on top of her head made her look witch-like and a bit frightening. She had no colour in her cheeks. Grey, her face was; tear-stained and terrible. There were bits of food — coffee-skin, biscuit-crumbs — clinging to her quivering lips, and her splashy flower-patterned frock was strewn with the remains of an eggy breakfast.

'Pleased to meet you,' said Stephanie, holding out her hand.

Madge shook it gingerly and managed a watery smile. Then she curtsied.

'How do you do.'

'Stephanie is a very good friend of mine, Madge.'

'Just good friends. I see, dear boy.'

'She used to live in my parish.'

'Did you know John Betjeman?' Madge asked.

'No!' The idea struck Stephanie as preposterous. 'Nothing like that.'

'He was very, you know, churchy.'

'I'm not much of a church-goer,' said Stephanie.

'Very few are, I believe,' said Madge. 'What am I, Eric? A fellow traveller, wouldn't you say?'

'A very good one,' said Bartle, in a weirdly parsonical voice. He shut the front door and ushered Stephanie into the sitting room. The arrival of the girl made him see what a mess everything was once more. Try as he could, he found tidiness impossible. He had the bad habit of carrying things from one room to the next and forgetting why he had brought them there. A pile of unwashed shirts were draped on the piano stool. What was a tin of Ovaltine (no lid) doing on top of the television set?

'I just thought I'd look in and see how you were getting on,' said Stephanie.

'Oh, not so badly, are we, Madge?'

'Very badly indeed,' said Madge. 'I have to make rather a lot of rude noises, and I keep doing everything wrong.'

'Ah,' said Stephanie. 'Shame.'

'I behave like a complete fool, do you see. At the moment I don't know whether I should be walking about or lying down. Do you have this trouble of people saying one thing and doing another?'

'Why don't you have a nice lie down?' said Stephanie. 'Then me and Bartle'll bring you up some dinner.'

'I think that would be very nice indeed. Very kind.'

'Shall we help you get to bed, then?'

'I don't think I'm meant to get *on* the bed.'

'I'll help you, shall I?'

With a kindness which was immediately authoritative, Stephanie took Mrs. Cruden's arm and led her towards the stairs.

'Now I shall have to make sure that I start off on the right foot, otherwise everything goes wrong.'

'Got a bad foot, have you?'

'I never remember which foot I'm meant to start out with.' Polite self-deprecating laughter. 'That's when the real disasters start to occur.'

'That's right, one step at a time.'

Bartle did not join in the procession upstairs. It was typical of Stephanie that she had been able immediately to accommodate herself to the rather crazy set-up. While she was upstairs he devoted himself to some tidying. He seized the shirts from the piano-stool and stuffed them inside the piano. He moved a pile of old newspapers from the table to the window seat and then back again to the table. He was still clutching an Ovaltine lid (where on *earth* was the tin?) when the girl returned.

'Poor old soul,' she said.

'So now you see it,' he gestured with the lid; by 'it' he meant, and she understood, the whole situation.

'I missed you,' she said coyly.

'And I missed you.'

'I wanted to apologise – about Uncle Lenny. He should never have come. I just felt awful when he said he'd been here. And the things he said!'

'Didn't you get my letter?'

'No. Not yet.'

'I've said it all in that. How it's all *right*. I can't imagine why you haven't got it. I posted it the evening of your uncle's visit.'

'I don't know what Uncle Lenny thought he was *doing*. He must be mad.' She looked at him with a long miserable look. 'Accusing you of being the father. Oh, Bartle, I'm sorry.'

'Don't be.'

Then he said, 'Golly! What a sad mess!' and he sat down on Madge's chair, feeling her saucer crack beneath his bottom.

'It's for you I'm sorry,' she said. 'Ever so sorry for what I've done to *you*. I don't love *him* – the father of my baby.' She came and sat on the arm of his chair and stroked his head. 'I'm the one who should be crying,' she said.

'Let's both cry.'

'Bartle, I want to tell you about it. Will you let me?'

He was about to reply, but when they looked up Madge had returned.

'Now, am I meant to be on my bed or aren't I?' she said. 'As usual I've done it all wrong.'

Stephanie stayed all day. For the first couple of hours they could not really talk. She helped him make a rudimentary dinner of fish cakes, tinned tomatoes, bread and butter and a tin of peaches. After they had all eaten some of it, Madge snored in her armchair and Stephanie did the washing up with Bartle. Once more, there was an enormous pile of it: sausagey frying pans, plates to which days-old bits of suet clung like warts.

'It's my boss.'

'Mr. Greenhalgh?'

It was remarkable that the man who had fixed Bartle's teeth should be the father of the baby, but what could have been more natural?

'I have been an idiot. I can see that.'

'How long has it been going on?'

'Ages. At first he said he wanted to get a divorce and marry me. I really believed him. I think he believed it himself. But then one thing and another happened, and his wife had another baby. I never wanted just an affair. I'm not that sort. Well, you know me.'

Did he? Stephanie's character had always been mysterious to him. He only knew that the more her character unfolded, the more painfully he loved her. These revelations, which should have had the effect of destroying his love, had quite the opposite effect.

'I had to tell Uncle Lenny. I had to. Mr. Greenhalgh – Tim –'

Oh, that hurt; that 'Tim'.

'What does *he* want?' Bartle asked. 'Mr. Greenhalgh?'

'Well, he was really furious, as if it was all my fault. Thought I was just trying to split up his marriage. He said – such things. He wanted me to have – you know.'

'An abortion?'

'But I couldn't, Bartle. Not my baby. I just couldn't.'

'So what are you going to do? Presumably you can't marry Mr. Greenhalgh?'

'I don't want to. I wouldn't marry him if he was free.' She spoke quite calmly.

'I'm going to smoke a cigarette,' said Bartle, as though this would solve things.

'Bad for your teeth,' she said automatically.

'Oh, Stephanie, Stephanie. Why didn't you come to see me *before*?'

'You stopped ringing up. I couldn't think why. I thought' – she smiled her old, deliciously flirtatious laugh – 'I thought you didn't love me any more. I just assumed that you were fed up with me, that's all.'

He made a vague sweeping gesture to indicate the mess, the house, Madge.

'There was all this.'

'I didn't really know, did I?'

'Stephanie, you know I'd have dropped everything if you needed me.'

'Well, once I'd found out I was pregnant, I . . .'

'When?' He tried to make frantic calculations but involuntarily they were racing through his head. When they had last had dinner at the Dear Friends, was she? . . . Had she and Greenhalgh just been? . . . It was too dreadful to contemplate.

'Oh, a few weeks ago now. And then, after I'd told Tim, I was definitely going to have my baby . . .'

'Must make things awkward at work.'

'I've left.'

'Oh.'

'That's when I had to tell Uncle Lenny. He went spare. So did Auntie Ray; throwing up a good job, I must be out of my mind. They wouldn't let it drop until I'd admitted it. That I was having a baby.'

On her lips the phrase 'having a baby' had its own sweet beauty. She said it as if it was all one word, with a high nasal, slightly cocknified emphasis on the syllable *babe*, which was almost, but not quite, *bibe. Havnabibie.*

'He didn't give me a chance to explain, Uncle Lenny. Just started shouting at me, really blew his top, and Auntie Ray was crying and telling him if he went on like that he'd do me an injury. He kept wanting to know who it was, the father, and I wouldn't tell him, and he said it was that vicar: that's what he calls you. Never likes it when I'm going out with you. It's that bleeding vicar, they're all the bleeding same . . .'

They both laughed as they automatically did when she quoted any utterance of Mr. Leonard Bernstein.

'That's when he came storming round here, presumably,' said Bartle. He told her about Mr. Bernstein's near assault on Simon, and about the ultimate insult: 'Call yourself a Reverend.' When their laughter died away he took her hand and said, 'I wish I was the father.'

'I wish you were, Bartle. I really wish you were. Oh, Bartle, what are we going to do?'

19

Snow came in the middle of January. Emma and Thomas went back to school. Marcus returned to his playgroup. Simon's communications with Monica became slightly more frequent. Chiefly, these took the form of letters. Monica wrote each day. Sometimes, they were little more than a few sentences. *I want to write to you, my own beloved, to tell you that I love you, and will love you Vsegda, as the Russians would say.* Sometimes she sent several pages, recounting books read, solitary walks through icy streets and deserted parks. Simon replied to most of these letters, which were sent in typed envelopes to his office and marked PERSONAL. It troubled him to note how the correspondence quickly developed its own existence and justification. It was almost as though they were both writing a novel about each other. It started to feel unreal. Unquestionably, there were, and remained, deep spiritual kinships between them. Through all the years these had been there, and the flowering of their love had merely put a seal on twenty years of laughing at the same jokes and liking the same kind of music. In the emotional turmoil of being discovered with Ruth Jolly at Fontainebleau, he had fallen in love with Monica, but, as the weeks of their separation passed, the prosaic and quotidian realities tightened their hold on his heart. If he were in love with Monica – what then? It now seemed incredible to him that he had actually contemplated giving up his job, and going to live with her in Paris. What would he *do* all day? And – there was no point in denying the importance of these ties –what of Sandilands, the children, not to mention 'the wife'?

I so understand your feelings that you can't face seeing R. until I have told her everything, he wrote in one letter. *I admire you for not wishing to do anything which is mean or dishonest, but . . .*

It was in that *but* that all the difficulties resided. He had been going to write *but we should not rush things.* But he knew, far from rushing them, he wished to keep these particular 'things' forever at bay. So he wrote: *but things at the works are very complicated just now. I have discussed the possibility of resignation with Brodie* [his joint managing director] *and his view is that with my various commitments it simply isn't feasible until we are well into the third quarter of the coming year.*

The lapse into the manner of business letters revealed a simple untruth. He had not 'discussed' matters with Brodie, nor with anyone else. One day over lunch he had remarked jocularly to his colleague that he was so tired, he ought to take early retirement, to which Brodie had laughed and said, 'Don't do that, Simon. Whatever you do.' That was all. The truth was, in this affair of Monica, he had bitten off more than he could chew. When she had first confronted him with his Fontainebleau-philandering he had been ashamed: not of his adultery, but of his own fickleness. He *minded* that Ruth Jolly meant so little to him: as little as all her boring predecessors. In his 'strange and fateful interview' with Monica, he had fallen in love with the idea that he might, after all, be capable of a great, enduring love. Now, when he woke up in the mornings beside Richeldis at Sandilands, he had to force himself to remember Monica. He kept telling himself that he was pining away for love of her, but it was not true. Absence makes the heart grow colder.

He had lapsed from his romantic ideal. Therefore he felt guilt about making love to his wife. He was not in love with Richeldis. She had managed to hold on to him by making it humiliatingly clear that she was not really in love with him. He still snapped at her when rummaging for shirts in the airing cupboard, and yawned at her tedious domestic narratives. The fact that he did not even like her much, if it registered, no longer seemed to hurt her. Moreover, he realised that *leaving* this woman who annoyed and slightly bored him would be an emotional impossibility. The prosaic and dull facts were that he was forty-eight years old, a father, a husband, and the director of a sand quarry. For years now he had regarded these facts as encumbrances, interruptions to life. (Life, he imagined, as a true Romantic, was what went on when he was listening to records of Brahms or fornicating with typists.) Now he recognised that the job and the family *were* life. Brodie was a crashing bore; so in quite a different manner was Richeldis: it was hardly exciting to talk about redecorating the spare bedroom or whether to pen a line to Emma's housemistress about her sore throats. But this was what life, in its concrete reality, was. There was nothing wrong with it. The leap which he had proposed to himself – going to Paris with Monica – had been, in effect, a desire to be detached from his real existence. He had been thinking of himself purely as a sexual being with absolutely no reference to his ordinary everyday life. He was trying to dismiss actual life in favour of an idealised version of life. Nor could he justify himself by claiming that his life was particularly hard. He had a warm house, a flat in town, pots of money. What more did he want? That he did want more was questionable. This mysterious more was somehow promised in the siren music of Brahms. He thought of Belinda, whom he despised. He thought of Bartle's wife, Vera, whom he supposed to be still alive. He thought of all the dozens of people who had been through the modern rigmarole of divorce. They had surely, most of them, been in pursuit of Romance. And quite inexorably, in the process of dull time, boring old porridgey Life had reasserted itself. With the new spouses, there had been the same need to get mortgages, choose wallpapers, book holidays, worry about schools. In some cases (no one, for example, blamed Vera) it was quite understandable that people found a particular husband or wife intolerable. But for the most part this was not what prompted break-ups. People *lived* with the most intolerable partners for years. What made them leave was the dream of Romance. Dull old, or dull young, anybodies were transformed by the alchemy of sex, for a few months (years if they were lucky), into Dante and Beatrice, Connie Chatterley and Mellors. And then, when they'd romped through the rain or fantasized their way into Paradise, there was still waking up, buttoning, zipping, shopping, paying, eating. He was not quite cynical enough to suppose that fondness did not last. But, if it did, one was lucky. None of the rest lasted.

He hated these realisations. They came to him as doubts might worry a devout clergyman. Romance, like Religion, pleaded not to be discarded. He would write *I love you and long for you*, to Monica. He was not lying when he wrote those words. He had once meant them, and he still longed for them to be true.

In the third week in January, she made another secret visit to London. The first day was spent mostly in bed. He wondered if she noticed that they now made love so repeatedly not because they had to, but because they had run out of things to say to one another. There were the moony little strolls around the Tate Gallery; restaurant meals; a concert at the Festival Hall. But, for the entire three days, he had known that he was enacting a lie. He hated himself when he saw the ecstatic brightness of her facial expressions.

'Just so long as we are together,' she said. 'I don't care *what* happens. If we have to go on in this unsatisfactory way a bit longer, then that is the way it will have to be.'

This was before getting her taxi for Heathrow.

'I shall think of you always and miss you,' he said, kissing her, and hating himself for the feeling of relief when, finally, she was gone.

The entire three-day spell had happened, once more, as in a vacuum. Almost Muscovite weather had justified the long stay in London. It was Richeldis herself, busy settling Madge into a 'home', who had urged him to stay in the flat rather than to take risks on the snow-bound roads. The painfulness of the three days was exacerbated by the fact that he had not exactly fallen out of love with Monica. He loved the smell of her; the shape and feel of her shoulders; her lips against his own, the softest lips of any woman he had known. But loving her did not *get* them anywhere. For all he knew, they would continue their secret love for ages. Everything was in such a muddle. Life itself, however, refused to be interrupted. It went on.

In this case, Life chiefly meant Madge's life. It had been obvious that she could not now continue to live in Rockingham Crescent, dependent on the inefficient ministrations of Bartle. 'Homes' had been visited, assessed, applied for. Richeldis spoke of them as if they were prep-schools. The more prestigious had waiting-lists. To hear her speak, you would think there was no chance of 'getting in' to one unless you had your name down since birth. There was the further complication of whether the 'nice' ones would take oldies who were incontinent or 'confused'. These places seemed to vary. Some were like very crumby amateur hospitals run with an almost pre-Victorian level of hygiene and discipline. Others were little more than genteel private hotels, which threw you out if you did anything so impolite as to wet your drawers or have a stroke. Others were good. And, by great good fortune, they found one which was good within driving distance: ten miles from Sandilands. It was expensive – £200 per week for a single room – but Simon agreed to make up any difference there might be when Madge's pension and 'estate' had been plundered.

Richeldis and Bartle between them managed the delicate business of moving a few of Madge's things, and finally Madge herself, to her new residence, which was called Birnham House. The transition was not an easy one. It appeared to set Madge 'back'. That is, she became rather madder again, and appeared to think that the perfectly nice nurses were in the hire of her persecutors. But at least, in the new place, she was cared for. They cleaned her up, laundered her clothes, did her hair, fed her.

Simon had been cowardly about going to see his mother-in-law, but after she had been at Birnham House for a while he consented, with Richeldis, to come on a visit. They left Marcus with friends one Sunday afternoon – one could not *always* be imposing on poor Mrs. Turbot – and drove through the undulating dull Bedfordshire landscape. There had been a slight thaw, but snow still lingered, on trees, hedges, rooftops. Richeldis, who by now had got into the routine of visiting Birnham, parked the Renault outside the front door, and let herself in. It was a large old Victorian house. The rooms on the ground floor were, for the most part, set aside for communal use. Simon had noticed, through the window, a circle of drooping figures propped in their orthopaedic chairs in front of a television set. The corridors smelt of overcooked vegetables and pee.

'Mother's room is upstairs,' said Richeldis, leading the way. They met a nurse who obviously recognised her. 'How is she today?' Richeldis asked.

'So-so,' said the girl.

Simon, who was instinctively assessing the girl – lovely hips, delicious hair – began to wonder if he had not been wrong to allow Life to win in its battle against Romance. This was Life – this was how it ended, heaving about our semi-capable bodies on walking frames, our minds, our bladders, everything gone. Surely any defiance of this was a good thing? And wasn't Romance the greatest defiance of all? The nurse, who saw him eyeing her over, blushed slightly and gave a little smile which Richeldis did not notice. Surely there was a deliberate wriggle of her bottom as she walked down the stairs?

'Mother's room is along here,' said Richeldis, almost as though she was trying to persuade her husband to live in it. 'It's got a lovely view of the garden.'

'Hullo, dears, I'm afraid you'll have to go at *once*,' said Madge. She looked much more like her old self: clean, a bit plumper, well-dressed, and this disconcerted Simon, because it was as if the magisterial Madge of the 1950s and 1960s was in a state of demented panic. 'All visitors forbidden, that's the latest decree.'

'We've just passed a nurse who said we could visit you,' said Richeldis, kissing her.

'Who's that?' asked Madge, pointing to Simon.

'Hullo, Madge,' he said.

As in the old days, which rather made one doubt whether she had ever been quite sane, Madge could not stop talking. Not content to provide them with her own monologues, however, she repeated large chunks of conversation which she had been having with her invisible inquisitors.

' "I suppose you'd like us to believe that you liked books." "*Books?* I published thousands." "Then you wouldn't subscribe to the view that History is bunk?" "Certainly not. You are thinking of Henry Ford Junior, who sold motor-cars. Quite another person, do you see. If you wish I could tell you some of the historians I have known. Maurice

Cranston once said to me ...'' "Novels! Hurry up! Name some novels!" "Well, I can't always *name* you the novels, do you see, because you will always say one thing and do another – but if you insist." "We do, we do." "Well, I would say *The Mysteries of Udolpho.*" "Is that because you admire Mussolini." "Certainly *not.*" "But you are a Crypto-Fascist." "Ezra Pound was a fascist," she bravely retorted to this group of persistent questioners, but they were too quick for her. "Ezra? Ezra? Some kind of yid?" "All right then, I am a yid" ' – for a moment she stopped the court proceedings and winked at Simon. 'That's foxed them,' she said. 'Then I was asked to carry a whole tray of foreskins down to the ... oh, that room.'

'The day room,' said Richeldis.

'No! Eric came,' said Madge. 'He brought, you know.'

'His girl friend?' asked Richeldis.

'Yup, Lilian Baylis I call her. They said, "You don't mean *The* Lilian Baylis," I most certainly do – Oh, dears, don't stay, it really *isn't* safe.'

'It's perfectly safe,' said Simon.

'Do *you* know who this is?' she asked Richeldis.

'It's Simon.'

'I know,' said Madge, 'and the other one, Eric, that's his brother. Got a new job, very pleased.'

'That'll be the day,' said Simon.

'Priest-in-Charge,' said Madge. 'They said, "What do you know about religion? You just make noises." I replied. "I know as much as Cosmo Gordon Lang." '

'Quite right,' said Richeldis.

'Quite wrong,' said Madge, laughing at her daughter's simplicity. 'He was a *very* learned man, and in case you haven't noticed I have turned into a complete fool.'

20

Returning to the habits of absolute solitude, Monica Cunningham discovered that she was angry, very angry, all the time. It is hard to be angry if you have no one to be angry with, but she managed. She made several furious little returns to her local street-market. Her interrogatory tones became shriller than ever as she asked her baffled greengrocer whether he considered *this* to be an artichoke. But yes, mademoiselle, and was it not you yourself who chose it? She held the thing out to him. It dripped, for she had boiled it and peeled off a number of leaves before deciding that it was insupportable. Likewise, in the post office, there had been uncharacteristic scenes. She had found herself tapping the heads of pensioners, and prodding shoulder-blades *blessés par la guerre*, and hissing, *Dépêchez! Pour nous autres, il faut travailler!*

A lie, of course. What was *her* work? She even found it hard to concentrate on the tapestry, these days. When she turned back to her books, she merely felt cross with the Russians. A common enough sensation in the West. There have been plenty of things to hot you up against them in the last thirty years: the annexation of Hungary, Czechoslovakia, Afghanistan; the persecution of the Jews; fibbing at Helsinki and at the nuclear arms talks. Monica's rage with them was more searching. Why have such a *stupid* language? I am *going* shopping. I *go* shopping each day; I am *going* out of the room; each year I *go* to Odessa . . . Other nations are content to use one word for all these varieties of going. Russians had literally dozens of 'go' words, depending on whether they intended to come back, or how they went. Bloody fools. And Agafya Mikhailovna had begun to get on Monica's nerves: the fact that lessons always started twenty minutes late while she spread out a tea-pot, lemons, books, cakes. Correction: little tea-pot, lemons, booklets and cakelets. All those whimsical diminutives. You had no sooner gone to the trouble of learning the word for window than Agafya would be telling you it was more *Russian* (how lovingly she said the annoying word) to say *windowling*, wee tables, little mothers, ugh! At first, Monica had felt in Agafya's presence a thrill, simply because she came from this infinitely large, distant place. Monica thought nothing of modern Russia, merely of *Russianness* as it had excited her in literature: white-painted dachas, wind blowing in birch avenues; faithful old footmen hovering by the samovar; lights twinkling before old silver-framed icons of the Mother of God; huge flat expanses of land; millions of toiling peasants, picturesque in their labours; troikas gliding through snow; monasteries with onion domes golden in winter sunshine; great cities, bustling with water-traffic, wet nurses, religious fanatics, sleigh-ponies, anarchists; vast palaces where a doomed royal family pursued their pathetically vulnerable lives. These vaguely-felt things were what thrilled her when she had begun to learn the language, with a view to reading the giants. How much she was going to enjoy it when the uniformed whiskery heroes returned from the Caucasus, fell in love with plump-armed girls and agonized about the Meaning of Life. Now she felt furious with it all and sat up, night after night, writing letters to Simon about how bad all Russian writers were. Dostoievski's mawkish cult of innocence utterly repelled her, she scribbled. So did the ridiculous frenzy of his books, the way everyone was dirty in them (you could smell them), dirty and bonkers: Raskolnikov's squalid lodgings, the drunken brawls of Karamazov, and the ghastliness of all those nutters in *The Possessed. Not* the sort of people you wanted to read about. What *would* Jane Austen have made of them all? In her next letter, Monica turned to Chekhov. With a hundred and fifty different words for *going*, those three dreary sisters still couldn't get up and go to Moscow. Why should we find them interesting? They were in no worse plight than the Bennett girls in *Pride and Prejudice* (the comparison kept intruding itself). The only difference is that the Russians were *bores*. If a playwright invented a world where nothing happened you at least expected him to be funny. If not, Mr. Anton Chekhov, as with artichokes, so with plays. May we please have our money back? Next it was Tolstoy's turn. So, *Anna Karenina* was supposed to be the best novel in European literature? Huh! Monica remembered the Garbo film in which there is a tragic conflict between Anna's love for her lover and for her little son. In Tolstoy's version, he forgets that she is meant to love little Seryozha and allows her to canoodle with Vronsky for years on end in Italy. Lucky pigs. Then when she comes home she just capriciously decides that he doesn't love her any more and sets off for the old 4.50 to St. Petersburgh. And what a *mess* the book is: all those boring excursions into the country, while Levin (the worst crasher in literature) muses about Life, its Meaning, while moving hay or quarrelling with the local *zemstvo*.

Her critique of the great novel (quite seriously felt) covered five sides. This time she got as far as putting it in an envelope. But these letters to Simon were not, quite, for posting. He hardly ever wrote now – the occasional postcard. Soon, she imagined, they would stop writing to each other altogether.

During her last visit to London, she had known that all was not well. During the first day, she had chided herself for her Karenina-style neurosis. Had he not begged her to come to London? Said that he loved her? What more did she want? Richeldis's head on a charger? Oh, she knew what she wanted, and it was obvious, now, that she wasn't going to get it. A month had passed in which Simon could have told Richeldis. The fact that he had *not* done so meant that he did not *intend* to do so. Monica was trapped. In the past, how silly she had thought those women were, who got involved with married men. 'If he's so wet that he can't chuck his wife, then you should chuck him.' Advice which she had given more than once to Lady Mason during one of *her* little disasters. Things and actions are what they are, and the consequences of them will be what they will be. Why therefore desire to be deceived? But throughout three days of lovemaking in Petersburgh Place she desired to be deceived. It would have been all right if she wasn't so in love. Silly thing to say, of course she would. No one in the *world*, she now realised, had been so all right as she was in October, with no mess in her life whatsoever. She had chafed at only being so-so happy. But she was happy, wasn't she? Her body had felt so completely contented in those days of solitude. She enjoyed feeding it, washing it, dressing it in sensible clothes. Above all she enjoyed feeding it. Now, she was permanently on edge and appetite had deserted her. She had begun to smoke cigarettes, and her lovely flat stank of stale Gauloises when she woke up in the morning. Her eating patterns had been so disrupted that she feared the development of an ulcer. As a prophylactic, she took nervous gulps of horrible French milk. She swigged it straight from the carton in the Frigidaire. The cold of it made her teeth ache. Gone were the days of her cheerful snacks, her happily solitary meals in restaurants, her chats with favourite waiters.

Sometimes, she tried reasoning with herself. Why could she not simply return to those days of happiness by an act of will? For twenty years now she had managed to live with the wistful knowledge that she rather loved Simon Longworth. It had even added a secret poignancy to her visits to England, her Harrods luncheons with poor Richeldis, her weekends at Sandilands. Nothing had *come* of this feeling. She survived. And then, suddenly, she had taken it into her head that this feeling must be acted upon. Well, she had not exactly taken it into her head, it had somehow got there. Was it beyond her powers to get it out again? She loved the man with the crazy abandoned passion of a teenager. When, during her last visit, she had lain in his arms, she thought that it was just as well that he was rather stupid about human relations and did not realise quite what power he had to hurt her. Such knowledge would distort a man, disfigure him morally. But her rational self demanded an explanation. What did she *mean* by saying that she was so much in love? If it was simply a matter of sex, then surely she should be able to go out and find herself another man. But it wasn't that. The sex was wonderful, heartbreakingly wonderful. By making love to her, he had, she believed, bestowed on her the greatest privilege which she had ever enjoyed in her life. She was aware that this opinion was unenlightened. It happened to be what she felt. But what she loved was something much more than the beautiful strong body of Simon Longworth. Surely not, either, merely the fact that he, too, liked Brahms, Elgar, Conan Doyle . . . Shared tastes would not create such feelings of weakness, such degrading adoration.

The trouble was, the more she reasoned, and worried with herself, the more these sessions of sweet silent thought turned merely into the reveries of the lover. What began as a seemingly rational inquiry – is it just his beauty which makes me love him? – became a meditation on that beauty itself. The attempt at a cold-headed rationalism – why should such a conversation be memorable – dissolved into a memory of the words themselves.

'Do you know something?'

'What?'

'I thought I'd been enjoying this all my life.'

'This?'

'Ouch. Let go! But now I realise I did not know what the word *enjoyment* meant.'

'Oh, Simon, words don't mean anything in themselves.'

'I love you, Monica.'

'I love you. Oh, how I love you.'

That conversation had happened in the motel near Dunstable. Or, there was another standing in front of Jan Van Eyck's *Marriage of Giovanni Arnolfini and Giovanna Cenami*.

'I do hope she's doing the right thing,' Simon said.

'She's doing just the right thing.'

'As well as all the repose in that picture, the homeliness of the little dog, the sensible daylight from the window, the delight in surfaces, and *things*, there's so much passion. Those discarded shoes.'

'You're the only person in the world apart from me who would see it,' she said. 'It's passion in the way Jane Austen is passionate, *n'est-ce pas?* Anne Elliott is quite as romantic a heroine as Jane Eyre or Cathy Earnshaw. It's just that she doesn't run about in bad weather, shouting . . .'

'You think if she'd gone up to Captain Wentworth's attic, she'd have found a mad wife?' he asked.

'Nowadays she might have found a sane wife, which would be worse.'

They stood, finger-tip intwined in finger-tip, surveying Van Eyck's masterpiece. Then she added, 'Just because everything is demure on the surface does not mean that underneath there isn't a swirling tempest.' She pointed with her free hand to the demure wife. 'She's swirling, just a little.'

Then Simon had leant close and whispered in her ear, 'I'm swirling a little, too.'

Ouch, ouch, ouch. If only she did not have such total power of recall. She could remember every word spoken, every glance which they had ever exchanged. She could remember the intensity of these early moments with him and compare them with the *last* visit to London. Her eyes no longer quite met his. His protestations of adoration came a split second too late to be believable. There was something forced about the lovemaking itself. But, by now, she was abject. She would accept him on *any* terms, however false or however cruel he chose to be.

In addition to her paragraphs of literary analysis, she also wrote Simon pages and pages of love letters. Some days she wrote as many as six of these wretched epistles. She knew that there was no point in posting them. She allowed them to pile up on her writing table. He would never again write to her in such terms. And, if he did, he would be lying. She knew this, but it did not diminish her childish optimism. She would wake at four a.m. in a twitter of excitement, knowing that, in a mere three and a half hours, M. *le facteur* would leave his bicycle against the shutters and put some letters in her *boîte*. If there were so much as a post-card, oh, the weakness of joy.

The next letter with a Bedfordshire postmark, however, was from Richeldis.

You must be wondering whether had lost use of limbs, rabbited that round familiar hand, *but quite honestly hasn't been a mo since Christmas and correspondence sadly neglected!! Thanks a mill for your cards and presents. Marcus loved the whistle. Wish you had come to Sandilands for Christmas. In the end it was just the five of us having a v. quiet time which think Simon needed because he's been going through a lot. Monica, this is going to be a difficult letter to write . . .*

Miss Cunningham's hand shook as she read on.

. . . but just know you are feeling awkward about mother. Quite honestly, Monica, you're really not to. Her breakdown was very definitely not your fault.

Her fault! Could Richeldis seriously suppose that Monica had really thought Madge's illness was her fault? What *was* she talking about? Monica re-read the previous paragraphs to see if there was any way in which they could be taken as some subtly damaging hint that Richeldis really knew about the situation with Simon. Was this bilge about Madge just a 'cover'? Or what? Could Richeldis really be so thick?

It was one heck of a year with mother, but we have at last got her settled in a v. nice home. Unfortunately it's just a little far but she's in excellent hands and to tell the truth, Monica, her sense of time is so wonky, am never v. sure whether she notices how long it is between visits. She lives in a dream world, tragic really, and has given up reading.

Oh, dear, somehow Monica could feel what was coming next.

For the first time in weeks am really feeling have a bit of freedom again and have had an absolutely brill idea which hope appeals, viz that Belinda and self BOTH come to Paris Feb. 7 –14 and have thoroughly self-indulgent hen party. AGES since we did so – real touch of Oakers!! – and entre nous (must brush up my French!) Linda really needs break. Anyone could have told her that Jules is queer as a coot but it honestly hadn't crossed her mind and humiliation terrible partic. since man he's gone off with (same panto at Swindon) is apparently beyond words ugly (literally back end of a cow – that's the part he's playing in panto!!). Simon is being frightful about it and says Belinda has probably got the dreaded AIDS. Just to be serious for a moment, this is no joke, but let's keep fingers crossed. Everything else crossed too, Simon says. Incidentally Simon v. grumpy about our Paris plans but why should he always be the one who swans off to foreign parts? Mrs. Turbot is being a total saint and having Marcus for a whole week. No question, by the way, of your putting us up. Have booked rooms at Hotel Scandinavia which Simon says much nicer than last hotel he stayed in – very businessy apparently. Belinda so depressed that even she tried to pooh-pooh the idea of our all getting together, which is unlike her. Lots of love, R.

So, she was to spend St. Valentine's Day with the wife of the man she loved, reminiscing about jolly old Oakers, and hearing in lurid detail the end of Belinda's affair with Jules. By rights it should have made her

weep, but she felt herself convulsed with whoops of quite uncharacteristic laughter.

*   *   *

Things moved very rapidly for Stephanie and Bartle, once all the
confusions had been sorted out. He was asked to Sunday dinner with
Uncle Lenny and Auntie Ray. It was not a riotously successful
occasion since, although they accepted Stephanie's assurance that the
dirty vicar was *not* the father of her baby, this made his willingness to
hover about her all the more unaccountable. Also, while everyone
round the table was determined to like one another, it somehow
didn't work. They found Bartle's voice off-puttingly posh, and rather
resented his ceaseless questions about their religious observances.
O.K. All right. So they were Jewish. Was that a reason for quizzing
them about the Feast of Tabernacles over their Sunday dinner? They
weren't *that* Jewish, why rub it in? Bartle for his part, while longing
to ingratiate himself, found Auntie Ray extraordinarily boring. It
would not be true to say that she had any conversation, as such. She
kept up a sort of commentary on the meal; words poured from her
mouth, so that no one else got much of a word in. But conversation it
wasn't.

'Thought I'd do some carrots, well, they're easy and everyone likes
carrots: well, hope you like carrots, Mr. Longworth.'

'Auntie Ray, he's called Bartle,' Stephanie protested.

Her aunt sniffed as if no sane person would altogether believe this,
and continued, 'Beef and carrots, go together, don't they, beef and
carrots. Then I thought I'd do a few potatoes.'

'Like a nice spud,' put in Uncle Lenny.

'Spuds, that's right,' said Auntie Ray.

Nothing she proposed could be gainsaid. There were indeed beef,
carrots, potatoes.

'I notice you eat butter,' said Bartle with an oecumenical smile.

'Well, load of old cobblers, if you ask me, Bartle. All this
cholesterol. Pull the other one. I mean, people have been eating
butter for centuries and not having heart attacks.'

'But it's on the table with the meat,' said Bartle. 'Does that mean
you're Liberals . . .'

He hesitated to call anyone a Jew to their face even thought he
found the whole thing so fascinating.

'Really, Bartle,' said Auntie Ray playfully, 'are you a vicar or a
rabbi?'

'Lovely beef, Auntie Ray,' said Stephanie.

It genuinely interested Bartle that you could be Jewish, but not so serious as to worry about the dietary laws. Was this the equivalent of being C. of E. but seldom, or never, going to church? Auntie Ray and Uncle Lenny thought his line of talk a little bit offensive. What interested them was what was he playing at? Did he intend to make an honest woman out of Stephanie in spite of her misfortunes? She was a nice girl, Stephanie. They didn't want any more older men messing her about, like that so-called dentist.

Had they felt able to broach them, these would have been the questions they would have asked him. But, after Lenny's disastrous attempt at a show-down with Simon, Ray had implored him to play safe. Bartle, on the other hand, was under the impression that a frank discussion of their religious differences would be a 'way in' to an explanation of his behaviour. But it was no good. The time for explanations was not ripe. Even Stephanie, as it happened, remained in the dark. She believed Bartle when he said that he loved her, but did he really *fancy* her? The religious rules by which he felt his life to be governed made it rather difficult to know. He couldn't make love to her unless they were married. It made her heart dance when he had begun to explain this. In spite of everything he was prepared to marry her. But then it turned out not to be so easy as that. Although he was legally divorced, Bartle did not consider himself entitled, as a priest of the Church, to marry again in his first wife's lifetime. Stephanie was vaguely under the impression that in recent years these rules had been relaxed. There surely *were* divorced clergymen who got married again. He'd talked some gibberish about Charles Williams and the doctrine of coinherence, and said he was perfectly prepared to set up house together. On what? He appeared to have no money, and how could she work once the baby came?

The problems appeared to be insuperable. She was not trying to run away from them by suggesting a change of scene. The idea came to them as they were walking hand in hand one day past a travel agent; within ten minutes they had gone inside and were poring over brochures. Bartle had £512 in his current account and largesse easily overtook him. They would have a week in a cheap hotel in Paris. Stephanie, who had never been to Paris, was completely captivated with the idea; what could be nicer? Tickets were bought, Stephanie, a hardened traveller, had an up-to-date passport. Bartle *thought* his passport was up-to-date, but after two days of frantic searching for it in the house at Putney they found it had expired in 1967. There followed a happy, time-wasting day of squatting in photographic booths and queueing up in the post office for a temporary passport.

Some decaying guidebooks to the French capital, obsolete when they were given to one of Bartle's jumble sales years since, were also discovered. 'Should come in handy,' he said, myopically surveying the tram fares. In the few remaining days they made lists of all the things they most wanted to do and see. They both felt very happy when, lovey-dovey, they snuggled together in the Paris boat train and pulled out of Victoria Station.

*   *   *

Monica was ashamed of her own cowardice. Other members of the human race bravely survived earthquakes, war and plague. Surely, she told herself, it ought to possible to endure a visit from her two oldest friends? Yet she devised every possible means of putting them off. Had she thought of a plausible excuse she would have done. Slate-grey skies, arctic winds, steely sleet dominated the first part of the visit. On the third day, Richeldis thought she must have eaten something – not in Paris, a difficult accomplishment – and was confined to her bedroom with diarrhoea. While she, green-faced, lay swigging kaolin and morphine in the Hotel Scandinavia, Monica had wandered with Lady Mason in the Jeu de Paume and heard the full Jules saga. The story altered with each repetition. When she first poured it all out, she confessed herself to be completely flabbergasted and, evidently a Jules phrase, freaked out, by the discovery of his proclivities. By the time they were staring at the late Monets, it was, 'Of course I knew, and quite honestly Monica, I couldn't give a *damn* about his *past*; it was the fact that he *lied* which hurt so much.'

Darling Belinda. Monica knew too well how much love hurt. Belinda, of course, had asked how things stood with Simon, but Monica had been non-committal. Belinda was sure that Richeldis didn't know a *thing*. But Monica was never sure, in all the years that followed, how much Richeldis knew or suspected. Nobody could be *that* thick, or could they? Life really seemed impossibly bleak, so full of possibilities of pain. Now that they were all together a collective sadness descended. The more they tried to recapture their lost youth, the further away it all seemed.

'Anyway,' said Belinda, 'that's enough of Jules. My dear, do you remember Edward.'

'Edward Wharton?'

'No!' Belinda laughed scornfully, as though anyone would remember Edward Wharton. 'Edward Maxwell.'

'Oh, horrible Edward.'

'Wasn't it awful that you used to call him that.'

'You were the one who called him horrible Edward. And he was.'

Horrible Edward had been one of those men who hovered about Oakmoor Road in the old days. A moustachioed man in a three-piece suit (second-hand, Linda had guessed) who was not all that he seemed. Was he the one with the frightful spots? Monica, with her unenviable powers of recall, remembered an hilarious evening when he had bored Linda 'rigid, my dear' by an account of how he was being put up for the Beefsteak. From time to time over the ensuing years, Lady Mason would announce that Edward had 'reared his ugly head' and taken her out to a meal in a restaurant. His visits to London were infrequent. Monica remembered that he had gone to teach at Fettes.

'Has he become a headmaster?' she asked.

'However did you know? Did you see it in *The Times*?'

'People of our age *are* becoming headmasters.'

'The other day he rang me up out of the blue. He was in London for a conference.'

'He reared his ugly head, in short.'

Belinda laughed all earlier estimates of the man aside. 'I thought he was frightfully interesting. He even promised to take me to an evening at the Royal Geographical Society. I felt rather honoured he remembered me. He was a huge success at Fettes and as you saw he's just become head of Pangham.'

'He never married, I suppose.'

Even if he had, there was always a second time or, in Belinda's case, a third. Oh dear, headmasters and managing directors. They were the sort of men they were falling in love with now. It would not be so very long before they were all fifty. Life had simply *gone*. Richeldis at least had children. The other two had – well, nothing. Just arthritis and the geriatric ward to look forward to. After that, extinction. Belinda was astonishingly capable of optimism. Even in the midst of her grief for Jules she could seek fresh woods, and – horrible Edward in prospect – pastures old. Monica had never guessed, even in moods of wildest despondency, to hear Belinda describe Edward as 'witty', 'interesting' or – as they were coming back in the taxi – 'rather a pet'.

The next day, kaolin and morphine had done some kind of trick, and Richeldis, bright as a button, emerged from her room, determined to enjoy the rest of the week to the full. She wanted to know if the others could guess what surprise she had in store for them.

'No, what?' asked Monica, who had had her fill of surprises.

'It occurred to me that I'd never seen Fontainebleau.'

The silence in Monica's drawing room was icy. Belinda, rather embarrassingly, blushed. Monica peered at Richeldis, at her open, smiling features, still pale though no longer green, at her (now) dyed hair, cut slightly too short for her plump face, at her kind, insensitive eyes. Did she know or didn't she?

'You know,' said Richeldis, 'the forest of Fontainebleau and the palace where the kings lived. I've been talking to the hall porter in the hotel and he says there's this marvellous 'bus tour you can take. They drive you to Barbizon, where the painters were, and Brie, and lots of lovely places. It would be nice to have an outing, particularly if the weather picks up.'

'There's not a lot to see at Fontainebleau' said Monica guardedly. 'Mainly bad Italian stuff, I seem to remember.'

'It will be so relaxing to go on a 'bus,' said Richeldis.

'There's always Versailles,' said Belinda, getting out her Falstaffs and fiddling in her bag for a lighter. 'There's much more to *see* at Versailles.'

'What have you got against Fontainebleau?'

'There's nothing against it,' said Monica.

If this was a test of nerves, she was determined to pass it. She once remembered Belinda, in a quite different context, saying, 'Married people tell each other *everything* in the end.' Could it be? The whole story, from Fontainebleau to St. Petersburgh Place?

'Oh, yippee,' said Richeldis triumphantly as she opened her bag, 'because the porter bought us three tickets for this afternoon.'

*   *   *

Some time before going away Bartle had received a letter out of the blue from his area bishop. It was an extremely friendly little note, hoping that all was well, and asking him to telephone the bishop's office should he have time. The communication threw Bartle into a quandary. Should he tell Stephanie? Would she understand that he wanted both things – to live with her, loving her for ever and ever, and to get back to being a priest? If only they could get married! Of course, he did tell her, and at her prompting he rang the bishop, explaining that he was just off to Paris.

'Lucky you,' said the episcopal tones. 'Listen, my dear' – for some reason, the bishop called everyone 'my dear' – 'I've been wondering about you. What are you doing?'

'I rather assumed that I'd been put out to grass.'

A lot of fake laughter. 'Listen, my dear, I couldn't possibly lure you back into the vineyard with a little *very* light pastoral duty?'

The old Mission Church in Kentish Town where Bartle went to confession was, it transpired, in need of a priest in charge. It was a place which nowadays attracted a tiny congregation. There were only twenty-nine people on the electoral roll and the duties would be minimal.

'But does this mean that Father Trownson is ill?' Bartle feared the worst. Had his beloved Father Trownson died?

'I must be candid with you, my dear, the future of St. Matthias's is very uncertain. Old Alfred Trownson is a darling but he's been there for years and he really thinks he's had enough, he's seventy-four.'

'Did he suggest me?' Bartle knew that there was no other way the bishop would have remembered him. He hedged, however, and blahed on a good deal about the problems of the inner city. Then he moaned about the obscurantist Victorian society which had tried to stop the church being made redundant. 'But we must face facts,' said the bishop. There they left it. The bishop offered Bartle the charge of St. Matthias for a year. There was no vicarage, but a flat (two bedrooms) came with the job and would Bartle please get in touch with the bishop as soon as he returned from Paris. ('Give my love to St. George's'.)

This was a turn up for the books. Bartle in demand! Stephanie felt pleased with him, proud. He said he would only take the job if she stayed with him. If necessary, they could undergo a civil wedding. The twenty-nine on the electoral roll could make what they would of the fact that their priest in charge was living with a pregnant young woman. His defiant certainty that all would be well, and all manner of things would be well, made the days in Paris very happy ones for Stephanie. There were dreadful problems ahead, but who minded? They would face them together. Arm in arm, and happy, they had traipsed about Paris, not caring in the least about the bad weather, or the funny smells in their cheap hotel near the Place de la République. Nor had they only eaten at Chinese restaurants. Indonesian, even Vietnamese, food had been savoured, as well as sustaining little late night snacks at a crêperie near the hotel.

'An excursion' had been Stephanie's idea of making happiness complete. Bartle's initial unwillingness to leave Paris, his feeling that he wanted to squeeze every ounce of wonder and excitement out of the city itself, evaporated, as hand in hand, they sat on the coach together, that Valentine's Day, and rolled through the forest. On either side, trees were still wintry; but the black twiggy expanses were in bud. Snowdrops, early crocuses, were in flower. For the first time that week, it had stopped raining. There was even a little watery sunshine in the air. Stephanie made Bartle so happy. He could feel no regrets. The burden of regret had been lifted from him. In her company he felt simply happy. Of course, it grieved him, that they could not be married, as he wanted, in church. But even this brought a sweet sort of pain. He could not resurrect any feelings of bitterness towards Vera. He hoped she was happy with Keith. He could not wish her dead, just to gratify his own happiness. Somehow or another, he knew that from now on he was going to be happy. With Stephanie, everything would be all right. And, although the legal niceties were problematic, inside it felt all right with God. They had nothing with which to reproach themselves. He left all in God's hands. Stephanie was his gift from heaven. Even Mr. Greenhalgh's baby was a blessing. They now spoke of it as their own.

'If it's a boy, we'll call him Matthias,' she said. 'After your church. Matthias Lenny. Oh, Bartle, look at the flowers. Isn't it lovely when life comes back to the earth?'

She leaned over and kissed his cheek.

'You are my springtime,' he said.

'I don't deserve you,' she said.

'That's what Vera used to say, in a very different tone of voice.'

'Oh, you know what I *mean*.'

'Deserving doesn't come into it,' he said.

'Isn't it lovely to be away – just the two of us – away from all the tension, away from Uncle Lenny and Auntie Ray.'

'Away from Madge. I love her, but, oh, the strain.'

The whole expedition was proving an unqualified success. They both gasped with wonder when the coach wound through the little street, and the château at length came into view. By the time they clambered out, there was a suspicion of warmth in the sunshine. When they climbed the swooping stone staircase which leads to the grand entrance of the palace, Stephanie felt that she was entering a fairy-tale, and that she and Bartle were going to live happily ever after. She neither worried about him nor doubted him. As she kept saying, sometimes aloud, sometimes to herself, she could not believe her luck. Wide-eyed and hand in hand they ambled through each gilded room, joyfully aghast as such splendour, and feeling that they were stepping forward into their own golden future. It was in Napoleon's throne room that she felt Bartle's grip tighten in her hand.

'It *can't* be,' he said.

At the far doorway, she saw three women.

'I'll have to get used to this sort of thing when you're a vicar again.' She took them for parishioners from a former existence. They looked that sort of age. One of the old women – well, not old, but late middle-aged, with short dyed blonde hair – was waving and shouting, 'Coo-ee!' And the other two stood by with a funny sort of look on their faces, as though they had seen a ghost.